SPICED AND ICED

A CALLIE'S KITCHEN MYSTERY, BOOK 2

Jenny Kales

To all of the people who inspired this series...you know who you are.

Thanks for the stories.

"There are some people who want to throw their arms round you simply because it is Christmas; there are other people who want to strangle you simply because it is Christmas."

ROBERT STAUGHTON LYND

"Christmas is a season not only of rejoicing but of reflection."

WINSTON CHURCHILL

"Kala Christouyenna"

MERRY CHRISTMAS IN GREEK

Contents

One

"Why does *anyone* think it's a good idea to have their bridal shower right before the holidays?" grumbled Natalie Underwood, her long red curls bouncing pertly as she rushed about the room. Her slim figure, decked out in a short, sleek dress and dark-colored tights seemed to bristle with consternation as she straightened silverware and adjusted the festive Christmas centerpieces in The English Country Inn's waterfront dining room.

"Because they enjoy making everyone as stressed out as they are?" Calliope Costas responded, but with a smile. Her friends and clients called her "Callie," but her Greek father normally stuck with "Calliope."

As the proprietor of Callie's Kitchen, a Mediterranean meets Midwest from-scratch meals business, she'd had her fair share of demanding clients. But customers were customers. Anyway, Callie knew she was more able to tolerate self-absorbed brides now than she used to, now that she had a new special someone in her own life.

As the two women chatted, Callie was rushing alongside Natalie, placing mini boxes of her famous Greek snowball cookies, aka, *kourabiethes*, at each place. The inn had its own chef, but occasionally Callie contributed an extra sweet treat to events at the inn at the host's request. To celebrate the season, Callie had spiced the treats with ouzo, the flavorful Greek liqueur, and had placed a fragrant clove in the center of each cookie. She wished that Natalie would eat a cookie – maybe the combination of booze and melt-in-your-mouth texture would cheer her up.

1

"Okay, that just about does it." Natalie straightened a final centerpiece and glanced out the huge expanse of windows overlooking Crystal Bay's namesake waterfront. She leaned forward a bit, squinting at the view. Callie kept placing boxes of cookies at each place. If anyone was out there, it had to be a duck who had forgotten to migrate: who else would brave the 15-degree temperatures?

The day was a bit overcast, but nothing unusual for Wisconsin in mid-December. The lake looked icy and gray, but even the lack of sun couldn't take away from its beauty. So far the month was unusually cold, even for Crystal Bay. Unlike previous years when warm temperatures prevented the water from icing over completely, it looked like this year the bay and surrounding waterways were experiencing an early freeze. The ice fishermen and ice skaters would have a field day.

Inside, the airy dining room glowed with soft Christmas lights and so many fresh pine boughs and tiny white fairy lights that it felt like walking through a winter forest. Large windows framed the pleasant vista of Crystal Bay. Delightful. Callie inhaled the pine-scented air deeply before turning to Natalie once more.

"Anything else that I can do to help right now?" she asked.

The young woman shook her head. "Not that I can think of." Natalie was, by all accounts, exceptionally good at her job as the head of events at The English Country Inn, a Crystal Bay mainstay for the last 40 years. The midsized boutique hotel was situated directly on the water, making for charmingly picturesque views. The interior décor reflected its namesake with inviting floral sofas and wallpaper, plush carpet and warm paneling.

The inn was also famous for a spectacular English-style Victorian tea service, presented only at Christmastime. Locals and tourists alike flocked to partake of the tender cucumber tea sandwiches, rich, flaky scones and spicy gingerbread. Callie had planned to attend the tea event with her grandmother, Viv and her 10-year-old daughter,

Olivia. She was even toying with the idea of inviting the British-born detective she was seeing. Would a detective enjoy a tea party?

Callie glanced again at Natalie who appeared to be white with fatigue. "Natalie, come on. Let's sit down for a minute. You look run off your feet."

"I can't," Natalie responded firmly. "You're sweet to worry about me but there is just so much to do."

"Let me help you then. I need to go back to work soon, but I can stay a little longer. Why not take advantage?" Callie smiled.

Natalie smiled back, but weakly, so it seemed to Callie. "Thanks," she said with a sigh. "Maybe I will take a short break. This particular bride is not my favorite and I really can't let my feelings show."

"Oh?" Callie asked, handing over one of the *kourabiethes*. Natalie dropped into a chair with another gusty sigh and munched glumly on the cookie.

"I'm surprised you don't know the story," she said. "These are good by the way. A little spicy, but buttery."

Callie smiled. At least her *kourabiethes* hadn't lost their ability to cheer people up. "Thanks. Now – what story are you talking about?"

"Well, this is the second bridal shower I've planned for the bride. At the first one, she and some of her relatives got, shall we say, a little too argumentative and the groom ended up ditching her."

"I didn't know that." The bride, Lexy Dayton, was a regular customer at Callie's Kitchen, and she had insisted that the Greek cookies be on the menu at her bridal shower. "That's terrible. Poor Lexy!" Callie offered, reluctant to criticize a loyal client – and Greek cookie lover.

Natalie rolled her eyes at Callie. "I can't say I blame her ex. The Daytons appear to be ever-so-elegant on the surface, but they know how to wreck a party. Believe me. In any case, Lexy blames me for her relationship gone awry. Logic is not her strong suit."

"I'm inclined to agree. Why on earth would she have her bridal shower at the inn if she blames you for ruining her last engagement?" Callie asked, raising her dark eyebrows.

Natalie finished her second cookie before answering. "The Daytons are loaded, so they really could afford to have the shower anywhere. Though, I suppose this setting makes sense to them. Apparently, Dayton brides have been fêted at The English Country Inn since forever and they are intent on keeping the tradition alive. I only hope that the groom doesn't dump Lexy today. I could lose my job!"

Natalie slumped back in her chair and frowned at her beautifully manicured fingernails. "To make matters worse, I went to high school with Nick Hawkins, Lexy's new groom. He had a crush on me way back when, but I think he's forgotten about it. Not Lexy, though. She's probably got a spreadsheet of every woman that Nick ever glanced at."

Callie laughed. "Oh, Natalie. No wonder you're tense today! Don't worry so much. Everything looks beautiful, the food will be delicious and you can just cut them off early if they hit the bar too often. Hopefully, the Christmas Spirit will help too."

Natalie stood up, smoothing her navy dress, accented with a flowing scarf, tied into a loose bow. To Callie's eyes, the dress looked like an expensive designer number that Callie had drooled over online. Was it Kate Spade? Either it was the real deal or a very convincing knock-off. Natalie must be doing well for herself if she could purchase *that*. Callie could only afford to dream of such clothing.

"You're probably right. And thanks for talking," Natalie seemed a little more calm and some color had come back to her attractively freckled face. "If you're sure you don't mind, I think I will ask you to do something for me. Will you see if the coat check person is here? The guests are arriving any minute and I forgot to do something."

"Of course," Callie agreed, inwardly relieved to be given such a minor task. She had been up early and was feeling tired.

"Thanks for all of your help today," Natalie smiled at Callie before lowering her voice to a near whisper. "I know you probably wouldn't but, please, don't repeat my story about the Daytons."

"No worries, here," Callie responded. "We've all dealt with bridezillas."

Natalie giggled and started walking quickly down the hallway. "See you in a minute," she called over her shoulder.

Callie checked her watch and strode to the lobby to look for the coat check person. She didn't see a soul, not even the concierge, Melody Cartwright.

Perhaps Melody wasn't working today – she was the type to have a lot of irons in the fire. Besides working part time at the inn, the forty-something Melody ran a tea party business for children and was about to have her first book published – it would include tea party tips and recipes. Callie thought the book sounded wonderful. There was even talk of her being a guest on a national talk show. Melody was Crystal Bay's closest thing to a celebrity these days.

"Melody!" Callie called, but no one answered. She headed back near the coat check area and was relieved to see a young woman standing behind the half-door.

"Oh. Hi there. I'm helping out today for the Dayton shower and Natalie Underwood just wanted me to check to see that you'd arrived," Callie explained.

The young woman nodded and smiled. "Well, let her know I'm here and I'm ready when the guests are." She smoothed her long blond hair back from her face. "Is everything okay? Natalie usually checks in with me personally before an event."

"Oh yes, everything's fine," Callie said, relieved that her tasks were nearly finished. Her assistant, Max, was working but she needed to get back to her shop for a pile of food prep. "Natalie is just really busy today. I'm Callie Costas, by the way."

"Kayla Hall," the coat check girl said, extending her hand. "I know you – you run the Greek food business downtown. It's really good."

"Thanks!" Callie felt herself blush a little at the praise. "You look familiar to me, too. I hope you can come to Callie's Kitchen again soon. We've got some great Christmas goodies. I even decided to do Kringle this year."

Kayla's eyes lit up at the mention of the classic Danish pastry, a Wisconsin Christmas tradition. Callie was about to elaborate but stopped when she noticed that Kayla suddenly looked strained, a forced smile painted on her face.

"Welcome to The English Country Inn," Kayla said perkily to someone who stood just behind Callie. "May I check your coat?"

Callie stepped aside for a tall, model-thin woman in her mid-fifties with a short, chic gray haircut. Without a glance at Callie, she handed a fur coat across the door to Kayla. She didn't look as if she ate much Christmas Kringle but looks could be deceiving. Callie had learned that sometimes the thinnest people had the best appetites.

"Thank you," the woman addressed Kayla in a brisk tone. Her voice was deep and resonant, like a newscaster. She was wearing a bright red jacket and matching pencil skirt that set off her athletic build. Her Christmassy outfit was set off with dangling earrings in the shape of small, sparkly snowflakes.

Abruptly, she turned to Callie. "Are you working the Dayton bridal shower? I need to speak to someone about the seating."

Ah. The famous Dayton mother of the bride. She certainly appeared to be elegant and put together. Callie tried to imagine her in the type of family brawl that Natalie had described and failed.

"I'm not the event planner, if that's what you mean," Callie began, but the other woman cut her off.

"I know that. Natalie Underwood is the event manager." The Dayton woman took a step closer, enveloping Callie in a cloud of expensive perfume that smelled like the *La Vie Est Belle* Callie's best friend Sam had gifted to her at her last birthday. *Life Is Beautiful.*

However, this woman appeared to be thinking just the opposite about life, at least at the moment. She glared at Callie and started tapping her foot. "Do you work for Natalie? I need to go over a few things. But perhaps Natalie would be the best person for me to deal with."

Anxious to get back to her own place of business, Callie decided the best thing to do was be gracious. "I'm sure she would be able to assist you. I just provided a few treats from my food business, Callie's Kitchen. Your daughter may have told you."

"Oh yes, Callie's Kitchen." She didn't look as if she thought much of her daughter's taste in food providers. "All right, then. Please see if you can find Natalie. The guests should be here in half an hour and I want everything to be perfect."

Getting a sympathetic glance from Kayla, Callie attempted to soothe the nervous mother of the bride. "Of course you do. I'll go look for her right now."

Grateful for an excuse to leave this woman's towering and intimidating presence, Callie scooted off in the direction she'd last seen Natalie. There was no one in sight but a few housekeeping workers and they had no idea where Natalie – or Melody Cartwright, the concierge – had disappeared to.

Callie started to sweat. The last thing she wanted was a confrontation with Mrs. Dayton who, despite her polished appearance, became somewhat overbearing once she spoke. Natalie was in for an interesting afternoon.

Finally, one of the bellboys took pity on Callie and directed her to Natalie's office, situated near the kitchen, where succulent odors of roast chicken were wafting through the doorway. Her stomach rumbled but this was no time for food.

"Natalie," Callie said, knocking on the closed office door. "The mother of the bride is looking for you and she seems a little tense."

The door swung open but instead of Natalie, it was Melody Cartwright who emerged from the office. "Hello, Callie," she said. "I was looking for Natalie, too."

"Oh!" Callie was startled. "I wondered where you were. The Dayton party is arriving and you might want to get out there, pronto. The mother of the bride had some things to discuss with Natalie and she looks like she means business."

"Oh my," Melody said, a frown creasing her forehead. "The Daytons want a perfect event, that's for sure. Where can Natalie be?"

Perfect. There was that word again. Despite enjoying the fee that came with supplying food for an event, Callie was glad she wasn't running this show. Everyone seemed a bit too uptight and combined with what Natalie had shared about the Daytons, the event had all the potential of a reality TV episode, complete with overturned tables and hair-pulling.

Melody ran a hand over her smooth dark hair, pulled back in a low bun. She looked conservative, but sophisticated, quite a different look than when she dressed up as a princess or a fairy for the children's tea parties she hosted. Melody pulled her ivory blouse more securely over her hips and smoothed her black trousers as she started down the hallway.

"If you're finished, you can feel free to go," she called over her shoulder to Callie. "I'll find Natalie. Thanks for your help!" Melody disappeared around the corner.

Callie let her breath out in a whoosh and headed back to the dining room to collect her coat and any stray cookie boxes. She heard a hubbub of voices in the lobby and realized that the guests would be entering the dining room any minute. No need to stick around for the bride – leave that pleasure to The English Country Inn.

As she re-entered the dining room, the windows framed a winter wonderland of white, fluffy snowflakes that descended gently from the sky. The scenery was certainly holding up its end of the bargain. Hopefully the calm winter scene would pacify any edgy guests – or hosts.

Callie located her belongings and looked out the window once more. The snow was really coming down now, a harbinger of slippery roads. Instead of taking a chance on running into Mrs. Dayton again, Callie decided to go out the dining room door that led to the patio, a popular spot in warm months. It was closer to the parking lot, anyway, she rationalized. She put on her coat and braced herself for the cold.

As she stepped outside, Callie felt some of the stress lift from her. Snow was a pain to drive in, but a white Christmas was so romantic and this year she would have someone to share it with. Gazing out at the water and inhaling the cold, head-clearing air, Callie relished the chilly beauty of the scene, but a flash of color in the water near the large boathouse attached to the hotel caught her eye. Squinting, she took a closer look.

Just visible through the fluffy white wall of snowflakes was a burnished orange blob. That was odd. Did somebody drop something in the water? Callie was ready to shrug it off and head for the warmth of her car, but something made her take another look. A prickle of apprehension made the hairs on the back of her neck stand up.

Callie started walking toward the object. It was slow going. The snow was starting to become slippery and ice patches were already on the ground. The falling snow was starting to obscure the ice patches, making them even more dangerous.

Callie stumbled a bit and with a struggle, righted herself before she fell. She glanced longingly back towards the parking lot, but her curiosity was getting the better of her. She felt silly and vowed to head back to the car if she slipped one more time. For all she knew, it was a stray buoy, left behind when the piers were taken up and stacked like Tinker Toys for winter storage.

Cautiously now, Callie stepped closer. From this vantage point, it was clear the item wasn't a buoy. *What was it?* The colors sharpened as she got closer. Callie started to quicken her pace, slipping a bit, but focused now. The outlines of a human body were now coming into view. Callie caught her breath in a gasp. An icy sensation began at her scalp and continued to her toes.

Forgetting the dangers of the ice and new-fallen snow, Callie made a beeline to the water's edge and the unidentified object floating in it. What she saw made the back of her scalp tingle and her stomach lurch. She screamed.

Natalie lay face down in the water. The thin ice must have broken when she fell, revealing the icy depths underneath. Callie shuddered and shrieked, tears springing to her eyes and momentarily blinding her. *No. Not again. Please.* She wiped her streaming eyes with a mittened hand and forced herself to look again.

Natalie's beautiful hair fanned out like seaweed. The back of her head was a bloody mass and the ends of her long, coppery locks were already starting to become covered with a fine coating of powdery snow.

Cautiously, Callie leaned down and nudged Natalie, loudly calling her name to no response. With one huge push, Callie turned the event planner over and then fell back onto the patio. Freezing water splashed onto her jeans and her hands felt like they'd been dipped inside a flash-freezing machine.

Natalie floated with her arms outstretched in the frigid water, her long designer scarf speckled with blood. Her normally rosy, freckled face was now grayish white and her wide-open eyes were glassy and devoid of the spark of life.

Two

Callie struggled to stand up, nearly falling as she scrambled to brace herself on the icy ground. "Help! Help!" she shrieked. Her brain couldn't reconcile the image of Natalie's lifeless body floating in the icy water with the pretty, young, vibrant woman who had been eating cookies and chatting with her such a short time ago.

Trembling with cold and fear, Callie felt panic closing her throat. Repeatedly, she told herself to remain calm and seek help. But before she could do so, loud footsteps pounded furiously behind her, growing closer and closer. Terror crept down her spine in an icy trickle as she whirled to face her assailant, her arms and legs tense.

But it was only Bix Buckman, the groundskeeper at The English Country Inn and a sometime date of her best friend Samantha. "Are you okay?" he asked. She could only point at the form floating in the water.

"No! I'm not! Please, Bix!" Callie finally found her voice. Her eyes were still streaming with hot tears that seemed to freeze on her face in the chill. "It's Natalie Underwood," Callie managed to croak. Bix stared at her before running to Natalie's body.

Callie cleared her throat. "I just found her. It looks like somebody hit her on the head." Her voice sounded hoarse and low.

Bix was already dragging Natalie out of the water, yelling her name and shaking her. Callie watched, numb with shock and shivering as he began performing CPR on Natalie's limp form. Images started to blur around the edges and for a minute she thought she might black out. Bix's voice brought her back to reality. He turned around long enough to shout: "Go get help. Hurry!"

Stumbling across the patio near the water's edge, Callie felt her feet skidding for about the millionth time and steadied herself, unable to face a dip into the freezing water. She ran to the door she had just exited but it was locked.

"Help!" she cried. "Let me in!" She pounded on the door as loudly as she could. "Let me in! There's an emergency. Call 911!"

Callie was just about to raise her fist to the door once more when Lexy Dayton threw it open, a disgusted look on her face.

"What's the matter with you?" she hissed.

"I need help. There's somebody out there, in the water," Callie heard herself wail, her voice taking on a note of hysteria. Images of Natalie were flashing in front of her eyes. Horrifyingly, those images were alternating with images of Drew Staven, a colleague and new boyfriend whom she'd found murdered in his home earlier that year. Again, she felt a wave of dizziness sweep over her and she grasped the doorjamb.

"Oh my God," Lexy said, her face blanching. "What? Are you serious?" Her voice grew shrill.

"Natalie Underwood is in the water," Callie repeated, her voice rasping hoarsely. She was still shivering uncontrollably. The warm smell of cooked food, which had made her hungry less than an hour ago, now threatened to turn her stomach. She started to push past Lexy into the inn, but finally Lexy seemed to gather her wits.

"Callie, you're white as a ghost," Lexy was saying. "Get in here before you freeze to death, pass out or both." She took Callie's arm and practically pulled her up the steps. "Sit down," Lexy said, leading Callie over to one of the soft-cushioned chairs that lined the room and guided her into it. Callie shook her head. They had to get moving. But as soon as she was seated, her legs seemed to turn to rubber. Lexy leaned forward, her hair swishing. She smelled like floral perfume.

Eyes still blinking back tears, Callie stammered out an explanation, her voice sounding odd to her own ears. "Bix is out there with her – but please. We need to get help. Now."

"What's going on?" asked a grating voice. Callie looked up to see Mrs. Dayton looming over the two of them, her eyes narrowed. She tapped her foot impatiently.

"Mom..." began Lexy, glancing at Callie who was taking deep breaths and struggling to stand up. Someone had to call 911 and these two didn't look they were going to do that anytime soon.

Callie tried again. "Natalie Underwood is out there in the water. Floating out there, in fact. I think she's dead. We have to call 911," she said loudly.

"Somebody's dead in the water?" Mrs. Dayton's modulated newscaster voice had risen to a shriek.

That did it. The guests seemed to go silent for one brief second, but then the hubbub of voices became overwhelming. Callie used the moment to escape from the clutches of Lexy and Mrs. Dayton. All she could think of was getting help for Natalie, though it looked too late for that.

Callie pushed her way past Lexy and into the dining room where bedlam was quickly ensuing. Dressed in their Christmas and bridal shower best, guests clamored to the windows, some of them emitting high-pitched screams to match Mrs. Dayton's wails. Callie rushed to get another glimpse of the scene. Bix had Natalie lying flat on the patio now. It looked like he was pumping her chest in attempts at CPR, but Callie had seen her. Natalie was surely gone.

"Where's Melody Cartwright?" Callie asked each person as she ran past them looking for the concierge. Most of the women simply stared at her with stricken expressions, so Callie finally stopped rushing back and forth and started fumbling for her cell phone.

Suddenly, out of the mass of people emerged Nick Hawkins, groom-to-be. He walked purposefully towards Callie and took her arm.

"I saw her go that way. Come on, let's go find her. I'm coming with you," he added. Callie nodded and they ran to the hotel lobby, Nick already dialing 911 on his cell phone.

"The police and an ambulance are on the way," Nick said, once he'd ended the call. "They wanted me to stay on the line, but what could I tell them? We need to find Melody anyway."

"I've got a friend on the force. I'm calling him now." Callie realized she should have called Sands immediately, as soon as she found Natalie. She realized that she wasn't thinking clearly at all – she must be in shock. *Who could blame me?* Callie thought. Finding two bodies in such a short time was discombobulating at best, completely sinister at worst. Callie wondered if she was just unlucky or if the two separate deaths had something to do with her. *But why?* She started to shiver in the warm, noisy room.

Callie pulled herself together enough to tap Sands' number into her cell phone while Nick went in search of hotel staff. There was no answer to her desperate phone call: the pleasant sound of Detective Sands' voice on his voicemail message prompt was her only reply. She left a terse message and rushed to join Nick who was behind the desk with a confused-looking Melody. Callie didn't see Kayla Hall but maybe she was buried in coats.

"Melody, I'm sorry but I have some bad news. It looks like Natalie's dead." Melody stood there, her mouth half-open and started shaking her head from side to side.

"Where were you? Did you see anything?" Callie persisted.

"I was behind the desk. I didn't see ...." Melody faltered and her face turned pure white, her eyelids fluttering.

"Nick, I think she's going to faint. Help me out here." Callie knew how Melody felt. Fortunately, Nick caught the concierge before she fell. Together, Callie and Nick gently dragged Melody to a soft chair covered in cabbage-rose patterned fabric where she slumped limply.

"Some bridal shower, huh?" Nick said, his mouth twisting into a grimace. He was about thirty years old, with the broad shoulders and tall stature of a former high school football player. His hair was short, brown and parted on the side. His dark brown eyes blinked as he looked at Callie.

"Are you sure she's dead? It can't be true." He shook his head slowly. "I knew Natalie. I've known her since we were kids. I can't believe this."

"I'm so sorry," Callie whispered. She didn't know what else to say.

Luckily, they had a task at hand – trying to bring Melody back around. Callie dashed to the ladies' room for paper towels soaked in cold water. When she returned, Nick was kneeling next to Melody and fanning her face as she started to awaken.

Callie blotted Melody's face and neck with the wet towel. "Feeling better?" she asked. Melody's face had lost its ghastly whiteness and she was sitting up straighter in her chair. Her face was like a tragedy mask.

"Yes," Melody managed to say. "Is Natalie really dead?"

Nick stared at her, his eyes beginning to well up with tears. He bent his head and swatted angrily at his face.

Callie tried to comfort him by placing a hand on his back. She felt his sobs before she heard them. She glanced at Melody who was sitting with her face in her hands. At least her fainting spell seemed to have passed. Callie didn't know which one of the two she should attend to first. *And I'm not doing so great myself.*

But there was no one else to look after these folks – just Callie. She steadied herself and assessed the situation. Melody was definitely the larger problem, since she'd just fainted, so she started towards her. Before she could reach the concierge, a blur of red and green rushed past Callie and nearly knocked her over.

"There you are, Nick!" Lexy Dayton folded Nick's stocky body into her arms, smiling with relief. "I'm so glad you're all right!" But suddenly, Lexy's eyes narrowed as she registered that her husky fiancé was crying.

Callie appraised the bride-to-be's floral dress, something she hadn't noticed before in her daze after discovering Natalie's body. The A-line dress was printed with what looked like poinsettias. Given the gruesome scene she had just witnessed, the red splotches reminded Callie of blood. *Ugh.*

"Honey, I'm fine. See? Don't cry!" Lexy held Nick's head to her ample bosom and embraced him even more firmly. After a few seconds of being smothered to Lexy's chest, Nick disentangled himself from her grip and wiped again at his eyes, his face taking on a bright red hue.

"I'm glad you're okay, Lexy. It's just...I've known Natalie since forever. This is all a really big shock." Nick took some deep breaths and smiled half-heartedly at his fiancé.

Callie had never actually seen someone's mouth fall open in disbelief, but there was no other way to describe it: Lexy was gaping at Nick like a big-mouthed bass. "You're *crying* over *Natalie Underwood*? I'm sorry she's dead, but – I thought you were worried about *me!*"

Now Lexy resembled a turtle. Her generous mouth closed with a snap and she pressed her lips together, her face turning bright red. She closed her eyes and suddenly the big-mouthed bass returned.

"Mom!" she yelled to Mrs. Dayton, sprinting past Callie, who was shoved rudely into Nick.

Lexy whirled around. "Excuse me, Callie. I didn't mean to bump into you." She glared at her fiancé and, turning on her heel, headed into the direction of the dining room.

"Sorry about that." Nick took a tissue out of his pocket and dabbed his eyes. "Lexy gets very excitable at times."

"It's understandable in this case," Callie said, trying for diplomacy. Lexy was a client of Callie's Kitchen, after all.

"You found Natalie, didn't you?" Nick asked quietly.

"I did find her. Yes."

"Did she..." Nick's face was red and he looked like he was suppressing an overwhelming emotion, either anger or embarrassment. He spoke through his teeth. "Did she appear to have suffered?" His voice wavered on the last word, his teeth still clenched.

Callie shook her head. She didn't know, of course, but she assumed she had, at least somewhat, considering the manner of death. And why did Nick need to ask about *that*, anyway?

Before Callie could find a proper response to this delicate question, she heard purposeful footsteps walking behind her, followed by a familiar and entirely welcome voice.

"You rang?" Detective Sands smiled down at Callie, his hazel eyes crinkled with affection and unfortunately, a tinge of annoyance.

* * *

"Another murder, Ms. Costas," Sands said, his English accent more pronounced, something that occurred when his temper was piqued. The two of them were sitting in a small conference room off the lobby of the inn, the sunny space now the site of police interviews. Sands sat back easily, his long leg crossed over his knee. He wore one of his rumpled suits but his errant lock of light brown hair for once was lying flat. Sands' handsomely weathered face was gazing kindly at Callie, so whatever was angering him, she assumed it was not her.

"It does look that way. Unfortunately." Callie wiped her eyes again and sniffled. She needed a tissue. Looking up, she was heartened by Sands, who wordlessly handed her a handkerchief from his pocket. She almost smiled; who carried handkerchiefs anymore?

Callie gulped and continued her tragic tale. "I was speaking to Natalie not half an hour before I found her. This is just unbelievable to me. Where are Lexy Dayton and Nick Hawkins, by the way? They must be devastated. In fact they got into an argument right before you arrived." Fresh tears filled her eyes and she wiped them with Sands' kindly donated handkerchief.

"Now, now, Callie." Sands patted her hand. "You'll be all right. You're safe now. Right? But allow me to ask the questions," Sands said, with another small smile at Callie. "I'm sure the happy couple is fine. We've got everyone in the dining room, waiting to be questioned."

Callie nodded. Fleetingly she thought how funny it was that she called her new beau by his last name, even in her private thoughts. His first name was Ian, a perfectly nice name, but for some reason "Sands" suited him better. After all, that was how she had first gotten to know him, as Detective Sands.

"Right, time to focus," Sands cut into her reverie. "Tell me everything you saw, heard, felt. Let's start at the beginning."

Callie wiped her eyes once more and steadied her voice. She told Sands about her morning, including the fact that Natalie had seemed stressed but overall, perfectly fine. She hesitated. She'd promised not to betray Natalie's thoughts about the Dayton family but at this point, did it matter?

"What is it? You must tell me everything if we're to find out who did this."

"I know. It's just so surreal. Natalie asked me not to betray a confidence, not two hours ago, and now she's dead."

"I understand, but any confidence she relayed to you is null and void at this point," Sands said gently but firmly. "Out with it."

Callie looked him straight in the eye. "Natalie didn't like the Daytons. Or rather, the Daytons didn't like her." She explained the story of Lexy's first doomed bridal shower and Natalie's nerves about dealing with the Dayton's in the same context once more.

Sands just shook his head. "My, my. Well, that does put the Dayton family in an interesting light. Any sign of Mr. Dayton, the bride's father?"

"No, I think he's deceased. I seem to remember reading that in the paper quite a few years ago. The shower was women only, although Nick was in attendance. That's the way a lot of showers are these days – the groom makes an appearance, but usually not any other men."

Sands gazed thoughtfully at her for a moment. "Right. Well, I'm sorry you had to go through this. Again." He was referring to the bizarre way that they had met months before – at the murder scene of Callie's former boyfriend, Drew Staven, a successful bistro owner.

Callie nodded at Sands. Natalie's murder was calling up far too many bad memories of her recent ordeal with Drew. She didn't want to admit that to Sands, but from the look in his eyes and the tone of his voice, she knew that he was aware of her feelings. He often seemed to know what she felt without her having to say it. It was a little bit disconcerting.

Suddenly Sands adopted a business-like tone. "It's time for my next victim, so you're free to go. Can you send in Melody Cartwright?"

He softened his tone with his next question. "I'm sorry but for obvious reasons I have to cancel our date at The Elkhorn tonight." He was referring to their dinner plans later that evening at The Elkhorn Supper Club, a popular spot just outside of Crystal Bay. "The best thing you can do tonight is stay inside, doors locked."

The thought of hiding inside of her home from a killer was simultaneously tempting – and stifling. She waved off his apology. "Please – no need to worry about that. It's been a terrible day." She sighed, a wave of exhaustion making her blink her eyes. "Samantha is probably going to be there. She dates Bix Buckman and his jazz band is playing tonight. I wonder if he'll cancel, especially after what happened today." Samantha, her tough-talking but elegant best friend, was a criminal attorney with a hectic work schedule and sporadic dating life.

"Samantha is dating a musician?" Sands raised one eyebrow.

"No judging, now. You know he's also the groundskeeper here. He's a good guy – tried to give Natalie CPR. Still, not her usual type, I admit." Sam was attractive and smart, but many of the guys she met were minor felons, since she was a criminal attorney.

"What kind of a name is 'Bix'?" Sands asked. "I never did get the chance to find that out when I was questioning him today."

"Bix Beiderbecke was a famous jazz musician. I think Bix's parents are music buffs and they decided to give him a musical name. Sam said he used to get teased about it a fair amount, but I think it suits him." Who was Callie to question a person's name? Her full name was the seldom-heard "Calliope" and most of her Greek relative's lengthy names weren't exactly common in their neck of the woods.

"You see. There is something musical about you after all. You know some music history, at least," Sands said, smiling at Callie. Unlike most people she met, Sands knew that she was named "Calliope" after the Greek muse of music. The irony of it was that she didn't play any instruments and only sang in the shower.

"We can talk more later, but in the meantime, I want you to be careful. I don't like that you were the one to find Natalie. It makes you a potential target until we get this thing cleared up."

"I know," Callie said, standing up. "I may just collapse on the sofa the second I'm able to." Still, part of her wished that Sands could offer her a shoulder to cry on tonight, of all nights, but his job made that scenario an impossible one. *Too bad.* Dismayed at her own selfishness, Callie squashed down that thought. She wasn't the clingy type and she wasn't going to start now.

She patted Sands on the shoulder as she passed him on the way to the door, wanting to give him a kiss but wondering if that was unprofessional since he was officially working. He solved the dilemma by standing up abruptly and giving her a very proper peck on the cheek.

"I'll call you later," he said close to her ear and sat back down, already scribbling notes.

* * *

Melody Cartwright and Kayla Hall were conversing in heated whispers as Callie entered the hallway. The both looked up sharply and stopped talking when they registered her presence.

"Melody, the detective said to send you in next."

Kayla and Melody exchanged a look before Melody entered the room briskly, closing the door with a sharp "click."

"I don't know anything about what happened today," Kayla whined. "I want to go home. I didn't see anything – I was checking coats! Anyway, it's creepy thinking about a dead body at the inn."

"It certainly is creepy," Callie answered, "but the police have to question everyone." She also wanted to go straight home but instead, she had a full day booked at Callie's Kitchen.

Kayla sighed, then pulled a compact out of her purse and looked at herself in the tiny mirror. "At least the detective is kind of cute," she said. "And that accent."

"Yes, isn't he," Callie said wryly. *Oh boy.* She said goodbye to Kayla and headed towards the dining room once more, her curiosity getting the better of her need to go to work and cook. As she reached the hostess stand, her cell phone rang.

"Callie!" boomed the hearty voice of Hugh, her ex-husband.

"Hugh, now is really not a good time." *That was putting it mildly.* "Can I call you back?"

"I guess so." Hugh sounded hurt. "I just wanted to share some news with you."

News? Callie remembered a previous conversation she'd had with Hugh's new wife, Raine, who had disclosed that the happy couple was looking to procreate. Wincing, she braced herself for the inevitable. *Could this day get any worse?*

"Fine, but can you make it quick?" Suddenly, Callie wanted nothing more than to escape.

"Sure, sure. I just wanted you to know that Raine and I are looking for a home in Crystal Bay! We really want to be closer to Olivia."

Callie was well and truly stunned. She'd thought an hour away from Hugh was too close. Now he was moving to Crystal Bay – her own turf?

And then there was this latest murder. *Crystal Bay might not be such a good choice, buddy.* Callie decided it would take too long to explain about the murder to Hugh – he'd find out soon enough – so she asked the next question that came to mind. "What about your job? Raine's job?" she spluttered.

"The commute isn't that bad. Anyway, we're hoping to find jobs closer to Crystal Bay. I've got a few leads already. Raine does too."

"I see." If it were possible, Callie felt even more drained. "I really can't talk right now, I'm sorry." She hung up before he could argue with her.

Callie slowly placed her cell phone back into her purse and shuddered. Thinking of Hugh and Raine in Crystal Bay was too much to take in right now.

Taking a moment to collect herself, Callie scanned the dining room curiously. Most of the guests were seated at their appointed tables, eating lunch and talking. Practicality wins, Callie thought. Probably, the Daytons had decided to serve the food as long as they had already paid for it. In any case, it would take hours to question everyone so perhaps the police decided to at least let them fill their bellies. A couple of uniformed police officers held watch, making sure, no doubt, that every guest stayed until they had given a statement.

The food smelled tantalizing but the stunning view provided by the floor-to-ceiling windows had taken on a sinister air with the recent removal of Natalie Underwood's body from the icy water. Despite their earlier obnoxious behavior, Callie's heart went out to the Dayton family. Two disastrous bridal showers weren't something she would wish on anyone.

She felt badly for Nick Hawkins, too, who was seated glumly at a table in the center of the room with Mrs. Dayton and Lexy. The two women spooned what looked like the inn's signature French onion soup into their mouths, but Nick only sat there, his back to the window, staring into space. Outside the window, Callie could see a bundled-up Bix Buckman standing in the falling snow and waving his arms toward the water's edge, most likely explaining his intervention to the small group of law enforcement officers assembled around the crime scene.

The sound of someone clearing their throat startled Callie.

"I'm sorry. Callie, isn't it? I can't find Melody Cartwright or Natalie Underwood. Do you know where they are?" The man smiled as he spoke so rapidly, revealing perfect, white, even teeth.

Callie took in the man's dapper appearance with a puzzled look before his identity dawned. Jack Myers, one of the main suppliers for The English Country Inn.

"I'm so sorry, I'm a little flustered," Callie stammered. "I didn't recognize you at first." Jack was normally dressed in the Crystal Bay winter uniform: heavy puffer jacket, pants and sturdy boots. Today, he had on a sleek sports coat and dress pants with a white shirt – no tie, of course, being Jack, who was more likely to be chopping wood and ice fishing than "dolling up" as Grandma Viv, Callie's Irish maternal grandmother, would say.

"The room looks beautiful, but why does everyone seem so, I don't know, subdued? The groom didn't run out this time, did he?" Jack cleared his throat and attempted to stifle a small smirk. Clearly he was aware of the Dayton's previous bridal shower troubles.

"Wait a minute," Jack said, peering closely at Callie's face. His large, dark eyes widened. "You're eyes are all red and puffy. Have you been crying? Or is it just allergies to evergreens and holly?"

"You must not have heard about Natalie," Callie said, stifling a groan. Apparently, she was going to be the one to break the news to Jack that his colleague had been murdered.

"Heard what? And what are all these police doing around here?"

"Natalie Underwood is dead. I'm sorry to tell you this, but it looks like she was murdered."

Jack blanched. "Murdered?"

"I'm so sorry," Callie said gently. "The police are here right now and all of these guests are waiting to be questioned."

"How horrible," Jack murmured, clearly trying to regain his composure. "Natalie is...was.... What I mean to say, it was a pleasure to work with her." Callie nodded, thinking of a way out. She didn't want to be rude to another mourner, but she had to get to work.

"Jack, Melody is talking to a police officer. Why don't you wait in the lobby for her? Hopefully, she won't be long."

"Thank you. What a rotten situation. I'm sorry to intrude." Jack looked around the dining room. "I'd better check with the staff first and see if there's anything I can do to help."

"That's a nice idea. I'd offer to join you, but I have to get going." Callie said goodbye to a pale and shaken Jack and retreated through the back doors of the dining room. She hesitated, and then headed back out to the patio once more. She couldn't help but glance at the spot where she'd found Natalie. Police and crime scene officers were still swarming the patio but Bix Buckman was gone.

A policeman near the back door walked up to Callie as she stood there, contemplating what had been a tranquil winter scene just a few hours before. "No one is allowed out here," he informed her. "If you're a guest, you need to be questioned before you can leave."

"It's all right, I've already been questioned. You can check with Detective Sands. I'm Callie Costas. He told me I could go."

"Okay, then. I'd do what he said. Now."

"You bet," Callie muttered under her breath. It was going to be a long time before she could enjoy the beauty of the water without thinking of Natalie's fate.

Three

The snow came down thickly as Callie maneuvered her small car back to Garden Street and Callie's Kitchen. The alley behind her shop was as yet unplowed, so Callie carefully drove through the slippery coating of fluffy snow until she found a parking space. She was not looking forward to sharing the news of yet another murder with her employee Max, she thought as she locked the car. She flipped up the hood of her coat against the swirling white flakes and strode quickly to the back entrance, hoping to avoid any inquisitive customers who no doubt, already had their cell phones buzzing with Crystal Bay's latest tragedy.

Stepping inside her shop, which felt positively steamy after the being out in the freezing air, Callie stomped snow off of her heavy duck boots, hung up her coat and washed her hands. The clean white walls and sparkling stainless steel workspace were a balm to her spirit after her frightening brush with death. The sweet scents of cinnamon, sugar and ginger permeated the air: Max must be baking the gingerbread cakes she'd prepped before leaving for the inn. This spicy essence of the Christmas season lifted Callie's spirits just a tiny bit above dismal. The ugliness and shock of Natalie's icy death had chilled her from head to toe.

She heard Max's voice through the half-door that separated her workspace from the main customer space. It sounded like a normal business transaction and Callie let out a sigh of relief. If it had been a reporter, Max would have put on his not entirely unwelcome pit bull act. Max, her twenty-something assistant with a spiky haircut and an array of colorful tattoos, was an excellent worker, but he was proud of his muscles and he didn't mind using them. Or, at least, threatening to use them. Still, he was no loose cannon, just protective.

Callie had begun peeling potatoes and slicing lemons for a Greek chicken dish, when Max banged noisily through the door, carrying several large stainless steel trays used to display baked goods.

"Oh, great, you're back. Business is picking up again," he asserted. "I think our new Facebook page and website are really helping get the word out. These trays were full of *loukoumades* this morning. Check it out: empty!" He held up the trays for Callie's inspection before setting them down in the industrial-sized sink, where they made a terrific clatter. He turned on the hot water faucet full blast. "This cold weather has been great for us. People are stuffing their faces more than ever!"

"I hope so," Callie answered, pleased that her Greek doughnuts were still a crowd pleaser. "Piper did a terrific job with the social networking and web site. I'm so happy you connected us."

Max blushed a little as he heard his girlfriend praised by his employer. "Yeah, she's something else, isn't she?"

"She is indeed," was Callie's reply. Piper was Max's girlfriend. She was a bit quirky – for example, she dressed in vintage attire whenever she could – but she was a whiz on the computers. She also had a nice touch in the front of the house where she pitched in serving and ringing up customers. Callie enjoyed the young woman's intelligence and willingness to work free for college credit, but she could be a bit flighty and intrusive, truth be told.

Max added soap and scrubbed vigorously at the empty trays. "Hey, how did it go this morning? Should have been a piece of cake – sorry, cookies," Max laughed at his own joke.

"Things didn't go exactly as planned," Callie replied. *No kidding.* In her mind's eye, Natalie's lifeless face was once more gazing up at her. Callie started shivering so hard that she dropped her knife right in the middle of prepping potatoes.

"Oh, no. What is it?" In an instant, Max was by her side. "What happened?" His brow was furrowed, eyebrow ring and all and he looked at her with friendly concern. Not for the first time, Callie was thankful to have such a kind co-worker.

Callie hesitated before looking Max straight in the eye. "You're not going to believe this, so I'm just going to come right out and tell you. There was a murder at The English Country Inn this morning."

"No. Not again. You're kidding, right? Playing a practical joke? Well, it's not funny." Max slowly went back to the large pans he'd been washing and started running water again.

"Natalie Underwood was killed," Callie said gently. "And it gets even worse. I was the one who found her."

"*What?*" Max dropped the pans into the hot, soapy water, saturating the front of his blue Callie's Kitchen apron. He whirled to face Callie. "No! Not Natalie!!" Max slapped a dishtowel against the counter and Callie saw tears in his eyes. "Natalie was a good kid. She had the prettiest red hair. Everybody teased her about it, but she didn't mind." He gave a shuddering breath and stopped speaking as he blinked back tears.

"Yes, it was beautiful," Callie said slowly, remembering Nick Hawkins' similarly stricken reaction to Natalie's death. Natalie, it would appear, had been something of a heartbreaker.

Max was shaking his head now. "This is just...really terrible news. Natalie was a few years ahead of me in school, but I remember her well. She was always just really nice and funny. Everybody knew her, because of her hair."

Callie nodded, remembering how Natalie's tresses had appeared in the water, the back of her head a mess of blood. Better not mention that to Max.

"I'm sorry Max. I liked her a lot too. It hasn't really hit me yet, to be honest. We had a nice chat this morning and then..." Callie trailed off. Then she remembered what Sands always said – don't discuss the case. "Uh, Max this is kind of awkward, but can you please not repeat any part of this conversation with anyone? Even Piper?"

"You don't like her, do you?" Max asked, grief perhaps making him more blunt than usual.

"It's not that at all. It's just that ... Ian... always says that you can hurt an investigation by revealing too much about it. I shouldn't have said anything." She'd been about to say "Sands," but that sounded so formal when speaking of him to others. "I'm sorry. I guess I'm just upset."

"Sure thing. I understand. Really." Max took up his dishwashing again, soberly this time.

"Hey, aren't you learning a lot about *detective work*, these days?" Max sounded sarcastic. "For all the good it's doing us. I can't believe it," he said, shaking his head back and forth. "Another murder. I really just can't believe it."

Callie went over to him where he stood at the sink, hanging his head. She patted him on the shoulder. "Max, I'm truly sorry that I had to be the one to tell you about Natalie. Just forget about the dishwashing for right now. We'll get to it later."

Max nodded somberly, wiped his face with a paper napkin and washed his hands, silently. Taking a deep breath, he headed back to the front of the shop to serve customers while Callie worked on her chicken and potato dish. She was pretty sure she'd seen him wipe another tear out of his eyes. She hadn't realized that Max would have taken the news so hard and she vowed to be patient with him over the next few days.

The tinkling of the bell over the front door as it opened to admit customers was a cheery, welcome sound, even on this terrible day. Callie remembered a recent lack of clientele that threatened to close her business after she'd been a suspect in Drew's death.

Being a murder suspect killed the public's appetite for your food, she had learned. Now that she had been exonerated, business wasn't

100% back to normal, but it was on a better track. Would finding another murder victim repel customers once again?

Callie shuddered and got back to work but her arm froze in the middle of slicing a fragrant, juicy lemon when she heard the unmistakable voice of her father, George, deep and raspy. After being in the U.S. for so many years, his English was nearly perfect but his accent remained strong.

"I've got a big surprise for my daughter," he was saying to Max. "Where is she?"

"In the back room," Max replied woodenly. Poor Max. Callie felt her hackles rise. Experience had taught her to wonder what George had up his sleeve whenever he dropped by on one of his "surprise" visits. Her father, unfortunately, had never warmed to Sands the way she had hoped, so she was apprehensive that he was planning to introduce her to yet another Greek or even part-Greek bachelor looking for a wife. George seemed to have an endless supply that he found through his connections at his diner, The Olympia, despite the fact that the Greek population of Crystal Bay was small. Callie wondered sometimes if he'd taken out personal ads.

Take the bull by the horns. Callie set down her knife. There was no way she was dealing with this right now. In fact, the full, ghoulish impact of Natalie's murder was starting to hit her. She would simply tell the nice bachelor that it was lovely to meet him but she couldn't chat during working hours. *Especially today.*

Squaring her shoulders, she walked into the front of the shop with a determined step. But instead of an awkward-looking guy in his mid-forties, a pretty, petite and slightly round lady in her sixties smiled back at Callie, her smile as warm and sweet as one of the confections on display in her bakery cases.

"Calliope! *Hrisi mou!*" George frequently used this affectionate term when speaking to his daughter. It translated roughly to "my dear."

"Look who I've brought to see you! It's my cousin, Glykeria, all the way from Greece! She's come to spend Christmas with us. I didn't want to tell you before – are you surprised? She just made it – snowstorms are cancelling the other flights." George's brown eyes crinkled at the corners, his smile wide enough to split his face.

"*Thea!*" Callie called running to her father's cousin for a warm hug. "Thea" was the Greek term for "aunt." Even though Glykeria was George's cousin, it was Greek custom to refer to your elder female relatives or even close friends as "aunt" and that's how Callie had always regarded her.

"*Yassou*, my dear," Glykeria said, grabbing Callie in a fierce embrace. Finally, she stopped squeezing and stood back for an appraising look. "You are beauty! I know this happen one day."

Callie blushed, remembering her last trip to Greece, at probably age 13, when she was experiencing an extremely awkward stage. It had been shortly after the death of her mother and the trip was intended to surround her with family and take her mind off of her troubles. Of course, it hadn't really worked, but Glykeria, which translated roughly in English as "Sweetie," had been especially kind to Callie. However, she hadn't ever been one to mince words.

"Thank you, Glykeria," Callie said, unoffended.

"Call me Sweetie," the older woman said, brushing back her thick, dark auburn hair, probably dyed, but it was very becoming to her. "Glykeria too hard for you to say, I remember."

Callie laughed. "I was only 13. I can say Glykeria now."

"Eh. Call me Sweetie anyway. Like you used to."

That settled, Callie asked the group if they'd like some Greek yogurt coffee cake and a cup of coffee.

"I always eat cake," Sweetie said, gesturing at her round figure. "You no need to ask next time." Callie laughed, remembering how she was constantly being offered food in Greece and to reject it was taken as an insult.

Max and Callie went to the back room to get the goodies while George and Sweetie found a table near the window. Their loud conversation in Greek, punctured by laughter, filled the shop.

"I don't think this is the right time to tell them about Natalie," Callie said quietly to Max. "They're so happy right now and they'll only worry. My dad will find out soon enough. Sweetie doesn't really even need to know."

Max gave her a sidelong glance. "I won't say a word." Max's normally spirited face was completely glum, his movements slow. Callie wondered if she should tell him to go home. There was so much work to do – she really couldn't. Well, maybe he could leave early.

The coffee break and family time were a nice respite for Callie, despite her internal turmoil. She was impressed that she was able to get through it without breathing a word about Natalie Underwood.

Soon, though, worry about the snowy roads prompted George to get his cousin back to his house where she would be staying for the next few weeks. Enthusiastic goodbyes and promises to see each other took up the next several minutes. By the time George and Sweetie were safely out the door, people looking for their ready-made dinners were starting to show up, despite the weather. Callie found that being snowbound made people hungry, and fighting through the storms drained them of energy for cooking at home – which was fortunate for her business. She glanced gratefully at Max, who was doing his best to appear friendly and cheerful.

As Callie and Max served customers and alternately checked on their baking and cooking in their backroom workspace, Callie's work phone rang. She hoped it was Sands, checking in, but her heart sank a little bit when she saw the Caller ID: Emma Cayden, owner of The English Country Inn. How was she going to console her friend?

"Emma, I take it you heard the terrible news," Callie said. "I am just so sorry. Natalie was a great person. It's tragic." She and Emma had been friends ever since the inception of Callie's Kitchen and had met through the Crystal Bay Chamber of Commerce.

"Yes, I heard all right. This has been a *nightmare*. Natalie was always a great asset to my team. She was really just a lovely person." Emma's voice broke on the last word and she was quiet a moment. "I don't remember if I told you, but I'm in Arizona right now. It was supposed to be a quick business trip but it doesn't look like that's what it's going to end up being." Emma sighed. "My flight was cancelled due to weather. Huge snowstorms across the country are making a mess of the airlines. Anyway, I've got a favor to ask you." Emma's voice crackled over the line.

"Yes, my aunt just arrived from Greece and apparently, she just made it ahead of the snow. What can I help you with, Emma?" Callie had a sinking feeling she wasn't going to like whatever it was.

"I'm devastated about Natalie, so don't take this the wrong way, but...well." Emma hesitated. "A scandal like this could destroy my business. You know exactly how *that* feels, right?" *Did she ever.* A business in jeopardy was a problem she could definitely relate to.

"I understand wanting to protect a business," Callie said. "But what would you like me to do? Shouldn't we let the police figure this one out?"

Emma sighed gustily. "I heard that you were the one who found Natalie."

"Yes, I was. Who told you?" Callie blinked, her mind wrenched back to the tragic scene of the crime. She gulped, not wanting to see the images that kept flickering into her brain.

"I can't remember who told me. Sorry. Everything has been so chaotic and I've been on about a hundred calls today. The thing is, until I get home, I need someone to be my eyes and ears at the inn. After what's happened, I'm not sure who I can trust. Can you do some digging on your own, ask around and just, I don't know, keep your ear to the ground? Please, I know I can trust you and I'm scared."

Emma's voice was tearful as she continued. "I don't want you to be in any danger. I would just really appreciate it if you would let me know about any new developments without letting anyone at work know that you're keeping tabs on them."

Awkward, as Callie's 10-year-old daughter Olivia would have said. Callie knew that Sands wouldn't want her involved, but Emma was an old friend and fellow business owner. It wouldn't be *that* difficult to just check in on things from time to time. She'd just have to watch her back – it was hugely unsettling to know that another Crystal Bay resident had been murdered. However, in this case, she couldn't say no to Emma. Callie of all people knew what was at stake for her friend.

"Of course I'll help you if I can. But remember, if I found out anything of significance, I have to share it with the police. That's my one condition."

"You mean, share it with your cute detective boyfriend?" Emma said wryly. "That's fine, just so long as you'll help me out."

"I will," Callie said, realizing that perhaps she agreed too soon. How was she going to explain her presence in and around The English Country Inn? Well, she'd just have to think of something.

The two said goodbye, one of them relieved, one of them stressed. Emma was a good and loyal friend, but Callie had that familiar feeling that she was about to get in way over her head.

Four

Several hours later, despite the fact that she'd felt the urge to curl up in the fetal position on the couch with her Yorkie, Koukla, Callie was seated in a cozy booth with her best friend Samantha. Samantha had insisted on taking Callie to The Elkhorn, a traditional Wisconsin supper club. Sam had been adamant about not letting her friend brood at home. She had also promised not to talk about the murder – unless Callie wanted her to.

After a lot of protesting and despite Sands' earlier warnings to "be careful," Callie had finally given in. Viv was entertaining her 10-year-old daughter, Olivia, and Callie felt that a little time with her friend might just make her feel human again.

Anyway, eating at The Elkhorn was practically the definition of "soul-soothing." Locals and tourists flocked to the supper club's friendly confines not only the delicious food, but for the spacious, wood-paneled dining room, set off by an enormous stone fireplace that went right up to the ceiling.

The Elkhorn was known for not only its tasty food and cocktails, but also for its festive and over-the-top seasonal décor. At Christmastime, Gary Schnittger and his wife, Doris, went all out. Two Christmas trees flanked the fireplace, along with numerous Santas, sleds, elves, nativity scenes and blinking lights. To the left of the fireplace, a small bandstand featured local musicians. The lobby separated the dining room from the barroom which featured a large, half-moon shaped bar, red leather seats and small booths. The wait staff wore Santa hats and overall, the dining room had the feeling of being at a Christmas party in somebody's home.

In such a festive setting, the tragic events at The English Country Inn softened a bit in Callie's mind, almost as if she were looking at a blurry photograph. Everything did seem a little bit off, however. Callie felt herself glancing around the dining room at The Elkhorn's patrons as they ate, drank and chatted. Could one of them be a killer? Would one of them be a victim? *Would she?*

Suddenly Callie felt very dizzy. She tried to bring herself back into the present by asking Sam how Bix was coping with playing a jazz gig after trying to revive Natalie. Sam had said that he was upset, but he couldn't cancel on The Elkhorn. Well, Callie certainly understood that. He probably needed the money.

Taking a sip of water, she breathed slowly and deeply and tried to calm herself. It wouldn't pay to fall apart. She felt the need to remain alert.

As the jazz trio headed by Bix Buckman played a soft tune, Callie felt her body relax just a little. Samantha had insisted on springing for steaks and potatoes and Callie was hoping the comfort food would help her forget her nightmarish experience earlier that day. She'd barely eaten anything all day after the shock of finding Natalie and to her surprise, she discovered that she was hungry – ravenous, in fact. Comfort food had its charms and there was no better place to indulge than The Elkhorn.

"I wonder if I should go up there and say hi?" Samantha said, nodding at Bix onstage. Sam was dressed in a fuzzy light blue cowl neck sweater, slim-fitting jeans and boots. As usual, her makeup was soft and perfectly applied, and her shoulder-length layered hair was attractively tousled. Her friend always looked well put-together, but Callie suspected she'd made an extra effort for Bix.

Callie appraised Bix's well-toned physique and chiseled features as he stood onstage. He'd been fairly calm and collected at the crime scene, something she'd appreciated at the time. For example, he hadn't hesitated to attempt CPR on Natalie.

SPICED AND ICED | 37

Just thinking about Natalie's lifeless form again made Callie shudder in the warm room. *Poor Natalie.* For the hundredth time she wondered if it had been a mistake to come out tonight. Suddenly, she longed to join George, Sweetie and Olivia at home, her Yorkie Koukla sitting warmly by her side. Sighing, she turned to Sam so that she could respond to her question.

Sam looked into her face. "Callie, are you all right?"

"Yes, I'll be fine. And of course you should go say hello to Bix. He's had a tough day, just like I have, so I'm sure he'd like to see a friendly face. Anyway, didn't you tell him that you'd be here?"

"I may have mentioned it." To Callie's surprise, Samantha had lost some of her usual poise and her cheeks were flushed.

"Wow, you've got it bad, don't you?" Callie asked, jolted out of her own apathy. Calm, cool Sam sure wasn't acting like herself.

"I don't know," Sam said. "We've gone out maybe three times. I just don't want him to think I'm following him around. I'm only here because Sands had to ditch you tonight and I didn't want you to be sitting around thinking about everything after what you've been through today." She nudged Callie good-naturedly.

"He didn't exactly 'ditch' me, "Callie knew Samantha didn't mean any harm but the words stung nonetheless. "He had to work a murder case, remember?"

"I'm sorry. I didn't mean for it to come out that way," Sam said, dunking a piece of celery from the classic "relish tray" into its homemade cheddar cheese spread. "Maybe I shouldn't have dragged you here tonight. Do you want to talk about Natalie?"

Callie swiftly shook her head "no."

Sam patted Callie on the arm and smiled at her friend. "I understand. Listen, I do think that Sands is a good guy. It's just – I know the long hours that guys like him are forced to work. I don't want to see you get hurt." She took a sip of her old-fashioned – a supper club signature cocktail. Like many other Wisconsin supper clubs, The

Elkhorn's "old-fashioned" cocktail was made with sweet and warming brandy, rather than bourbon or whiskey.

Callie felt her hackles rising. Why was she feeling so defensive about this? She willed herself to calm down. It wasn't like Sam to be so discouraging. There was also the possibility that the day's events had made her hypersensitive. Well, who could blame her?

Callie took a cracker from the bread basket, smeared the rich, luscious cheese spread on it and popped it into her mouth, in lieu of responding right away.

"I won't get hurt," she finally said after another cracker or two. "We don't have anything serious – yet. And anyway, I work long hours too, so maybe it's a match made in heaven." As she spoke, she realized that her tone was sharper than she had intended.

"Oh, just listen to me after the day you've had! I'm sorry," Sam said again and reached out to grab Callie's hand. "I know how much you like him. It's me. I'm probably projecting onto you. Bix isn't exactly the type of guy I usually go out with. I guess I'm the one who's afraid I'll get hurt." Sam sighed.

Callie smiled at her friend. "What's the harm in liking someone? Just say hello to the guy and then let's order something caloric for dessert."

"You're right." Sam stood up and smoothed her sweater. "Order us anything you want – just so long as it's chocolate. And why don't you order a grasshopper? I know they're your favorite." Grasshopper cocktails were another Wisconsin supper club specialty, a delicious relic from the 1960s. The Elkhorn's version was rich and tasty. With a blend of chocolate and mint liqueurs, it was practically a dessert in itself.

"Deal," said Callie. She didn't need to see the "dessert trolley" to make her decision – she'd eaten at The Elkhorn dozens of times. Callie watched as her gorgeous friend walked to the stage and got Bix's attention, bemused to see her so smitten.

Bix's face lit up like one of The Elkhorn's multiple Christmas trees when Sam approached him. He leapt off of the stage and gave her a huge bear hug in full view of the supper club patrons. Callie stared at him. His distraught behavior over Natalie's body seemed to have evaporated. It could also be that he was trying to put a good face on things – the show must go on and all of that. Callie didn't know why she was making excuses for the guy. Everyone grieved in different ways.

Not wanting to seem overly interested in Sam and Bix's romantic moment, Callie signaled the waitress. She glanced again at Sam and Bix, who were chattering away, their conversation punctuated by intimate laughter. Finally, Bix gave Sam another wordless, close embrace and hopped back onstage to tweak the speakers and microphone.

Dessert arrived just as Sam was sliding back into the booth, a private smile on her lips. Callie grinned back at her. "I guess he was happy to see you," she said, gesturing at homemade chocolate lava cake. "Time for chocolate." The two friends grabbed their forks and dug into the piece of cake at the same time. Dark chocolate oozed out of the center of the cake and Callie made sure to scoop out some of the sauce.

"I don't mean to act like such a teenager," Sam said, blushing a bit. "Especially today. I'm sorry."

"Don't worry about it," Callie answered. But inwardly, she was a bit taken aback. Sam was normally the very picture of poise and she certainly didn't equate romantic success with personal success.

Sam was trying to take Callie's mind off of things, so that could be why she was focusing on "girl talk." Callie sighed and snuck another glance at Bix. She hoped he was good for her friend – she realized she didn't really know much about him.

The topic of Sam's dating life was interrupted as the man himself addressed the audience. "Welcome to The Elkhorn," Bix said in his mellifluous voice. "I'm Bix Buckman and we're 'The Tundras.'" With that, the band began to play a jazzy rendition of "Winter Wonderland."

"Great band name," Callie said to Sam, raising her voice to be heard over the music. "As in 'frozen tundra?'"

"I guess so," Sam said, shrugging. "It certainly fits Crystal Bay, in any case. We're living in frozen tundra for about 300 days of the year."

Callie looked around the warm room. Unless it was a true blizzard, snow, even heavy snow, didn't deter most Wisconsinites from venturing out into the world. You simply bundled up, scraped off your car or truck and got on with your life.

Tonight, The Elkhorn was packed, its cloth-covered tables filled with people of all ages sipping old-fashioneds, martinis and other classic cocktails, eating from the small but stellar menu and listening to the music. No doubt about it, Bix's band was a hit. Either that, Callie thought, or the locals had discovered that Bix had tried to resuscitate Natalie today and they were hoping for gossip. Probably a little bit of both.

Or it could be that they were afraid, as she was, and following the herd instinct – safety in numbers. Callie could identify. She didn't relish the thought of being home alone later that night with just her daughter and a dog – and a killer on the loose. The Elkhorn patrons may be attempting to keep calm and carry on, just as she was, but Callie had noticed an unusual number of whispered conversations and anxious glances around the room.

The band played a few more numbers and Callie sipped at her Grasshopper, the crowd continuing its quiet buzz as people contemplated their food and the music. Finally, the set ended with a flourish and Bix told the crowd that the band was taking a break.

Sam and Callie were still taking tiny bites of their chocolate lava cake, trying not to take more of their fair share. *Next time, I'll get a piece for each of us,* Callie thought. *Life is too short to share chocolate lava cake.* That was a lesson she was learning well these days. The dessert was served with a small scoop of creamy vanilla gelato on the side, in a pool of rich raspberry sauce and it looked beautiful on the plate, almost too pretty to eat. The Elkhorn prided themselves on homemade desserts and this cake was one of the reasons why.

"What do you think?" Sam asked Callie.

"Of the cake or of Bix?" Callie asked. "I'm just kidding. The cake is excellent – as was the rest of the meal. Thanks for going out with me tonight. I didn't think it was possible to have a good time after what happened today but I'm starting to feel a little better. And yes, Bix and his group were pretty good, too." Callie took another sip of her Grasshopper.

Just then, the sound of breaking glass made the two of them jump. "What the...." Sam began but was interrupted by raised voices near the bar.

"Don't mess with me!" The voice was deep, angry, familiar – and loud. "Just give me the money you owe me!"

Another crash made the dining room go silent, and Sam stood up to get a better look. Whatever she saw made her gasp. Nodding at Callie, she headed quickly towards the commotion without a word. Callie had no choice but to follow.

Callie trailed Sam into the Elkhorn's bar and did a quick scan of the familiar room. Two bar stools lay overturned and a sticky brown liquid dripped slowly onto the floor. Ice cubes and glass shards decorated both the bar top and floor with a dangerous mixture.

Bix and Gary Schnittger, Elkhorn owner, stood toe-to-toe in front of the bar, their fists clenched. Gary was a tall man with greying hair and powerful muscles, despite being much older than the equally fit Bix. Bar patrons stood well out of the way. Callie tugged at Sam's sleeve but her friend was glued to the scene.

"What do you say we calm down, gentlemen?" Wait, was that....??
No, it couldn't be. A stocky older man had stepped forward to address Gary and Bix. His Greek accent and the mulish expression on
his face were all too familiar. Callie nearly groaned aloud. *What was
George doing here?* And worse yet, why was he getting in the middle
of an ugly fight?

"Dad," she said urgently, but either he didn't hear or he was ignor-
ing her.

"No need to go upsetting everyone," George continued to address
the two men, folding his arms in front of his chest.

Callie assessed the damage. So far, it looked like the only violence
that had occurred was the overturned chairs and broken glasses of
whiskey. Neither Bix nor the bar owner had a black eye or bloody lip
– yet. She wanted to keep it that way. What was George thinking?

Callie grabbed Sam's arm once more. "What should we do?" she
asked, but before Sam could speak, the men jumped back into their
heated conversation.

"Stay out of it," Gary warned George and Bix grunted in agreement.

"You've got nothing to do with this, buddy, so take a walk." Bix
barely glanced at George, as if he were of no importance. Callie knew
from experience how well *that* would go over with her proud and
stubborn father.

"Gentlemen, stop this nonsense. Why not sit down, have a drink?
No fighting with ladies present, please." George nodded at a tall, silvery blonde-haired woman who was standing just behind him and
Callie squinted at her. Who was that? Callie couldn't place the attractive woman, but she and George looked well-acquainted.

Bix glanced over at Sam who he had just noticed standing nearby.
He appeared to be trying to reign in his anger but then his face slowly began growing red again. "You know what? This is a money dis-

pute and I can't let it go. This *gentleman,* as you call him," Bix sneered, "owes me for our gig tonight and won't pay me!"

"You owe *me* money!" Gary contradicted Bix. The two men advanced ever so slightly toward each other and to her horror, George stepped quickly between them.

"All right boys, enough. You go now. Yes?" He nodded at Bix and then looked around at the assembled crowd. "Before someone calls the police."

Bix cursed under his breath and took a step back from his adversary. "I'm not going to jail for this scum." He looked at George with disgust. "I guess you don't care if people don't get paid."

"I do care. I also care if people get hurt." George stared down the two men who looked at each other and then back at George. Finally, Gary clapped George on the shoulder.

"You're right, George," he said. Callie and her family had known Gary and Doris for years – fortunately. *Or else, George might have found himself in the snow next to Bix.*

Bix's face remained beet red but he seemed to be calming down. "You haven't heard the last from me – or my lawyer," he offered as a parting shot.

Gary only shrugged. "Whatever, Bix. Bring it on," he said in a low but challenging tone.

"All right. Enough. Good night. *Kalinihta,*" George used the Greek version of "good night" for emphasis as he pointed to the door. Shaking his head, Bix reluctantly started walking towards it, grabbing his coat and instruments from a nearby booth before stalking outside.

Callie and Samantha looked at each other. "What was that all about?" Callie asked.

Samantha seemed shaken as she stared at the door Bix had just exited. "I don't know. But I'm going to find out. I'll be back in a minute." Not bothering to grab her coat, she pushed past the crowds around the bar and followed Bix out into the snow.

That little drama having concluded without violence, patrons of The Elkhorn started buzzing almost immediately, but quietly. First a murder, now a fight in the family-friendly supper club?

George still hadn't noticed his daughter and had rejoined the tall silvery blond. *Well, at least he wasn't checking up on her.* Still, what was he doing here? Callie started towards him, intent on finding out.

"Calliope!" George cried, finally noticing his only offspring. Before she knew it, George had taken her to a small, comfortable booth almost near the back corner of the bar. It was no wonder that Callie hadn't spotted him when she first arrived. If not for the fight, her seat in the dining room would have prevented her from seeing him at all.

"I'd like you to meet someone," George was saying. "This is Kathy, Raine's aunt." Raine was the tall, bubbly, blond new wife of Callie's ex-husband.

George was continuing the introductions with enthusiasm. "Kathy is a realtor and she's helping Hugh and Raine find a house in Crystal Bay. Kathy, this is my daughter, Calliope. She was, uh...." Suddenly George seemed to realize the awkwardness of the situation.

"I'm Hugh's ex-wife," Callie said taking Kathy's extended hand. Hugh hadn't been kidding about wanting to move back to Crystal Bay. He obviously hadn't wasted any time looking for a home in the area, despite the fact that most people don't house hunt at Christmas time.

"Pleased to meet you," Kathy replied, her smile too white to be true.

Callie responded with as large a smile as she could, but inwardly she was reeling. Didn't George know how hard it would be to have to face Hugh and Raine every day in town? What was he doing, wining and dining their realtor – and Raine's aunt, at that – at a supper club?

Callie's father didn't seem to be aware of the emotions he was evoking in his daughter. In fact, George didn't seem to be aware of anything beyond staring at 'Kathy' with a goofy look on his face.

"Dad, what happened to Glykeria? Sweetie, I mean?"

"Oh, Sweetie was tired, *hrisi mou*." George used the endearment, which translated to "my dear" all the time, but especially when he was trying to placate his daughter. "Kathy came into The Olympia this afternoon when I was showing Sweetie around and introduced herself to me." George's diner, The Olympia, was his pride and joy and he still harbored dreams that Callie would take it over for him someday. "I recognized her right away, realized she'd been coming there for years." He beamed at Kathy who beamed back.

Oh...kay. "So how did you end up here?" Callie asked, genuinely puzzled.

"We got to talking about properties and soon it was dinnertime. Kathy suggested The Elkhorn and I thought, why not?" George shrugged. "Take a little drive. Live a little. By the way," George said, his voice growing sterner. "Kathy told me about the murder of poor Natalie Underwood. It's been all over the local radio station!" Callie felt fortunate she hadn't heard that report. She gulped.

George continued. "It would have been nice if you'd told me about it yourself – how did you come to find another person dead?"

How indeed? "Just bad luck. And the reason I didn't say anything to you earlier is because I didn't want to upset Sweetie," Callie made a quick excuse, and fortunately, George nodded in agreement.

"Very smart of you, Calliope. Sweetie just got here – no need to frighten her."

Kathy stood by looking uncomfortable and suddenly, Callie was too. The last thing she wanted to do tonight was hobnob with one of Raine's relatives. And she definitely did *not* want to talk about Natalie.

Looking to take her leave, Callie kept her tone upbeat. "I hope you enjoyed your dinner and I'm sorry to interrupt your evening out. I'm going to find Samantha so we can pay up and head home. She was checking up on Bix but he was pretty upset. She didn't even bring her coat with her and it's freezing outside. Below freezing."

"Samantha must be careful," George said firmly, finally tearing his eyes away from Kathy who was standing off to one side, gazing into a small compact fixing her lip gloss. "That Bix seems like an angry man."

"She's been seeing him, Dad. They've had a few dates, that's all."

"Samantha is dating that man?" George shook his head. "You can never be too careful who you let into your life. As you should know." George gazed at his daughter with a mixture of concern and frustration. Was he referring to Sands? To Drew Staven, whom she found murdered just a few months before? To the latest murder she'd stumbled her way into? Or to Hugh, her ex-husband? It was a long list.

Callie exhaled sharply. What about him? Was he letting this 'Kathy' into his life? Was he being careful? She didn't want her father to be lonely, but did he have to become affiliated with someone related to her ex-husband's new wife? Or maybe she was getting ahead of herself. Maybe they were talking real estate and nothing more. Callie didn't know, but she was too exhausted to analyze it at that moment.

Deciding she'd been involved in enough drama for one day, Callie answered her father in measured tones. "No, you can't be too careful, Dad."

Five

Callie was too busy at Callie's Kitchen to snoop at the inn the day after Natalie's death, but the following day, she promised herself she'd be there bright and early for a brief check-in. Sunlight made the snow glisten as Callie powered her car along slippery streets – at least it had stopped snowing, for now.

She tried to keep her mind on safe driving but thoughts of the last couple of days kept intruding. For one thing, what was up with Sam? Their dinner together had ended somewhat strangely, but Sam didn't seem all that concerned about Bix's behavior. Once she'd rejoined Callie inside the warm environs of The Elkhorn, she'd told Callie that Bix had apologized for creating a scene and had simply gone home. Sam seemed to think that was enough to smooth things over, but Callie wasn't so sure.

And Kathy – Raine's aunt? Where did she come from? For years, Callie had encouraged her father to meet women, to get remarried after her mother died. George had always begged off, claiming he was too busy, too involved in taking care of her and ultimately, happy with the way things were. It came as a shock to have this status quo interrupted even a little bit, Callie realized, and she chided herself for being silly.

Callie put those thoughts aside to contemplate the myriad other tasks that awaited her. Because she had promised Emma that she would check on things at the inn, she'd been trying to figure out a way to snoop around without seeming to be doing so. She couldn't very well tell Melody Cartwright, the concierge, and the rest of the staff that Emma, the owner, wanted her to check up on them.

So Callie turned to her secret weapon – food. She had wrapped up some Christmas goodies in festive holiday packaging and planned to tell the staff that she was dropping it off as a show of support for the recent tragedy they'd all suffered at work. It sounded relatively plausible to her. But would they see through it? She was fairly certain that Melody, at least, knew she was friends with the owner.

Finally, Callie saw the inn just ahead, looking like a picture postcard with its snow-covered roof, Christmas wreath on the door and silvery, snow-covered pines flanking the entrance. Callie pulled into an icy parking space and turned off the engine. Her breath frosted the air as she scooped up her Christmas treats and carefully made her way around the icy patches that led to the inn's front door.

Someone – Bix Buckman, probably – had sprinkled salt but Callie took her time. She didn't want another fall on the hard cement like she'd had just a few months earlier, after Drew's murder. Callie looked around nervously, but she was the only one in the parking lot.

"Here we go," she said out loud as she strode into the warm and highly-decorated lobby of the inn, holding her wrapped food treats in front of her chest like a shield.

Soft holiday music played in the lobby and the air still held the green, wintry scent of fresh pine. To all appearances, the hotel was in full Christmas holiday operation mode, murder or no murder.

Melody Cartwright, wearing a conservative but fashionably snug red knit dress, looked up with surprise as Callie came up to the reception desk. She smiled, but Callie got the impression that it was automatic. Behind her large but surprisingly becoming glasses, the eyes that looked back at Callie seemed a bit wary. Callie had the odd thought that the glasses and the red dress made Melody look a little bit like the cliché of the "sexy librarian."

"Why, hello, Callie. I wasn't expecting you today," Melody said with a small smile. "Shouldn't you be at work?"

Not exactly a warm greeting, but Callie ignored it and pasted a cheery look on her face.

"Oh, yes, of course. I'm just stopping here on the way." Callie gently set down her boxes of food and gave Melody a warm smile. "I brought you and your staff some sweet treats. Let's see, I've got gingerbread, Greek "snowball" cookies and a few other things."

Melody made another attempt at a weak smile and nodded her thanks. Callie forged ahead, trying a more somber tone this time. "I'm just so sorry about what happened the other day. I thought some fresh baked goods might be welcome."

"Yes, thank you. That's very nice of you." Melody looked a little pale.

"Are you all right?" Callie asked, concerned.

"No, I suppose I'm not. We're all just in a state of shock. It's all I can do to keep up with the demands of the guests. Fortunately, the hotel is still booked for the holidays. Still, the area behind the inn is a crime scene. I've got guests asking questions and I just don't know what to say."

"I can imagine," Callie answered.

"Between you and me, I can't even walk into the dining room without thinking about Natalie. You know, there's a view of the spot where she was found. That room has always been one of the best features of the hotel and now it's just gruesome. Yellow crime scene tape and all." She frowned. "And there's something else, but I really shouldn't tell you."

Callie prompted Melody. "What is it? Maybe I can help," she said gently.

"No, you can't, trust me. It's nothing, probably." Melody cleared her throat and smoothed her already smooth hair, perfectly coiffed in a sleek brown bun. "I'm sorry to burden you with my troubles. You must be suffering as well. After all, you found the...body." Melody blinked.

"Yes, I sure did." Callie didn't feel the need to replay that day's events.

"I'll get going in a minute," Callie said. "By the way, how is Kayla taking all of this? It must have been very difficult for her, losing a colleague, being questioned by the police...." Callie prompted. She thought back to the young woman's remarks about Sands' accent.

"She's devastated – and afraid," Melody admitted, looking away. "And of course, the Dayton family is *livid*. They're probably going to sue. Lexy's mother has been claiming that they and all of their guests were at risk and it's all the fault of the inn. It's a big mess."

She nodded at the stack of baked goods' boxes on the counter and seemed to be collecting hold of herself. She attempted to smile at Callie. "It was nice of you to bring us some holiday treats. I'm sure the staff will appreciate it."

"Any time," Callie said. "I'm always happy to provide food. It's a Greek thing."

Melody suddenly looked more alert. "You know, there is something you can help me with, come to think of it." She rummaged behind desk before placing a full-color brochure on the counter.

Callie peered at it closely. The festive brochure advertised The English Country Inn's annual Christmas Tea. "Oh, I just love this event," Callie gushed. "I was hoping to bring my daughter this year."

"The holiday tea party is stressing me out," Melody said glumly. "One of our usual food suppliers has messed up our bill and won't provide some of the ingredients. I know it's a mistake and I hope to get it cleared up. However, it may take a while to straighten things out with so much going on. And the holidays are such a busy time anyway." She paused. "You're such a good cook and baker. Do you think you could handle preparing some of the food? We'd pay you well, of course. Simple tea things like little cakes or maybe cookies. Do you think your schedule would allow it?"

Callie was taken aback.

"I think so," Callie said slowly. This might be just the way to be able to dig a little bit deeper into the inn's issues without appearing to be nosy.

"Thank you!" Melody seemed relieved. The phone started ringing. "I'd better get this," Melody said. "See you later."

"See you," Callie answered. She walked out to the parking lot, a bit dazed at having taken on yet another food project when her spirits were already so low. Still, clients had to be fed. It was a good thing the holidays only came once a year. Too bad murder was starting to become a regular occurrence.

* * *

Max was straightening Christmas lights when Callie returned to her shop. Piper was near the front of the store, taking pictures of food in the shop. She flitted from attractively displayed baked goods to the refrigerated cases filled with festively-wrapped take-home meals. A couple of Callie's Kitchen patrons photo bombed the pictures, but Piper only laughed.

Jack Myers was among the patrons, but he wasn't trying to get into any pictures. Callie wished she could grill him about what was going on at the inn, but he didn't look like he was planning to get a table. He had a cup of coffee in one hand and a box of Greek doughnuts, aka *loukoumades*, in the other. He nodded at Callie and gave her a dazzling smile, all white teeth and dimples, before heading out the door.

"Social media stuff?" Callie asked Piper, as she rolled up her sleeves and headed behind the counter, smiling and nodding at customers. Callie rang up some orders and Piper joined her behind the counter when the crowd thinned out a bit.

"I took some pictures for Instagram. It's a great way to show off your food," Piper answered, putting her iPhone back into her pocket.

"Great idea," Callie said. At least work seemed to be going smoothly. She was relieved to see a fair amount of customers bustling about the shop. While Callie watched, Max gave one final tug to the Christmas lights and then jumped down from his perch so that he could assist the customers beginning to assemble near the cash register. Who knew that Max would be so good at Christmas décor? He smiled at Callie and took a moment to admire his handiwork. Callie was happy to see Max behaving more like his old self. He must be feeling better. The lights sparkled and blinked, adding a warm and cozy glow to the shop's interior.

"Thanks for doing the lights, Max. I'll be in the kitchen," Callie called as she went through the French doors leading to the food prep area. She checked the calendar on her computer to see if providing food for Melody conflicted with any other big orders or events. At the rate she was going, it just might.

One event she knew about already and it wasn't making her feel any holiday cheer.

"Lexy Dayton holiday lunch," she read. Callie hated to get dragged into any more Dayton drama right now, but she needed to keep her customers happy. Lexy was certainly celebrating frequently this season. Callie wondered if she and Nick had patched things up since their scene the day of the would-be bridal shower.

Callie sighed and turned away from the computer, deciding to seek out a bracing cup of coffee. She'd barely slept a wink and could almost taste a cup of her favorite dark roast, loaded with milk and a couple of sugars for extra energy.

However, a peaceful cup of hot, fragrant coffee was not to be. The newspaper folded next to the coffee maker nearly made her break the cup she'd just taken from a cabinet.

"*Too Many Rooms at the Inn?*" *The Crystal Bay Courier's* headline read. "*Murder Frightens Guests Away from Popular Hotel.*" Had Melody been lying when she'd said that the inn wasn't affected? Or was the *Courier* exaggerating – not an unusual practice?

Max walked briskly through the French doors. "Where do we keep the rest of the Christmas lights? Looks like one of the strands I just put up is burned out."

Callie was absorbed in the article. "Uh...right. Lights. They should be in the storage closet. I've got a box marked "Christmas" above the extra cookie sheets." She barely looked up from the newspaper.

"Yeah, I used those already. I guess I'll have to get some more." When Callie didn't respond, he strode over to the coffee area. "What's so interesting?"

Callie finished reading the short article that gave the bare outlines of yesterday's murder at the inn and the supposed cancellations and held the paper up to Max. "Have you seen this?"

Max skimmed the headline and then looked back at Callie. "So? That's to be expected, isn't it? Look what happened to us after Drew's murder last year. We nearly had to close."

Callie sighed. "Don't remind me. No, what I mean is, I was just at the inn and I spoke with Melody Cartwright. She implied that business was pretty normal, despite guests asking questions. In fact, she mentioned that she was really busy trying to keep up with everything."

"Weird," Max agreed. "Maybe she didn't want to admit the truth about the crash in business, expecting that it could lead to more. But, in that case, who told the *Courier* that there were so many cancellations?"

"It wouldn't take much to get that kind of information. All you would need was someone inexperienced in dealing with journalists to answer the phone. Something could slip out before you even intended."

"Well, in that case, it could have been Melody herself. What experience does she have with journalists?" Max wanted to know.

"You're right. She could have been trying to cover her mistake by lying to me. Come to think of it, I didn't see a lot of cars in the parking lot...."

The bell over the front door rang. "I'll get that. Food prep can wait for a minute." Max turned to leave the kitchen.

"Wait. I'll help with prep. What are you making?"

"Just some *avgolemono*. It's not on the menu but I've had three customers ask me for it today. It seems to sell like hotcakes when it's cold outside."

"Got it. Maybe I'll just keep it on the menu permanently – at least for the winter months."

Max went to help the latest customer and Callie hunted in the walk-in refrigerator for the vat of homemade chicken broth she'd placed there recently.

Why would Melody lie? Callie shook her head, too preoccupied with soup and serving customers to figure it out at the moment. The woman was probably just confused, as anyone would be when confronted with a brutal murder at work.

Callie made her way back over to the coffee pot and poured a huge mugful. Melody wasn't the only one confused – Callie hoped the caffeine would kick in soon and clear her foggy brain.

* * *

The rich smells of chicken, homemade broth and lemon filled the kitchen with a mouth-watering scent. Callie had made a large quantity of soup and was working on cutting out some Christmas sugar cookies, a soothing process, when the phone rang. She almost hated to break her peaceful state of mind by answering, but she wiped off her hands and picked the phone reluctantly.

"Hi, it's me." On the other end of the phone, Samantha sounded rushed, as usual. "I've just got a minute but I wanted to apologize again for what happened at dinner the other night. Bix was totally out of line and I know he's sorry he reacted that way in front of you, me and of course, George. I guess he's had some problems with The Elkhorn but really, that's no excuse."

"Just so long as you're all right, Sam. That's all I care about. Although..." Callie hesitated. She didn't want to come across as if she were criticizing Bix.

"Callie, come on. What's on your mind?"

"Well, are you sure Bix is someone you want to keep seeing? I know he's charming and good-looking and all of that but he seems a little volatile." There. She'd said it.

Silence.

"I'm not trying to criticize him," Callie hedged, concerned she'd upset Sam. "But I'm just calling it like I see it."

"Yes, I know." Sam finally answered tersely. "Look, I didn't call to dissect Bix's character right now. I just wanted to say I'm sorry. And I am. But right now, I've got to go. Talk to you later." Sam's phone beeped and the call ended.

Well, that escalated quickly, Callie thought. She sighed as she returned to her cookie dough. If only she could iron out her problems – and her friend's problems – as easily as she rolled out her smooth, buttery dough.

Callie had another thought as she cut out whimsical Christmas cookie shapes and placed them gently on baking sheets. She was already checking up on the situation at The English Country Inn for Emma. Maybe Bix could bear an even closer examination. She wouldn't tell Sam of course. But it wouldn't hurt to find out more about this man who had her intelligent and logical friend so obviously smitten.

Six

Returning home that evening, Callie was determined to relax. Sands had called from the office but only to say hello and that he hoped to see her in person, soon. *That makes two of us.* Callie hadn't realized how much she was starting to rely on Sands' company and his absence these last few days had thrown her feelings into stark relief.

Olivia, her 10-year-old daughter was home from a visit with her father and his new wife, Raine. And her 6-year-old second "child," Koukla, her Yorkie, was curled up on the couch next to her. As far as she knew, Sweetie was still at home dealing with "the jet lag," Grandma Viv was no doubt involved in one of her many activities and George was who knew where?

Olivia sat on the other side of Callie, also curled up close. They were watching a movie and her daughter seemed to be enjoying it hugely. Callie tried to stay present, but considering the events of the last few days, her mind was wandering.

She was struggling to stay awake and Olivia was poking her, pointing out things in the movie that she was missing, when the doorbell bonged and startled her.

"Who could that be?" she asked over Koukla's loud, excited barks. Secretly, she hoped it was Sands showing up for a cozy night in. A part of her was apprehensive – she didn't usually receive surprise guests and with a killer at large, who knew who might be on her doorstep? Would a killer announce their presence by ringing a doorbell?

She peeked through the peephole and breathed a sigh of relief before throwing the door open. Bundled up against the weather and already covered with a fine coating of snowflakes, were Grandma Viv and Glykeria, aka "Sweetie."

"Let us in before Sweetie freezes. She's not used to the Wisconsin cold." Viv had her arm wrapped around the diminutive Greek visitor.

"Eh, I fine," Sweetie protested, but Callie noticed that she sped into the house as quickly as her short but shapely legs would carry her.

"Nice house. That beautiful girl your daughter? *Tou, tou!*" The Greek custom (well, really superstition) of warding off evil spirits by pretending to "spit" on beautiful children was something that Olivia was used to from George. Olivia was soon enveloped in Sweetie's tight embrace.

Callie ushered Viv into her home over Sweetie's exclamations about Olivia, Koukla, the house and the cold weather. Now fully awake, she was happy to see the two women and guiltily, she was glad for an interruption from the movie.

"Olivia, can you pause that for a minute?" she asked and Olivia glumly started to point the remote at the TV.

"No need for that," Viv said smoothly, holding her coat out to Callie, who placed it next to Sweetie's somewhat thinner coat on a chair near the door. "We just thought it would be nice to stop by and see how you're doing. We heard about the murder at The English Country Inn." Viv whispered this last part, glancing at Olivia.

"I figured you would have," Callie said, nodding at her daughter to continue watching her movie. Olivia beamed and returned to the TV. But where was George? It was unlike him to miss out on family time, especially with his cousin in town.

"I bring cookies," Sweetie said, holding up a container. "I no sleep at night. The jet lag. So I bake for you."

"Thank you, Sweetie. That's so nice of you!" Callie enthused. "Why don't we go in the kitchen and I'll make some coffee to go with the cookies. Decaf. So you can sleep." Callie smiled at Sweetie. "Olivia can join us in a bit."

The trio walked into Callie's small kitchen, one of her favorite spots in the house with its white cabinets, cheery pale-lemon walls and the matching pastel yellow Kitchen Aid sitting on the countertop. She gestured to the women to sit down at the table while she made a pot of decaf and got out plates for the cookies. Carefully, she opened the container that Sweetie had brought with her and a delightful smell wafted out. Mmmm. *Koulourakia,* the famous "Greek twist" cookies.

"These look delicious," Callie enthused, setting down some coffee cups and joining the ladies while the coffee brewed.

"Is nothing," Sweetie said with a shrug. "I like to do."

"Where's George?" Callie asked the two women who looked at each other, then down at the table.

"Well? What is it? Is he all right?" Callie asked again, growing alarmed.

Sweetie was the first to speak up. "He all right, dear. He out with woman, but he ask me first if it fine with me. I tell him, go, go. I visit Calliope. Viv nice enough to call and ask me here."

"What woman?" Callie asked, pretty sure she already knew the answer.

"Her name is Kathy," Viv answered, with a wry smile at Callie. "And she's..."

"She's Raine's aunt. Yes. I believe I just met the lady yesterday, while she was with Dad. They're out together again?" Callie found that hard to believe. After all these years, George Costas was giving somebody the rush? And of all somebodies – a woman related to Raine!

"Let's not jump to conclusions," Viv remarked with the wisdom of her 80 years. "They may just be friends."

Callie was ashamed of her petty feelings. "It's not that I don't want Dad to date," she hedged. "It's just that ... someone related to Raine? It feels...I don't know." She couldn't finish. Surely she wouldn't resent George if he found someone she truly liked. However, she was uncomfortable with the rush of conflicting emotions flowing through her. Besides being annoyed by the Raine connection, she had to admit it did bring up feelings about her mother's death, something she thought she had gotten over long before now.

"It feels like a betrayal?" Viv asked gently, picking up Callie's train of thought.

"Yes. I guess so." Callie looked at Viv. "I know how stupid that sounds."

"Not so stupid," Viv said softly. "Don't be too hard on yourself. Anyway, you know George doesn't want you unhappy. That's the last thing he wants."

"Let me get straight," Sweetie broke in, already on her fourth cookie. She brushed crumbs off her sweater and continued. "George date woman related to ... who? You ex-husband?"

"Yes," Callie said, her face growing hot. "Sorry. I don't mean to air all of our dirty laundry. The woman dad is out with tonight is the aunt of my ex-husband's new wife. It's a little confusing, I admit."

Sweetie looked perplexed for a minute and Callie was worried that the convoluted way she had described the relationship was bumping into a language barrier. But, Sweetie's next words erased that theory. Unfortunately.

"So." Sweetie said, narrowing her beautiful dark brown eyes and tossing her shoulder-length dyed auburn hair. *Uh-oh,* Callie thought. "George date woman related to evil woman who steal you husband? He act like donkey."

"No, Sweetie," Callie was embarrassed. "It's not like that at all. No one stole my husband. Let's wait and see what happens. Maybe we're way ahead of ourselves."

"OK," Sweetie agreed, but looked skeptical. "But I talk to George for you, if you want."

"Thank you, Sweetie, but no. That's not necessary." Callie didn't want to imagine the fireworks that would ensue if these two got into a discussion of how George should live his life. Anyway, Callie didn't want to be selfish and hypocritical. If she didn't want George interfering with her way of life, then how could she interfere with his?

"Let's change the subject," Viv offered and delicately took another cookie off of the plate. Callie had already inhaled two of the delicious cookies and was contemplating a third. Sweetie was some baker. "Not that this is a cheerier topic," Viv said, lowering her voice a bit. "But what happened the other day? Can you tell us anything about the murder of poor Natalie?"

After another large gulp of coffee for fortification, Callie gave Viv and Sweetie the basic details of Natalie's murder and her role as witness.

Viv shook her head and Sweetie managed to look grim, while chewing what had to be her sixth cookie. "How terrible," Viv said. "And that poor couple engaged to be married. I hope this doesn't poison their happiness."

"I hope not," Callie said, recalling that their argument in the aftermath of the murder hinted at an unhappiness already present.

"So what now? Who do the police suspect? And what does Detective Sands have to say about all of this?" Viv wanted to know.

"I would imagine there are many suspects," Callie answered. "Probably too many. However, this time I'm not one of them, thank goodness. That's really all I can say. I'm sure you know that Sands wouldn't want me to discuss the details with anyone outside of the investigation."

"Oh, my dear, of course not, though it was more informative when you could discuss such things with us. The pitfalls of dating a law enforcement officer!" Viv's bright blue eyes twinkled at Callie.

She liked Detective Sands, unlike George, who was wary of him after he had suspected his darling daughter of murder fairly recently.

"Well" Viv said, sipping her coffee. "Let's hope the police take care of this and soon. And you stay out of harm's way," Viv said pointedly to her granddaughter. "No more bumps on the head or worse," she intoned, obviously still upset at Callie's involvement in a previous Crystal Bay murder.

"I'll try," Callie said wryly. "But, there are one or two odd things that don't add up." She told the two women about Melody Cartwright, the *Courier* article and the fact that Melody appeared to be lying about the business status at the inn.

"That's a little bit strange," Viv agreed. "But look at it this way: Her colleague has just been murdered. Maybe you can talk to her again in a few days when she's calmed down." Viv frowned, apparently deep in thought, and suddenly, brightened. Callie could nearly see the light bulb go off over her grandmother's head.

"I know," Viv said with triumph in her voice. "Sweetie and I can talk to Melody. Didn't you say she puts on tea parties for young girls? Maybe Olivia would like to have one. That way, we can cozy up to Melody and maybe she'll talk to us."

"I perfect for job," Sweetie chimed in. "People think I no understand English. Maybe I hear something good!"

Callie had to laugh at her two enthusiastic amateur sleuths. "I don't know, but thanks for the offer. I'm already helping Melody with the annual Christmas Tea. It could be great publicity for the baked goods at Callie's Kitchen – and you never know, I could get some inside information. Or maybe not," Callie said, thinking about Melody's closemouthed approach that afternoon.

She sighed as she considered her options. "I agree that we have to find some way to get Melody to open up. I think she might be downplaying trouble at the inn because she's got her new book coming out. Anyway, with the holidays, her tea parties are probably already booked for the season. And I really don't want to involve Olivia in all of this."

The three women sipped coffee and were silent for a moment, thinking. Koukla trotted into the room and batted Callie's ankles with her paws until Callie absently picked her up and placed her on her lap. The dog promptly curled herself into a ball and sighed with contentment.

"Wait. This might work," Callie said after a few minutes of furrowed brows and anxiously nibbled cookies. "Why don't I offer to do something for Melody's upcoming book? Like a launch party or something like that. Maybe I can offer to host it at Callie's Kitchen and I can make some of the tea party foods she talks about in her book. She'll probably be busy and would welcome the help – especially with the food. The only thing is that her book comes out very soon. Do you think it's too late to ask her?"

"Only one way to find out," Viv said briskly. "It's a wonderful idea. Melody will probably be flattered by your interest. Plus, it will give you an excuse to talk to her."

"I like," Sweetie said, motioning to Koukla to come sit with her. Koukla wiggled until Callie placed her on the floor. The little Yorkie ran to Sweetie and was quickly nestled in her warm embrace. Callie was pretty sure she saw Sweetie sneak a cookie piece to her dog but she didn't say anything.

"That's it, then. Our plan, such as it is," Callie said, pouring more coffee. "I really do like Melody and would like to help her with her book launch. I guess this way I can kill two birds with one stone – help her AND get info."

Viv shuddered. "Ugh. Don't say 'kill.' I'm still in shock about Natalie. Such a sweet young woman and always kind to me."

"I didn't know you knew Natalie," Callie said, though she wasn't surprised. Viv and George knew just about everyone one way or another, having lived in Crystal Bay so many years.

"I did know her, but not well. We attended the same ballroom dance class at that new studio over the dress shop in town. It was only for a few weeks but it was a hoot!"

"Ballroom dance class? Did Natalie have an occasion she was preparing for? That's usually why people take those kinds of classes, though not always," Callie asked Viv, puzzled.

"She came to the dance lessons with a tall young fellow. He was quite handsome and had a strange name. He wasn't super-friendly to the group, in my opinion, but they certainly looked like they were having fun together. Laughing, talking, you know. Her young man may have even stolen a kiss now and then."

Callie felt Sweetie's delicious cookies turn to stone in her stomach. "His name wasn't Bix Buckman by any chance, was it?"

"Yes, that was it! Bix. Why do you ask, dear? Do you know him?"

"Uh, sort of," Callie said, wanting to protect Sam.

Bix Buckman and Natalie? Really?

Nick Hawkins, Lexy Dayton's would-be groom had clearly had a soft spot for Natalie. So did Max. And now Bix? Who knew who else? Natalie had inspired much admiration from Crystal Bay's young men. But had she also inspired anger – enough anger to kill?

* * *

Olivia had finally been asked to join the women, consuming her fair share of cookies and two cups of hot chocolate. The little group had chatted and laughed with no mention of murder, George's romantic life or other controversial topics. No doubt about it, having Viv and Sweetie there had lifted Callie's spirits considerably. It was late when Viv and Sweetie bundled themselves up against the elements and headed home, with promises to keep in touch.

"I like Sweetie," Olivia said sleepily as Callie tucked her in. "She's funny."

"Yes," Callie agreed. "I like her a lot, too. In fact, I visited her when I was just about your age. In Greece."

"I know, you told me. You'll take me there someday, right?"

"Yes. I hope so. Maybe we can even stay with Sweetie."

"OK," Olivia mumbled, pulling the covers up to her chin. Suddenly her eyes popped wide open.

"What is it?" Callie admonished. "Time to go to sleep."

"I know, but I forgot to tell you something. Dad thinks that he and Raine might have found the perfect house!"

"Oh they did?" Callie tried to keep her voice neutral.

"Yup! And guess what – it's only two blocks away from our house!"

Seven

After Olivia's bombshell about her father's house-hunting activities, and unwelcome images of Natalie's lifeless form in the water, Callie didn't think she'd be able to sleep. However, exhaustion caused her to sleep like a log. Her alarm woke her at 6:30. It was still dark outside and the house was cold. Callie was disoriented. She'd slept so soundly that she had nearly forgotten the horrific events at the inn and to wake up was to remember anew.

Heaving herself out of bed, Callie turned up the thermostat and made herself a cup of coffee while trying not to think about Hugh. She couldn't tell him what to do or where to go – but she sure wished that she could.

The air was so glacial that Callie felt as if she were inhaling icicles as she started up her car, after seeing Olivia to the school bus. Callie was wearing her warmest down jacket, a hat, thick gloves and boots, but still she shivered as she scraped ice off of her windows.

On the ride to work, Callie's mind wouldn't stop churning. She had taken on too many projects. Emma was a good friend and she wanted to help her. However, her own business wasn't exactly out of the woods after recent difficulties. She needed to take care of her clientele, spend time with her daughter – and she missed Sands. Why had she agreed to help figure out what was rotten at The English Country Inn?

As she pulled into a parking space near work, she realized that she wanted to help find the killer, not only to help Emma, but to find justice for this young woman who was struck down so tragically. She was shaken and angered by Natalie's death. It just wasn't right.

Callie unlocked the back entrance of her shop and walked in to find Max and Piper perusing food pictures on Piper's phone that she'd taken earlier that week.

"Hi Callie," Max said. Today he wore a tight blue T-shirt with the Callie's Kitchen logo and well-worn, ripped jeans. They were fashionably tattered, but Callie smiled as she thought of what Viv would say: *Can I help sew those jeans for you? It looks like they've been through a shredder.*

Max seemed excited about something. "We've got some good shots of the food. Piper's going to load them onto Instagram."

"Some of the customers were getting in on the act the other day," Piper explained, scrolling through pictures of *loukoumades*, the Greek doughnuts that Callie's Kitchen was famous for, along with photos of iced gingerbread loaves, especially for the Christmas season, and buttery mini coffee cakes. Callie smiled at her customers' antics – she was so thrilled to have them back, she didn't care how many pictures they photobombed!

"I can always crop the people out of these shots," Piper was explaining. As usual, she was wearing colorful vintage clothing, including a red A-line dress topped with a black cardigan sporting a vintage Christmas tree pin. Her dark hair was pulled back in a sleek ponytail. Callie squinted at the pictures, surprised to see Nick Hawkins in the background of one of them. She didn't remember seeing him, but put it down to being preoccupied.

"Hmmm," Callie considered. "Maybe we should keep a couple of these as is. After all, people like to see and hear about themselves on social media."

"I'm impressed," Max said, only half-teasing. "You're finally catching on to the ways of the 21st century."

Callie decided to ignore his innocent jibe. "So what's the status so far today?"

"I've got some more gingerbread cake in the oven and we've got *pastitsio* in the coolers out front." Piper smiled at the mention of the delectable dish, a delicious mélange of ground meat, tomato sauce, spices and a luscious topping.

"Great. I guess I'll get a head start and make the beef stew and biscuits for tomorrow." Besides offering her favorite Greek dishes, Callie's Kitchen was known for serving up Midwestern comfort food classics. Callie had eaten both styles of food growing up and loved them both. "Max, I could use you out front when you're done here."

"You bet." Max stood up and Piper jumped up with him. "I'd better go," the young woman said with a regretful look at Max. "I need to get to class soon, anyway."

Piper was a student at Crystal Bay College and worked at Callie's Kitchen for college credit in social media and communications, which was one reason she was constantly updating the Instagram and Facebook pages for Callie's Kitchen. It was a dirty job, but somebody had to do it – that is, if you wanted to compete in today's marketplace.

Wrapped in a fluffy fake fur coat, Piper said goodbye to Max and then called to Callie. "Now that you've seen the pictures, I'll go ahead and load them onto all of our social media."

Callie nodded her approval. "Thanks, Piper!" A blast of freezing cold air blew through the kitchen, which was warm and fragrant with the smell of gingerbread, cinnamon and lemons for the gingerbread icing, egg-lemon soup and just about every other dish at Callie's Kitchen. She truly could never have enough lemons on hand.

Alone in the kitchen at last. Callie started browning beef cubes for her stew. She added onions, a smidge of garlic, stock and a bay leaf, and then covered the mixture to cook at a slow heat. She was just chopping up some carrots and potatoes when Max stuck his head in the kitchen door, a wry smile on his face.

"Someone to see you," he said. "They said they really need to talk to the owner."

Terrific. "OK, just a second," Callie said, wiping her hands on her apron, a small knot of anxiety building. And just when she had gotten into a peaceful cooking groove, too.

But when she entered the front of her shop, the anxiety disappeared and was replaced by an equally troubling reaction. Butterflies.

Sands was standing expectantly behind the counter, a small poinsettia plant in his hand. Callie glanced at Max who was grinning back at her.

"Good one, Max." she said with a smile. "You had me going there for a minute."

Max shrugged. "Don't look at me. It was his idea."

Callie went around the counter to join Sands, who was wearing one of his dark wool coats, snowflakes still melting on the lapels. He leaned down and kissed her cheek. "I missed you," he said.

"Alrighty, then, I'll just go, uh, check on the gingerbread," Max said, uncomfortable with the public display of affection. He walked quickly through the half-door and Callie heard him ostentatiously singing to himself, as if to prove he wasn't paying attention to them, while he moved around pots and pans.

Callie smiled up at Sands and took the proffered poinsettia plant. "Some Christmas cheer for you," he said. "Although, this place already has quite a bit of it. And that's not even including its lovely owner."

Callie looked around her shop, seeing it through the eyes of a customer – or Sands, for that matter. Max and Piper had done a beautiful job bringing a Christmas feeling to Callie's Kitchen. The entire space sparkled with white Christmas lights and live mini-Christmas trees on every table. The front window display had a red wooden sled to hold cake stands filled with baked goods. Glittering faux snow with miniature trees, reindeer, candy canes and Santas sparkled from glass mason jars throughout the shop. The effect was festive, whimsical and inviting.

Callie brushed the remaining snow off of Sands' lapels and he caught her hand in his.

"I've missed you, too," she said. "But you've got a job to do. I understand that."

"Ah, yes. The job. It *has* kept me busy." Callie noticed upon closer inspection that Sands' eyes were blood-shot and he could use a shave. She was touched that he had taken the time to bring her a present when he should have been resting – or more likely, working.

"Thanks, this is beautiful," she said, setting the red flowering plant on a nearby table. "It was thoughtful of you."

"Sorry that I've been like the Invisible Man lately," Sands said, smiling at Callie. He squeezed her hand and slowly released it.

"Well, I'm glad you've been busy working on Natalie's murder. It's scary to think that there's a killer out there, wandering around." Callie shivered. "Anyway, I think I may have found a way to combine your work with us getting to spend some time together."

"How so?" Sands asked, narrowing his hazel eyes. "Callie, what are you up to?"

Callie filled him in on the connection between the ballroom dance class, Bix Buckman and Natalie, the murder victim.

"Viv says she saw them together at the dance class," Callie said. "I was thinking that we could join the dance class and see if we find out any information. So even though we'd be socializing, you'd be investigating Natalie's murder. I looked into it and there's a lesson this Sunday afternoon."

Sands gave her a look that was equal parts irritation and admiration. "Well, well Ms. Costas. Very enterprising." He was silent a moment, mulling it over. "I don't see the harm in it. But it's a pity Natalie wasn't in a football-watching club."

"You mean soccer?" Callie said, thinking he was talking about the British usage of the word.

"No. I mean football, the American kind. I may be from the UK but I live in Wisconsin, don't I? And that's where my heart is now." He crinkled his hazel eyes at her and she felt her stomach flip-flop and not necessarily in a good way. His heart was here? That thought was somehow simultaneously pleasing – and strangely uncomfortable.

"The Packers are playing the Bears on Sunday," Sands was saying. "But in the interest of detective work – and ballroom dancing – I think we can work something out."

"Great!" Callie hugged him spontaneously and he returned his embrace. Sands was just leaning down to give her a kiss when Max walked back into the room.

"Oh geez, can't leave you two alone for a minute," he mock-scolded and disappeared again. The bell over the door jingled, announcing another customer and reluctantly, Callie and Sands sprang apart.

"I'll text you the details," Callie said as Sands started towards the door.

He smiled at her, waved and walked back out into the snow. She watched him go, and then turned her attention back to her customers, cheerily directing them toward the day's specials. But inside, she was in turmoil.

Was Sands starting to get serious about their relationship? Was she? And if she was, did she really want to be vulnerable again, after all that had happened in the last few years? Callie catalogued the disastrous romantic incidents that had comprised the last several years: separating from Hugh, Hugh's remarriage, the untimely murder of her boyfriend, Drew Staven and his secret life.

It was all very confusing. Not for the first time, Callie was happy she worked with food. Food was usually predictable, provided you followed the recipe. It was too bad that the same couldn't be said about relationships.

* * *

Business picked up a bit that afternoon and Max and Callie were busy. It warmed Callie's heart to serve hungry customers. People seemed to be loading up on carbs in particular – cookies, quick breads and Callie's Greek yogurt coffee cake were flying out the door. Max had put it down to people "stress-eating" after Natalie's murder. Callie had noticed some customers looking askance at her while having whispered conversations, but luckily, no one had yet asked her about the fact that she'd found yet another murder victim. Could that be Max's doing?

Callie glanced at her co-worker. With his imposing physique and height, he wasn't someone that you necessarily wanted to cross. Of course, Max was a complete teddy bear at heart, but he could be fierce when warranted. Thank goodness for that, Callie thought. It never hurt to have someone like Max in your corner.

Callie had just wrapped up a ready-to-eat Callie's Kitchen special – *avgolemono*, Greek roast chicken and lemon potatoes and handed it to a customer – when she noticed a commotion across the street. It was about 4:30 p.m. and nearly dark, but she could make out two figures that seemed to be shouting at each other. As the customer left her shop and opened the door, she heard an aggressive-sounding conversation, punctuated by shouting.

"Lexy! Please! Just forget about it. Nothing happened! Can you just please stop this!" Callie glanced at Max as she walked to the storefront window to get a better look.

"It's Nick Hawkins and Lexy Dayton," she told him, squinting for a better view. "Wow, they're having a huge fight about *something*."

"You think?" Max said, sarcastically, joining Callie near the window. "Poor Hawkins. She's really letting him have it."

Callie bit her lip, trying to decide if she should intervene. It really wasn't any of her business, true. But it was devastating to see the young couple appear to be so miserable. Callie's maternal instincts won out. "Max, I think I'm going to see if I can help."

She dashed into the back room for her coat. When she emerged, shrugging it on hurriedly over her bulky sweater, Max was already wearing his ski jacket, his spiky hair covered by a wool knit cap.

"Let me go with you," Max said. "You never know."

"Fine," Callie said, thinking about her earlier appreciation for his abilities as impromptu bodyguard. "But let me do the talking."

The couple was still arguing heatedly as Callie and Max made their way across the street.

Callie was momentarily distracted by the fact that Nick and Lexy were fighting in front of a new gourmet tea shop. The month-old shop had opened after Minette's Chocolates, owned by her two college friends, had closed. She'd meant to introduce herself to the new owner, but she'd just not had time. Or maybe, she confessed inwardly, it had been too difficult to face the new owner because of her painful experiences with the previous ones. Callie nudged Max and for a moment they both stared, helplessly, at the screaming couple.

Lexy had been crying. Black mascara oozed down her face and her eyes were puffy and red. Nick's face was red and his breath was coming out in short, steaming puffs in the frosty air. He looked like a bull about to stampede.

"Uh, Lexy? Nick? Please. Is there anything we can do to help?" Callie asked.

"No!" Lexy said bitterly, barely glancing at Max and Callie. "Nobody can help."

Callie and Max looked at each other and Callie nodded at Nick.

"Hey Nick," Max said, gently steering him a little bit away from his fiancé. "Let's go across the street. I'll get you a coffee and you can take a break, calm down for a bit."

Surprisingly, Nick agreed, but he didn't look happy about it. Max gave Callie a look that said *you should have let me do the talking.*

Fair enough. "Great idea," Callie said enthusiastically. "Max, give him something to eat, too. You guys can do me a favor and taste-test the new batch of Greek butter cookies that I just made. And Lexy, why don't we go in here?" Callie was talking to the engaged couple like they were younger than Olivia, but they were so upset they didn't seem to notice. She gestured at the new tea shop. The sign on the window said "Tea for Two."

Lexy sniffled and wiped her eyes, but it only made the mascara mess worse. "I really don't care what Nick does." She sniffed again and turned her back on the two men. "Let's go, Callie."

Nick stared back at Lexy with a hangdog look on his face as he walked slowly away, but Max was already chatting to him, leading him back across the street to Callie's Kitchen. Callie turned her attention to her charge. "We won't stay long. Let's have some tea and relax," she said in what she hoped was a soothing, not patronizing tone.

"Ha!" Lexy answered bitterly, but at least she was going along with the plan, opening the door to Tea for Two, and stomping over the threshold. Once inside the warm and fragrant shop, she turned to Callie with a sneer on her face. "Would you be relaxed if you found out your fiancé was in love with someone else?"

Speechless for a moment, Callie looked around helplessly, trying to find a suitable answer. As she did, she noticed something she hadn't seen before in all of the confusion. Mrs. Dayton, mother of the bride, was parked outside of Tea for Two in a snow-covered SUV. She was looking right at Lexy and Callie, a smirk on her face.

Eight

Callie sipped at her tea, a delicious blend that the owner, Christy, told her was from Greece. It was herbal and slightly floral and she found it calmed her frazzled nerves.

Lexy, who had fixed her face in the ladies room, was looking more normal, but it was obvious that she was still highly agitated. She twisted her long wavy hair around her finger as she sipped her Earl Grey and couldn't sit still. Callie had decided to wait until the tea came before bringing up the argument but she'd waited long enough.

"Why do you think Nick's in love with someone else? Do you have proof?" Callie asked gently, bracing herself for another crying episode.

Lexy set her teacup down with a bang. Earl Grey sloshed over her cup and onto her pink sweater. She muttered under her breath as she dabbed at the stain with a paper napkin. Finally, she turned her attention to Callie.

"Proof? I don't need any. Nick's been totally depressed since Natalie was murdered. He'll barely look at me. They dated, you know. Nick and Natalie." Lexy narrowed her eyes and Callie was taken aback by the look of anger and hatred in them. "Nick and Natalie," Lexy repeated in a sing-song. "Too cute for words, isn't it?"

Callie took another sip of soothing Greek tea and tried again. "It could be just the shock, Lexy. If he did know Natalie and dated her for awhile, then he probably just feels terrible about it. It doesn't mean that he was in love with her."

Lexy sighed and the tears slid down her face again. Callie offered her another paper napkin.

"I know," Lexy squeaked. "That's what I want to believe. It's just that my mom is driving me crazy. She's putting all sorts of thoughts into my head, telling me that Nick isn't good enough for me and that I shouldn't marry him."

I can relate to that, Callie thought, although, thankfully, George's over protectiveness didn't extend to unkindness.

"Well, Lexy, I know you want to please your mother, but at the end of the day, it's your life. If you love Nick, that's really not for your mother to decide."

Lexy sipped her tea and put the cup back on the saucer, gently this time. "I don't mean to be like this. So nasty. And babyish. It's just that – after my last fiancé left me, I have a hard time trusting my judgment. You know?"

"I get it," Callie said. *Did she ever*. "But you and Nick need to talk, heart to heart. Forget about everyone else, just for a minute. It's not about them. This is about you two and the rest of your life."

The two women sipped their tea while Christy, the owner, rang up orders and tidied up her shelves. The new tea shop was adorable, with exposed brick walls painted white, beautiful teapots for sale and loads of packaged gourmet teas. In addition, the shop served brewed tea but thankfully, no food. At least, not yet. Callie wondered what she would do if Christy started to offer baked goods and sandwiches. No doubt the competition would be hard on her business, especially since she had just found her footing again.

On the bright side, Christy, owner of Tea for Two, seemed perfectly nice. Blue-eyed with dark, chin-length hair, fair skin and rosy cheeks, she looked exactly as you would imagine a tea shop owner to look: Sweet, pretty and kind. Callie hoped she was the latter. You couldn't open a small business in Crystal Bay without a will of steel – it was still hard to make a go of things.

Never mind, Callie thought. That worry could wait. It was enough that she was playing amateur relationship counselor. Fleetingly, she wondered if Max was getting any info out of Nick.

Despite her attempts at helping Lexy and Nick, she wasn't getting paid to counsel couples, Callie thought ruefully. And who knew? She could be doing more harm than good. In any case, she'd accomplished one small mission: she'd calmed Lexy down. Now, it was time to get back to work and wrap things up so she could get home at a decent hour. Snow was coming down at a rapid pace, and she fretted as she thought about Viv, who was watching Olivia for her. She wanted Viv to get home safely.

Finishing her tea, Callie stood and pushed back her chair. "Lexy, I'm glad we were able to talk, but I've got to get back to work, then home to my daughter before this blizzard gets any worse. I hope I've helped at least a little bit."

Lexy, who had also finished her fragrant cup of tea, walked around the table and gave Callie a hug. "I'm so embarrassed about what happened between Nick and me. Thanks for talking. I'll...I'll try to take your advice."

"Good. Keep me posted, OK?" Lexy nodded in agreement.

Callie and Lexy waved goodbye to Christy and then the two women parted in front of Callie's Kitchen. Mrs. Dayton's SUV was gone. Callie wondered where Mrs. Dayton had gone and why she'd been parked nearby, watching the couple fight without trying to stop it. It seemed an evil thing to do to a beloved daughter.

Max was alone when she returned to her shop. "Well?" Callie asked, taking off her coat. "Did you find out anything from Nick? Lexy says she thinks he was in love with Natalie."

"Yeah, he told me. He also said that's not true, but that Mrs. Dayton has been trying to get rid of him for months."

"That's what Lexy said, too. Any idea why?"

"Well, I'm not sure." Max frowned. "Between you and me, Nick seems a little bit unenthused about getting married. Not that he would admit to it. He just said that Mrs. Dayton doesn't like him. Personally, I think he could be using his mother-in-law to be as an excuse. Something seems a little bit off about him, if you know what I mean."

"Hmm. That's troubling," Callie replied. She liked Nick but she hadn't had the heart-to-heart that Max had had with him. "In his defense, I don't think Mrs. Dayton wants to let go of her daughter. She seems a little, um, controlling?" Callie rolled her eyes.

"Yeah." Max looked skeptical. "Maybe he doesn't want to get involved with a bad family situation."

"It's definitely possible," Callie said, thoughtfully. Was she behaving that way as well – not wanting George to have a social life with whomever he chose? Perish the thought.

A few late stragglers came in for ready-to-go meals, so Callie cleared up the kitchen and finished some more food prep while Max rang up the customers. Finally, they were ready to lock up and go home, both of them promising each other to drive safely on the slick roads.

Callie was almost at home when her cell phone rang. Emma. Sighing, she answered her phone, which was hooked up to a hands-free system. No way was she holding a cell phone on these slippery roads – that was asking for trouble.

"Callie!" Emma's voice crackled over the line. "How are you? Is this a bad time?"

"I'm in the car and it's a little icy, but I can talk. How's the snow in Arizona?" Callie decided to go for a weak joke.

"You've got me there. But snow is causing a different sort of problem for me. I still can't get a flight. There's some type of major blizzard that's blanketing the Midwest. In fact, it's headed your way."

"Isn't there always a major blizzard headed our way?" Callie quipped. "It *is* December, after all."

"You're right. But that's not why I called. Do you have any info for me? I'm going crazy with worry out here."

Callie decided to pull over for just a few moments so that she could concentrate on the call. "Just a second." She parked on a side street just off of Main.

Also, she was buying time. She did have information to report, but she wasn't so sure that it behooved her to burden Emma with all of it, if it didn't pertain directly to Natalie's murder. After fierce internal debate, Callie decided to tell her what she knew – well, most of it.

"I've found out a few things." Callie hesitated.

"Well? What is it?" Emma asked.

"Remember, these are just observations," Callie hedged.

"Yes, yes, of course," Emma replied impatiently. "What's up?"

"First of all, Bix Buckman seems to be a little volatile. I witnessed him having an altercation at The Elkhorn Supper Club."

"In other words, a fight. What happened?"

Callie gave her the bare details, leaving out the part about Samantha and Bix dating. What good would that do?

"That's just great," Emma grumbled after Callie finished telling an abbreviated version of the bar fight story.

"There's more. A very good source revealed to me that Natalie and Bix were most likely in a relationship at some point."

"You don't think he killed her, do you?" Emma gasped. "I don't even...I mean, I can't...." Callie interrupted her friend.

"I don't know, either Emma. I just thought I should mention it."

"Yes, thank you. You definitely should have. I almost hate to ask – but is there anything else?"

Callie decided to skip the part about the supplier non-payment mix-up Melody Cartwright had told her about. That was an issue for

Melody to take up with her boss and anyway, as a fellow business owner, Callie didn't want to embarrass Emma.

"There was a newspaper story. It said the murder was causing people to stay away from your inn. But when I spoke to Melody Cartwright the other day, she said everything was normal and that she was very busy with the guests. I have no idea who spoke to the reporter, by the way. She didn't say a word about that."

"Yes," Emma answered, her voice low. "I already heard about the newspaper article. I get the Internet edition of the *Courier* sent to me via e-mail every morning – unfortunately. So you're saying that Melody lied? I can easily check on that."

"I wouldn't go that far. Maybe she just didn't want me to know. She could have been protecting you – and the inn. Plus, she's got a book coming out. She might not have wanted bad publicity surrounding anything she's involved with right now."

"Yes....that makes sense." Emma was sounding more defeated by the minute. "Well, thank you, Callie. You've certainly been busy. I do appreciate it."

"You're welcome." Callie decided that Emma needed a little cheering up, so she changed the subject. "Melody asked me to contribute to the Christmas Tea – did she tell you about that?"

"No! But I think it's a wonderful idea. Will you do it?"

"I told her I would."

Emma sounded more chipper. "Please make those snowball cookies. You know the ones. They're not exactly a British teatime cookie, but that's all right. They'll be perfect for the party."

Callie was relieved that Emma's mood was brightening. It must be horrible to be stranded so far away from your place of business while it was undergoing a crisis. On the other hand it wasn't so great to be stuck in town with yet another killer. But she kept that thought strictly to herself.

The two exchanged a few more pleasantries and ended the call. Callie put on her turn signal and was about start driving home again when she saw a car speeding towards her on the opposite side of the street. It was a large SUV. Callie squinted at it, sure that she had seen it somewhere before. The thickly falling snow made it difficult to be certain.

Horrified, Callie watched as the SUV began weaving from side to side as it grew closer to her car. Suddenly, it veered directly towards her. Callie screamed, but the vehicle lurched in the other direction just before it would have hit her and kept going down the road at a fast pace.

Callie sat for a minute, trembling with fear at the near-miss. The worst part of all was that she'd recognized the other driver: Mrs. Dayton. What was she doing out here, driving like a bat out of hell?

* * *

The next day dawned bright and sunny, the snow sparkling like sugar spilling out of a bowl. Callie got to work early, still slightly shaken about the incident with the out-of-control car the previous evening. She'd debated calling Sands to report Mrs. Dayton's erratic driving right after it happened, but in the end she decided it was wiser not to make an enemy of the woman. It was only today that she regretted not reporting it. Mrs. Dayton could have killed someone.

Max wasn't coming in until later that afternoon, so Callie was alone but for customers seeking out breakfast breads and lunches to take to work. She decided to work on some prep for the Lexy Dayton holiday party, scheduled for only a few days away. She wasn't sure what she would do when she encountered Mrs. Dayton at the party but one thing was for sure – she definitely wouldn't get in the way of her moving car.

As Callie rolled out cookie dough, stirred soup and started another pan of *pastitsio*, the good cooking smells soothed her as always. Stopping for a moment, she inhaled deeply. A mélange of appetizing scents swirled through the kitchen – butter, cinnamon, cooking meat and the sweet/sour tang of lemon. Call Yankee Candle Company: Callie's Kitchen scent would be a hit.

The bell over the door jingled and Callie looked up in surprise. "Sweetie!" she greeted her relative. "It's so nice to see you. What are you doing here so early?"

"I bored," Sweetie said, joining Callie behind the countertop. "I no can sleep, I only bake so much. George and I no eat all I cook. So George asks me to come here, see if you need any help. He drop me off just now."

"Oh!" Callie said, unable to hide her surprise. If George wanted to give Sweetie something to do, she wondered why he didn't insist on her joining him at The Olympia. Could it be that family togetherness had its limits? And why hadn't he stopped in to say hello to her? It was almost as if he were avoiding her.

Maybe, Callie thought with a sinking feeling, he doesn't want Sweetie to know how often he's seeing Kathy. He mentioned that Kathy visited his diner, The Olympia, quite a bit. Also, if he didn't see Callie, then she couldn't ask him about his new love interest.

Never mind. She'd put Sweetie to work and with her help, she could finish food prep before Max arrived for his later shift, giving her time to visit Melody Cartwright once again and offer to host a book launch party.

"Sweetie, I was thinking of making *spanakopita* but I think the phyllo dough is still frozen. I've got spinach, eggs, feta cheese, and onions – all the good stuff. Do you think you could make something with that?"

"You kidding?" Sweetie asked, a broad smile showing off the dimple in her left cheek. "I have just the thing. I call it lazy *spanakopita*. You will like."

"Go for it. I trust you."

Sweetie put a blue-and-white Callie's Kitchen apron on over her dark sweater and skirt and went to the back room to create her dish. Soon, the delectable scent of melting butter wafted through the shop.

Callie turned back to the Lexy Dayton party menu and got to work on the prep, but inwardly, she was fretting about the revelations from Lexy and Nick's fight the previous evening. Lexy certainly didn't seem like someone who was ready to be married and Nick, well. She hadn't wanted to say anything to upset Lexy, but he seemed to be preoccupied, albeit tolerant of Lexy's up-and-down moods. Could he have been in love with Natalie – and was he now coping with a broken heart?

Or was it even worse than that? Was mild-mannered Nick the killer?

Nine

Sweetie finished her "lazy spanakopita," which consisted of a luscious spinach-feta-onion mixture bound together with a bit of flour and eggs, then baked into warm, flavorful squares. Callie decided to call the dish "Spinach Squares" and she praised George's cousin to the skies before offering her a ride home. "Bless your hands," she said in Greek, and Sweetie beamed. "Thanks – I'm sure my customers will love this."

"You welcome," Sweetie said, taking off her apron gratefully. "This cooking tiring. Maybe now I take nap."

Max had already arrived, so Callie told him she was going out for a bit and bundled Sweetie into her car, looking carefully into the alley behind Callie's Kitchen before walking past it. She no longer parked her car behind her shop after the events of just a few months ago – maybe she would be able to park there again, someday, but for now she felt safer out in the open. Her plan was to take Sweetie home and then stop by The English Country Inn for a *tête-à-tête* with Melody Cartwright about the possibility of hosting a book launch for her.

"How's my Dad," Callie asked casually as she and Sweetie powered over the snow-covered roads.

Sweetie gave a knowing glance to Callie. "You mean – he still with that woman?"

Callie felt her cheeks grow warm and attempted to laugh it off. "No, I really want to know how he is. He seems to be avoiding me."

"I don't know if he avoiding. But you two a lot alike. Strong. Stubborn." Sweetie smiled to soften her words. "You know George, he proud man. He tell you what he think, when he ready."

"Ha!" Callie said, steering her car around a snowbank. "I'm not worried about Dad telling me what he thinks. He does that very well already." She was quiet a moment, focusing on her driving. "I'm so used to him checking on me, nagging me. I guess I just miss him."

They pulled up in front of George's cozy house, its roof covered with fluffy white flakes and his evergreen trees sporting big dollops of snow that looked to Callie like scoops of whipped cream.

Sweetie turned to Callie. "Stop by and see your Dad anytime. Or call him. He worry, you know. With a killer in town."

"You're right," Callie answered. "I'll check on him." Maybe George was avoiding her, maybe he wasn't. Either way, she would check on him – and soon.

Sweetie opened the door to George's house, then turned around and waved. Callie slowly drove off in the direction of the inn, gathering her thoughts about what she would say to Melody.

* * *

As she navigated the icy roads, Callie found that she had to convince herself yet again that she was doing the right thing by helping Emma. The murder of Natalie had her well and truly spooked. All too soon, she was walking through the door of the inn and she had to suppress a shudder. The sound of Christmas music playing softly and a fully-decorated Christmas tree displayed in the lobby served as a great contrast to the recent tragedy staged there.

Callie scanned the hotel lobby, which opened up into the formal dining room of the hotel restaurant. The dining room had been re-opened but appeared nearly empty, while a couple of guests milled around the gift shop, a small nook to the right of the hotel lobby. No question about it, the hotel definitely lacked its usual "buzz."

Melody was on the phone, talking quietly in anxious tones to someone but she hung up quickly when she noticed Callie standing there.

"Hello," she said, her smile a bit strained. "What can I do for you today? Or do you have more food for us?" Her tone was kind but a bit cool.

"Well, there's actually something that I'd like to do for *you*," Callie said brightly.

"Oh," Melody asked, puzzled. "What's that?"

"I'm so happy for you regarding your book launch. I was wondering if I could host a book launch party for you. I was thinking that Callie's Kitchen would be the perfect spot. I could serve some food from your book and we could have a blast!"

"Why, I..." Melody's cheeks flushed even deeper than the pink blush that she wore. "Thank you! Are you sure you have time? I know you must be busy. My publisher told me I should do a local launch, but I haven't really planned anything yet." Melody sighed. "This situation with Natalie has me stressed and frightened beyond belief. I've hardly had time to even think of the launch. There are so many things to do and, well – it's just that not everyone is as supportive as they might be." She frowned.

"Really?" Callie was taken aback. "I would imagine that everyone is very happy for you."

"Not everyone," Melody said, darkly. She composed her features and looked up at Callie. "I have a confession to make. I was considering asking Tea for Two if they wanted to host my book launch, considering I've written a book on tea parties. However, I don't see why you can't serve some food and Christy can bring the tea." Melody smiled at Callie. "Would that be all right?"

"Sure!" Callie said agreeably. It might make it a little more difficult to uncover Melody's secrets with Christy around, but she'd figure out something. She'd have to speak to Melody alone at some point, right? Anyway, it might be a chance to get to know the new proprietor of Tea for Two a little bit better.

"I think that sounds good. We can have the launch at either venue. But we'd better plan quickly. We want to make sure you have plenty of time to advertise."

Melody chewed her bottom lip. "I know. I'll get back to you. I promise. Just let me figure out what I want to do. Once I get that settled, I'll give you a call."

Callie produced her business card and passed it across the counter to Melody, who took it and placed it in a drawer, out of sight.

She wasn't lying about being stressed. Callie noticed that Melody's normally perfect nails looked chewed and in need of a manicure. Well, put that down to the last few days. Callie couldn't imagine that Melody was having an easy time dealing with Natalie's murder, even without a book launch hanging over her head.

Just then, Jack Myers, dressed in his usual flannel shirt, jeans and boots combo strode out into the lobby. His stubbled cheeks gave him a rakish air.

"All set, Jack?" asked Melody, giving him a big smile. Hmmm, Callie thought. Was prim and proper Melody flirting?

Jack returned her smile, albeit not as enthusiastically. "I think so. Per our previous discussion, everything seems to be a go." He nodded at Callie. "Hi, there. Hey, thanks for the food delivery the other day. Melody shared some stuff with me. Very good." He gave Callie an appraising look. "A beautiful woman who can cook. Not a bad combo."

"Uh, you bet," Callie said looking from one to the other. "Thanks." She felt her face growing warm. Even though she enjoyed Sands' company – more than she wanted to admit – he *was* a little distant lately. It was nice to have some male attention. Immediately, Callie felt disloyal to Sands. You couldn't fault him for being hard working.

A glance at Melody revealed an unhappy expression on her beautifully made-up face. *Maybe I'm getting paranoid*, Callie thought before the lightbulb clicked.

Could it be that Jack was the supplier that Melody had been complaining about the other day? That would definitely be enough to cause tension between the two of them. Not sure what to make of this unexpected insight, Callie decided to cover some different ground. "Has Bix been in yet today?" she asked, looking from one of them to the other.

Jack and Melody exchanged glances. "Yes," Melody said. "He's been here. He's super busy. I think he's working out near the boathouse. I know he was supposed to spread salt on the back entrance of the hotel, right behind the dining room. Some guests use that entrance and it's pretty icy on the patio right now."

"Oh my goodness," Callie said, blanching. She didn't want to revisit the scene of Natalie's murder. No need to bother Bix right now.

"Thanks, I'll catch him later." She walked out before anyone could ask her why she wanted to talk to him.

On a whim, she turned around to wave to Melody and she noticed that Jack had joined the concierge behind her desk and was speaking softly and intently to her. Melody hung on every word.

Well, well, Callie thought. Was their tension truly about a financial disagreement...or was romance in the air for those two, as well? No wonder Melody looked unhappy when Jack complimented her. She wanted him for herself.

* * *

"Welcome, everybody, to *Let's Dance*," said the attractive, dark-haired young woman at the front of the large room. Located strategically, perhaps, for couples seeking dance training for their first wedding dance together, "Let's Dance" was on the second floor of Bette's

Bridal Shop. The instructor's hair was pulled up into a bun on top of her head and she wore a black dress with a full, swishy skirt.

"I'm Lina and this is my co-instructor and dance partner, Sean." The instructor bobbed her head at the lithe, muscular young man standing next to her. "We're going to teach you how to dance like you've been doing it all your life."

Callie smiled at Sands, who stood next to her in a long-sleeved white shirt and casual trousers. Her plan to drag Sands to the dance class once attended by Bix and Natalie had been a success. Sleuthing aside, she was happy to be away from the stove and finally in the same room as Sands, even though the reason for the outing – investigating Natalie's murder – was a grim one.

Sands smiled at Callie as the instructor spoke to them about leading, following, which foot to begin on and how to loosen up and find your "inner dancer."

Callie watched with the rest of the class as Lina and Sean – a compact, muscular 20-something with astounding thigh muscles encased in rather tight black pants – demonstrated a few warm-up steps to get the class moving.

Callie took stock of the rest of her fellow dancers. The class was a mish-mash of old and young, single and partnered. Many of the couples appeared to be practicing for their wedding dance, but just as many seemed to be there as a result of such shows as Dancing with the Stars.

It was a relief to be out with people who were smiling and laughing. Maybe this crew wasn't following Natalie's murder as closely as some of the Callie's Kitchen clientele was – she could hardly keep up with their requests for carbs. She was inclined to agree with Max's diagnosis of stress eating.

Loud music disrupted her thoughts. "It doesn't matter if you make mistakes," Lina was shouting over the din. "What matters is that you have a good time. Nobody was born knowing how to dance!"

"What about John Travolta?" Sands said under his breath and Callie shook her head.

"Gentlemen, face your partners," Sean announced. "Now, get in the 'dance stance.'"

Sands placed his arm around Callie's waist and took her hand. "We're in the stance," he joked.

"OK! 1-2-3!" Lina and Sean started swirling around the room and the class stumbled along as they followed suit.

Sands turned out to be a surprisingly smooth dancer. He held Callie in a firm grip and confidently steered her through the steps. She stumbled a bit at first but soon found her footing. Who would have thought that he would be such a good dancer – and why hadn't he told her?

"Hello! Hello!!" a voice from the doorway startled Callie. She whirled around to view the source and stopped dancing abruptly, causing her and Sands to collide with another couple.

"Sorry!" Callie gasped and Sands looked at her in concern. "Are you all right?"

He followed her gaze to the door and as he was still holding her firmly about the waist, she felt the rumble of laughter flow through him before she heard it. "You didn't tell me we were to be chaperoned," he chuckled. "Why, hello there, Mr. Costas!"

George nodded at Sands before turning to his daughter. "Callie! What are you doing here?" her father addressed her with a wrinkled brow. To Callie's dismay, the music had stopped and the entire class was watching their exchange. In a distracted way, Callie noticed that her father's curly, greying hair was carefully combed and he wore a sport coat and one of his nicer pairs of trousers.

Behind George was Kathy, who gazed upon the class with a demure smile. Callie noticed that she was dressed to the nines in a black, form-fitting sweater dress and high-heeled boots. How was she going to be able to move freely in that get-up? Callie wondered. But she had to admit, Kathy did look quite nice.

"I'm taking a dance class, Dad, same as you," Callie said with dignity. She wouldn't let George ruffle her feathers, but she was hurt that he had time for a dance class but apparently, had been AWOL as far as everyone else was concerned. "Hello, Kathy," she said to the older woman who stood next to her father, a bemused look on her face.

"You look wonderful, dear. And who is your charming partner?" Kathy was smooth, no doubt about it.

"Detective Ian Sands," he said holding out his hand. "Pleased to meet you."

"I'm so sorry," Callie said, addressing Lina. "This is my dad, George Costas and his friend, Kathy. I didn't know they'd be joining us tonight." She darted her eyes at Sands who looked as if he was holding back laughter.

"The more, the merrier," the instructor replied, pursing her glossy red lips. "George, you and Kathy can get up to speed by watching us do our first step. Join in when you're ready." She nodded to her dance partner to turn the music back on and Callie was flooded with relief as Sands whirled her away.

When they were on the opposite side of the vast room away from George, she finally spoke. "I swear. I had no idea he'd be here. I'm a little hurt at him, actually. No one but this Kathy seems to see him anymore!"

"Is that so?" Sands said, giving Kathy an appraising glance. "She's a nice-looking lady. Good for him!"

"Oh, you're as bad as he is," Callie answered, giving his foot a light stomp.

"Watch it," Sands said. "If you're seen having a tantrum, you'll be sent home."

Sands kept them both in step over the next few numbers and when the music ended, she found herself looking at him a bit in awe. "Why didn't you tell me you were such a good dancer?" she asked.

Sands' cheeks flushed and he cleared his throat. "I've had a bit of practice, you see. In the past."

"Oh," Callie replied. He must mean with his ex-wife. He also had a young daughter that had passed away but he never spoke of her and Callie felt that it might be prying to ask him. He'd tell her about it when he was ready.

Suddenly, their lighter mood felt like it was growing darker. Callie squeezed his hand. "Well, you're terrific," she said. He squeezed her hand back but didn't look at her.

The instructor clapped her hands, her nails bright with red lacquer to match her lips. "Wonderful job, guys!" she crowed. "So let's move on to the next step." She and her dance partner demonstrated the box step and the class followed along, albeit, not as gracefully. Callie noticed out of the corner of her eye that George and Kathy were moving smoothly together and she felt a rush of love for her father. *Please don't let Kathy break his heart*, she prayed.

She glanced at Sands as he whirled her around the room, still smiling at her, but seeming slightly preoccupied. She was startled by a sudden, unwelcome thought.

And please don't let Sands break mine.

Ten

Despite the unexpected drama with George, Callie enjoyed herself at the class and when Lina announced the last dance of the evening, she was surprised at how quickly the time had gone. George and Sands had exchanged partners at one point, but Callie and her father didn't have time for any sort of deep conversation. George seemed happy to see his daughter, if a bit abashed at being caught out on a date. She told him what Olivia had shared with her: that Hugh and Raine thought they'd found a home just a couple of blocks from her own.

"Eh, you worry too much, *hrisi mou*," had been George's dismissive response. "It may not even work out. Real estate – who knows?" He had something there. Real estate deals were notoriously dicey, especially in this market. However, she would have thought that George would understand why she didn't want her space invaded by her ex, cordial though she tried to be. She didn't get a chance to ask him. The dance had ended, George had returned swiftly to Kathy, and that was that.

Callie's stomach did a flip flop once she realized it was soon time to interrogate Lina about Bix.

The last remaining class members were still chatting and laughing with the dance instructor and her partner, but thankfully, they started to drift out the door after a few more minutes. Callie let out a sigh of relief as Sean, the other dance instructor, gave Lina two big cheek kisses and then went out the door as well. Here was her chance!

Callie sidled up to the fit young woman who smiled warmly, if a bit wearily, at her. "Thank you, Lina. This really was an enjoyable class. Sorry about my Dad – George, that is. He didn't mean to disrupt anything."

"No need to apologize. George is a darling! Don't worry about it! I'm glad you enjoyed the class." She gathered up her things as if to leave and Callie put a panicked hand on her arm. "I have a question for you. I hope you can answer it for me." Callie was aware of Sands standing nearby.

The dance instructor looked up at him and back at Callie, a concerned look on her face. "What is it?" she asked, disengaging from Callie's grasp.

"One of your former students was recently murdered. Natalie Underwood. I heard that she came here with a man named Bix. I'm a friend and colleague of Natalie's and I wondered if you knew anything about their relationship."

"Surely if you really are her 'friend' you would know more about it than me," Lina answered, somewhat sarcastically. "What are you – police?"

"Actually, I am," Sands said smoothly, stepping forward. "Callie here is just a ballroom dance fan. We don't mean to trouble you, Lina and we really were here to participate in your class. We just thought that you might be able to shed some light on a few things for us."

"You want to know about Natalie and Bix," Lina said with a gusty sigh. "OK. Well, Natalie was nice enough; I'll say that for her. Obviously, I didn't know her well, but that's how she seemed. I was devastated to hear about her murder. She was fashionable, funny, and polite. Bix on the other hand..." Lina raised a palm in the "stop" sign. "He thought he was God's gift to women." She sighed and sat down on the lone folding chair at the front of the room.

Callie looked at Sands and he nodded at her. "What do you mean?" she asked Lina.

"Bix and Natalie were definitely an item. I mean, most people who come here are engaged or at least in a serious relationship. Like you two, right? When's the wedding?"

Callie gulped and couldn't look at Sands. "No wedding yet," Sands said pleasantly and Callie's heart thrummed. "What about Bix and Natalie?" he urged.

"Sorry. Well, they acted really affectionate together. Hugging, kissing, laughing." Callie nodded – she'd heard as much from Grandma Viv's description.

"But then – get this." Lina narrowed her eyes. "Right after the last session of the class – Natalie had already gone to the car or some such thing – Bix comes up to me and asks me out! Seriously." She shook her head.

"What did you say?" Callie asked.

"What do you think I said? A big, fat 'No.' What a jerk. But truth be told, I've even had grooms-to-be ask me out. Kind of makes you lose your faith in marriage, you know?"

No need to go there, Callie thought. She glanced at Sands, who looked grim. "Anything else you think might be of interest?" Sands asked Lina.

"Bix tried contacting me after I rejected him. He emailed me a couple of times and somehow got my cell phone number. He texted me a couple of times, until I got smart and blocked his number. I guess he got the message. I ran into him a few days ago in town and he totally ignored me. Thank goodness."

"Right. I may need to question you again, more formally about this, Lina. And if you think of anything else, would you give me a call?" Sands gave Lina his crisp white business card and she nodded.

"You know what? For a cop, you're a pretty good dancer." Lina batted her eyelashes just the tiniest bit. "And I like your accent."

* * *

"That was interesting," Sands offered as they walked down Garden Street, past Callie's Kitchen, Tea for Two and the many Crystal Bay business district shops now covered in evergreen boughs, tiny white lights and all manner of festive Christmas decorations. Callie inhaled deeply of the cold but refreshing air. It had been a little bit stuffy in the dance studio. Fresh snowflakes fell softly on the two as they strolled together, and there was a hushed quality to the early evening.

Suddenly, Sands stopped and grabbed her hand. "I'm sorry I got a little funny in there. I loved dancing with you, you know."

Callie was embarrassed that he'd noticed her dismay while they were dancing. "Oh, don't worry about it. I understand that you have a lot on your mind."

"Let me explain anyway. I don't really talk about my past much, do I?"

"No," Callie admitted, her face flushing. "But I didn't want to upset you by prying."

"That's one of the things I like about you, Callie," Sands said, keeping hold of her hand as they started walking again. "You only pry when there's a murder mystery involved."

Callie was startled into laughter but she quickly grew somber. Whatever Sands was trying to tell her, he was clearly using humor to deflect some of the pain.

Sands seemed to be struggling to find the right words, but he hesitated and Callie saw his expression change. "It's nothing. I just used to dance with my ex-wife and it reminded me of some things I'd rather forget."

"Oh." Callie was taken aback. "Do you miss your wife?" The question popped out before she could stop herself.

"Ex-wife," Sands corrected her gently, giving her hand a squeeze. "I don't miss her. Please – it's not that. It's just reminded me of my life with my daughter. You know, before."

Before. Callie gulped. Sands had told her before they started dating, that his young daughter had died. He hadn't specified how and Callie had never asked. She debated asking now but didn't want to cause him any more pain.

"I'm sorry," she said, softly. "I never would have dragged you to a dance class if I thought it would bring up sad memories for you."

"Not sad, exactly. Well, I guess, so. If I'm honest. But listen," he said, facing her. "When I found out about Natalie being in the class, I would have been forced to go the dance studio to ask questions, with or without you. You provided a bit of moral support for me."

"Really?" Callie asked, taken aback. "Then I'm glad I was there for you."

"Me too," Sands replied and Callie felt her heart give an odd little skip. Suddenly, Sands light humor and seeming glibness about life made a lot more sense. In his shoes, Callie would be frantic.

"What about an Irish coffee or a beer?" Sands asked. "Maybe we can even catch the end of the Packers game."

"You bet," Callie answered. Someday she'd get the whole story about his previous life, but he didn't seem to want to share more right now. "After that, I'd better get back. Sweetie and Viv are watching Olivia tonight. They've really been helping me out a lot lately and I don't want to take advantage." In the back of her mind, she was worried about the three of them, alone in the house. A chill went down her spine as she thought of them, defenseless against anyone who might want to cause them harm.

But Sands was already steering her into the only pub on Garden Street, aptly and simply named, "The Pub." They also served pretty good food and Callie as always was interested in what the competition was doing. Callie stood back to let a couple pass and then let out a little gasp of astonishment when it registered who they were.

"Hi, Callie," chirped Piper, albeit a bit uncertainly. Instead of Max, Callie's loyal friend and co-worker, Piper's companion was none other than Bix Buckman.

"Evening," Bix nodded tersely. "Piper, let's get going."

"See you tomorrow, Callie," Piper called, following Bix quickly past Sands and Callie and out into the street.

Once the two were gone, Callie gaped at Sands who looked back at her with a raised eyebrow, his hazel eyes glimmering.

"The game is afoot," he said, a gleam in his eye.

"Sherlock Holmes would be proud," Callie answered.

Eleven

Callie felt drained the next day at work, but she tried to channel positivity into baking a huge batch of *paxemathia*, Greek "biscotti." She'd decided to place them in large, pretty glass jars with a red ribbon around them. Spiced with festive anise-flavored *ouzo*, they'd be perfect as impromptu Christmas gifts or hostess gifts at holiday parties.

As Callie gathered ingredients and cooking utensils, she found her mind ticking off the many odd experiences and revelations of late. As a whole, the events of the last few days had been not only tragic, but puzzling in the extreme.

Between nearly being hit by a wayward SUV, breaking up fiancé feuds, finding out that her best friend's current boyfriend was most likely a "player" and possibly a murderer, and having her Dad squiring a relative of her ex's new wife around town, Callie's brain was on overload.

Not to mention, trying to help her friend Emma keep an eye on her hotel, processing young Natalie's brutal murder and now – she was finding herself increasingly confused about her relationship with Sands. Could he still be hung up on his ex? He was a perfect gentleman, a smart, funny, dear companion. She blushed when she realized it didn't matter that her brain was telling her to slow down. No question about it. She was falling for him.

Exhaling in a whoosh, Callie brushed flour off of her hands and plopped onto a stool in the baking area of her kitchen. Max was out front serving customers, which was always a good thing. But thinking about Max made Callie think about Piper. And more specifically, it made her think about Piper and Bix, together. What was *that* all about? Maybe Piper liked guys that had an "x" in the last letter of their name. Callie shook her head at her own whimsy.

Break time over. Callie heaved herself out of her chair and started forming dough for the *paxemathia*. Just like biscotti, they'd be baked in small, delectable-smelling loaves before being cut into slices and baked again. As usual, working with food, especially baking, perked up Callie's spirits. While she shaped the cookie loaves and put them in the oven, she decided that she wouldn't tell Max about running into Piper and Bix. Maybe the two were just friends.

Except that Bix didn't seem to have female friends: He was either dating the women in his circle, trying to date them, or semi-stalking them. This last observation made Callie decide that she had to share some of what she'd learned with Sam. Now *that* was a conversation that she wasn't looking forward to initiating. Out of loyalty to her friend, though, she had to give Sam warning about the guy she was seeing. It wouldn't be welcome news, but she'd want Sam to do the same thing for her.

Or would she? Grimacing, Callie remembered her tense conversation with Sam at The Elkhorn regarding Sands and his frequent unavailability. She didn't like anyone criticizing the person she was seeing, true. Still, Callie rationalized; Bix just seemed like a man with too many secrets and too many women in his past – or possibly his present. Leaning down to check on her *paxemathia* loaves, she resolved to speak to Sam ASAP.

"Callie?" a hesitant voice jolted her from wondering if the cookies were browning too quickly. Easing the kinks out of her back, she straightened up and turned around. Piper.

"Can we sit down a minute?" Piper asked. Callie nodded and gestured at two stools by the long marble countertop that she used for rolling out cookies and pastry.

Callie busied herself with the coffee pot as Piper settled herself onto a stool. Finally, when the two of them were seated and sipping at the rich, dark roast coffee, Piper spoke.

"I wanted to explain about Bix and me," she said. Her blue eyes blinked at Callie and she licked her upper lip nervously. Callie sat and waited, tapping her foot against the metal rung of the stool. Today, Piper wore a retro-looking red knit dress with a white Peter Pan collar. She looked like a young, pretty Mrs. Claus.

"You don't have to explain anything to me," Callie began, but Piper cut her off.

"Yes, I do. I saw the way you and your boyfriend, that detective, looked at us last night. I like Max and I don't want him – or you – to get the wrong idea."

"Piper, what you and Max do is your own business. If anything, I'm more concerned about my friend, Sam, who's been seeing Bix." Callie wasn't sure if she believed Piper's story but she didn't want to get involved in a fight between her employees. That was a recipe for nothing but disaster.

"OK, well, there's nothing going on with me and Bix," Piper was saying, her eyes still blinking rapidly. "He wanted my help with social media for his band. I took the freelance job with Bix because I need the money," Piper explained, with a little shrug of her red knit-covered shoulders. "You know how it is. I need to pay for school."

Callie nodded encouragingly. "I know. You've done a great job. I'm not surprised that other people want to work with you."

Piper took another sip of coffee and stared into her cup as intently as if she could read her fortune in it. "There's something else. Max wasn't around last night, but Bix was. Because of Natalie's murder, I wanted a bodyguard. I didn't want to tell you this, but the other night, I felt like someone was following me."

"What happened?"

"Well, I was leaving class and even thought it wasn't late, it was pitch dark. You know how it gets around here – it's like midnight at 5 pm." Callie nodded encouragingly.

"So I was walking to my car and I heard footsteps behind me. The footsteps were soft, but fast, like they were jogging to catch up to me. I was alone and I started to panic. I carry pepper spray, and I was about to get it out of my bag." Piper's face was white as she relayed the incident.

"But just as I was about to turn around, a whole bunch of people came out of the student bookstore. It's right near where my car was parked. They were heading my way and I was about to call to them for help, when the footsteps stopped for a minute, and then started up again but in the other direction. Whoever it was ran away."

Callie let this sink in. Why would someone be following Piper?

"You probably don't believe me and I know you and Max are friends." When she looked up again, her blue eyes were wet at the corners. "I don't want Max to think I'm going out with Bix. Because I'm not."

Oh dear, thought Callie. *What have I gotten myself into?* "Piper, I'm not the Dating Police. Talk to Max if you like, about last night. I won't say anything."

Piper beamed at Callie, her lipstick bright red to match her dress. "Thanks, Callie."

"But I am going to mention this to Sands. This may be nothing, but you never know. Any ideas as to why someone would be following you?"

Piper shook her head just as the oven timer started beeping. "Hey, didn't you want me to take some pictures of your cookies?" she asked. Clearly, she was trying to change the subject.

Callie put on oven mitts and lowered the oven door. She'd leave the topic for the time being – but it was troubling.

"Yes, I would love that," Callie said, hoping to placate her co-worker. She set the cookie sheets on the countertop, being careful not to let the hot surfaces touch her. "Let me slice them first; they've got to be baked twice." Callie went about her business as Piper snapped what she called "action shots" with her iPhone, and finally took some stills of the cookie slices lying prettily in the pans before Callie returned the cookie sheets to the oven.

"The cookies look great," Piper said, flipping through her phone. "You'll definitely want to use some of these pics." Callie peered over Piper's shoulder at the photos and smiled at the images of her messy hair pulled into a topknot, and her floury apron and hands. One thing you could say for her: she looked like she was working hard.

"I like them," Callie said. "Go ahead and put one of them up on our Facebook and Instagram accounts." Callie was happy with how much she'd caught up with the social media challenges presented to modern small businesspeople. Piper had been a big part of that, she had to admit.

She turned to Piper who was busily gathering up her things and not looking at her. "Gotta go," Piper chirped, visibly relieved that the conversation was coming to a close. "I'll get your pictures up as soon as I can but I'll be late for class if I don't leave now. Especially with all of this snow."

"It's snowing – again?" Callie asked, following Piper to the door so that she could inspect the skies. Sure enough, fluffy white flakes were descending from oppressive gray clouds: a typical Wisconsin winter day.

"Bye!" Piper called, barely recognizable in her hat, coat and scarf that covered half of her face. In addition to snow, the temperature had dropped and it felt about 20 degrees outside.

"Be careful!" Callie called back and Piper gave her a thumbs-up sign. What felt like a wall of frigid air blasted her as she opened the door. Quickly, she slammed it shut and retreated to her warm kitchen.

Well, that was awkward. Callie slumped against the countertop. *And worrisome.* Frankly, someone following a young woman in a parking lot sounded an awful lot like reports she'd heard about Bix. Would he follow a woman he was interested in, in the hopes that it would drive her closer to him? If so, that was sick. Callie sighed deeply. And this was the guy her normally sane and sophisticated best friend was seeing. Sheesh.

The oven timer binged again. Worrying about her personal life and analyzing potential suspects would have to wait. *Paxemathia* were calling.

* * *

That night, after closing up shop for the day, Callie found herself driving the short distance to George's house for a family dinner. George had called her at work to invite her, just as she was pulling another batch of *paxemathia* out of the oven.

Sweetie and Viv would be there, of course, and Olivia was in the back seat of the car with Koukla, who her daughter insisted should be able to join the gathering. Olivia was chatting away about school and excited to be visiting Sweetie, her new obsession.

Callie had tactfully refrained from asking if Kathy would be joining them. Spending nights at home alone just didn't have the same charm it once did. Every creak of the floorboards, every lashing of wind, every bark from little Koukla convinced her that something evil was lurking. With resignation, Callie realized she'd probably feel that way until Natalie's killer was apprehended.

Callie's car crunched over the packed snow as she parked in front of George's cozy house. It was pitch dark and bitingly cold, but white Christmas lights on the evergreens, and the glow from the lamps in her father's picture window were inviting and warm. Olivia took Koukla gently out of her kennel that had been strapped and secured in the back seat, and grabbed her leash. The two of them scampered up the walkway, while Callie locked up the car. Carefully, she balanced the box of Greek biscotti she'd brought from Callie's Kitchen and took cautious steps up the pathway in her chunky-heeled leather boots, silently admonishing herself for not wearing her more practical, waterproof footwear.

Olivia had already pressed the doorbell, so Callie was quickly ushered into George's small living room. This was Callie's family home growing up and not much had changed – from the walls covered with Greek art, to the comfortable leather sofa, now worn around the edges, but sublimely comfortable. Callie took off her snow-covered boots and placed them next to Olivia's on a small rug by the front door while Koukla barked excitedly and ran around in little circles around everyone's feet.

Callie hugged her father tightly, then Viv and Sweetie, who smelled like butter. "Cooking again, Sweetie?" she asked with a smile and the older woman smiled, showing her one dimple. "For you – yes!"

"Hello, dear," Viv greeted her granddaughter with an embrace. "I'm so glad you could make it. Any news about Natalie?"

"Viv!" scolded Sweetie, with a smile. "We have nice dinner, no talk of murder."

"You're right," Viv said apologetically. "We'll talk about it after dinner," she said with a firm nod.

"Of course!" Sweetie nodded firmly. "But not now. Now we have nice time."

Those two. Callie left the two ladies to fawn over Koukla as she followed George into the kitchen. From her quick scan of the house, he didn't seem to be harboring any surprise guests. "Thanks for having us over, Dad. What can I do to help?"

"Nothing, all good!" George washed his hands. The rich smell of roasting meat coming from the oven was excruciatingly delicious. "I made Greek meatloaf, vegetables, *tzatziki*, and a little spinach pie left over from the other night. I've got bread, feta cheese, what else?" Even though *tzatziki* – a luscious cucumber yogurt sauce flavored with garlic – was a traditional summer dish, it was excellent on meats and pita bread and George served it year round.

"It already sounds like enough to feed an army, Dad." She put her arm around his shoulders. "Sounds great. Should I tell Olivia to go wash her hands?"

"Yes, everything is nearly ready." George gave Callie a squeeze and walked over to the oven to check his meatloaf. "Correction. Ready now!" He removed a gigantic roasting pan from the oven and placed it on a large trivet before turning to Callie. "Can you call everyone to the table?"

Callie gathered the troops and everyone seated themselves around George's rectangular table, covered in a beige cloth with an open crochet pattern, no doubt created by his mother years ago in Greece. *So,* Callie thought, relieved. *No sign of Kathy and no eligible bachelor for me to meet.* This might just be a nice, calm, family dinner after all.

George filled everyone's glasses with his favorite full-bodied red wine, while Callie poured grape juice in Olivia's tumbler. Before eating, he said a short grace, and then nodded at the group. "A toast! Here's to Sweetie for joining us all the way from the old country for Christmas."

They all clinked glasses and sipped their wine while smiling at Sweetie who was blushing prettily. Her hair was pulled back in a low ponytail and she was wearing a thick sweater with a reindeer on it. Callie looked more closely – it looked like it came from a local store in town. "I like your sweater," she said to her cousin, passing her a platter of roasted potatoes, zucchini and carrots that had been tossed in olive oil and lemon before going into the oven with the meatloaf.

"Thanks. Viv get it for me," she said, taking a generous portion of the vegetables before passing it to Olivia.

"Yes, Sweetie and I have been seeing quite a lot of each other," Viv said with a smile.

"Yes, we even go to The English Country Inn," Sweetie said innocently. "Just look around, no big deal."

"What?" Callie said. "You did?" She looked at her grandmother with exasperation. "They're going to get suspicious if we all start showing up there."

Viv waved her fork in the air, unconcerned. "Don't worry. I already thought of that. I pretended I wanted to have an event there and I ended up talking to Melody Cartwright. She's filling in for Natalie Underwood, apparently. She was very nice, if a bit harried."

"Okay, sorry. Did you find any new information?" Callie wasn't aware that she was leaning forward in her eagerness.

"I thought you didn't want us to investigate..." Viv teased.

"I didn't. I don't. But as long as you were there, I figured I might as well ask." Callie rationalized. "Besides tipping them off, I don't want you and Sweetie to get hurt. There is a killer out there, after all."

"I know, Callie. It *is* frightening, but I promise, we were careful." Viv had the good grace to look a bit sheepish.

"We fine," Sweetie said stoutly, forking a piece of *spanakopita* onto her plate. "Anyway, nobody think I understand English. But I no hear much, just Melody tell someone on phone to stop bothering her."

Didn't hear much? It sounded pretty juicy to Callie, though it could be as innocent as a reporter calling – or even a fight with a boyfriend. "Sweetie, not that I condone eavesdropping, but did you happen to hear who she was talking to?"

"I no hear." Sweetie took a huge bite of meatloaf and chewed contentedly. Swallowing, she raised her eyebrows and said eagerly, "I go back, hear more if you want."

"No, that's okay," Callie said quickly. She turned to Viv. "Look, I appreciate the help. I just don't want you two to get hurt. Promise me."

"Callie," Viv answered, looking a bit offended. "We were just talking to Melody. Don't worry. Anyway, do you think I would have lasted so many years if I didn't know how to take care of myself?"

"Sorry, Grandma. Of course not." Callie busied herself with her food. "Just look out, that's all I'm saying."

"I will, dear. And you as well."

George finally spoke up. "Glykeria, enough with the snooping. It's bad enough that Callie is involved. I didn't invite you here from Greece to play detective."

Oh boy, thought Callie. *Here we go.*

"George, you my cousin and I love you," Sweetie held her head high. "But is boring hanging around the house. I want go out, see Crystal Bay. Beautiful snow, nice people. You out working, with girlfriend, I find things to do."

The two exchanged some heated words in Greek. Callie thought she caught "donkey" and "nosy" but they were speaking too rapidly for her to get much more. Olivia looked at the two with interest, her gaze rapt. When George noticed his granddaughter taking in the argument with wide eyes, he stopped talking.

"Glykeria, I'll spend more time with you all. Sorry, I've been very busy." He cast a glance at Callie, who stared back at him. "Calliope, the same goes for you. The holidays are busy but family comes first."

"Don't worry, Dad," Callie answered. "The holidays have been busy at Callie's Kitchen, too. And no one begrudges you a social life..." she said slowly, trying to be magnanimous. Olivia interrupted.

"Yeah, Dad's busy, too," Olivia said, happy to have a topic that may be of interest to the adults at the table. "He and Raine think they found a house in Crystal Bay. Mom already knows, I told her about it." Olivia beamed. "Right near our house. I could see Dad every day!"

"Yes, you did mention that to me, honey. I remember. Dad," Callie said, turning to George, whose face was a bit flushed. "What does Kathy say about that? Any news on whether or not she found a house for Hugh and Raine yet?"

"Not really," George answered, looking away. "Well, how is the food? Olivia? Glykeria? Viv?" *Fine, change the subject, Dad.* Callie decided to corner him in the kitchen later, under the guise of dishwashing.

"It's great, Pappou," answered Olivia, scooping up more *spanakopita*. Koukla yipped and George tossed her a small piece of meatloaf.

"Olivia, you no eat nothing," Sweetie accused, looking at the girl's plate. That was what she always said, even though everyone had had seconds, if not thirds. Knowing the drill, Olivia shrugged it off. "I ate a lot, Sweetie," she said. "This is my third piece of meatloaf."

"OK, honey. Is dessert coming so you eat that, too. I make cookies and a honey cake."

George stood up. "I'll make coffee," he announced, apparently eager to get out of the conversation involving Kathy.

"I'll help you, Dad," Callie answered, gathering up a few empty plates. The two of them had a brief stare-down until George sighed resignedly. "Thank you, Calliope."

Callie followed George to the sink where he started running water, full force. She addressed him in a loud whisper, not wanting the others to hear, but needing to compete with the blast of the faucet. "Dad, you know I love you and I'm happy for you if you met someone. But I want to be honest. It's really hard for me to think of Hugh moving so close to my house. I've moved on, of course, and I want

Olivia to see her dad, but it's awkward. It's hard for me to understand why you might be encouraging this to happen."

George started filling the kettle with water for the Greek coffee he was preparing. He put it on the stove and turned to his daughter. "Callie, there is a reason for everything I do. Just trust me."

"What 'reason' are you talking about?"

"I said, I'll tell you later. Not now." George handed some dirty plates to Callie and she rinsed them in the sink.

Callie tried again. "Dad. Can't you at least give me a hint? And what about you and Kathy?" She hesitated and asked in a softer tone. "Is it serious?"

"Oh, Calliope. Everything is serious when you're my age. But you have the wrong idea. Kathy is a nice lady. Very nice. But that's all I can say now. I promise I'll tell more when I can."

Callie felt her anger bubble up like the water on the stove. "Fine. Well, I guess this is payback time for not liking the guy I'm dating," she blurted and instantly regretted it when she saw George's crestfallen face.

"No, Callie. You're wrong. It's not that at all. I'm disappointed you would think that." He filled the *briki*, the copper pot especially for making Greek coffee, with water and put it on the stove. Later, when the water boiled, he would add sugar and strong ground coffee. Only the thick, sweet top portion of the coffee would be drunk by the guests; the grounds would settle to the bottom of the cup.

By the set of his shoulders, it was obvious to Callie that George wouldn't say another word about the Kathy/Hugh conundrum. Wordlessly, Callie placed cookies and cake on a platter, got out dessert plates and brought then into the dining room to oohs and aahs. George gave everyone a cup of sweet Greek coffee and Sweetie offered to read the coffee grounds once everyone had finished the dark, rich drink.

When she came to Callie, she frowned. "You see this ledge? That means you go on a trip near water. This is boat."

"Do mine, do mine!" Olivia begged. She'd been given Greek coffee as a special treat and Callie hoped it wouldn't keep her up all night.

"Ah yes. See this ledge? This is bed. You sleeping here tonight." She smiled at Callie. "If okay with your mother."

"Yes, yes! A sleepover! Can I, Mom?" Olivia was bouncing up and down in her chair and Callie couldn't help but laugh, nodding her assent. "I should get going," she said. "Lots of baking tomorrow."

Everyone kissed and hugged goodbye, extensively, and then finally, Callie picked up Koukla and braved the cold.

The streets were dark and eerily silent, lulling a sleepy Callie, who was fighting fatigue despite the Greek coffee. She was approaching a stop sign when she became aware of lights filling the back window of her car. The vehicle was large and the headlights were so bright that Callie couldn't make out what kind of car it was.

When it didn't appear to be stopping or even slowing down, Callie swerved to the right to avoid a collision, but the roads were slippery and she'd swerved too sharply. Her car bumped and thumped into a nearby ditch. Callie screamed for Koukla and felt a large jolt to her jaw as the car came to a rocky halt.

Twelve

Callie was freezing cold and her jaw was in serious pain. Her brain felt sluggish and she wondered if she'd blacked out for a moment. "Koukla," she tried to shout, but her voice emerged as a weak half-whisper.

She turned her head, wincing, and looked back at Koukla, who was in her tipped-over kennel, wagging her tail and whimpering at her mistress. "Are you all right, baby?" she asked the little dog who gave a loud, piercing bark. She seemed all right, thank goodness. *Now – how to get out of the car?*

Callie considered her dilemma with a pounding heart. The car listed to the side and the driver-side door was jammed. Unfortunately, the passenger side was wedged against a snowbank.

It appeared that the hardened snowdrift had prevented a full roll-over and, for the first time in her life, Callie thanked the Wisconsin winters for being icy and cold. She realized that her jaw was so sore because the airbags had punched in her in the face when they deployed.

Where was the other car? Callie shook her head, causing a wave of nausea to roll over her. She looked out the windshield and saw red taillights blazing several hundred feet in front of her. A figure stood in the middle of the road. As Callie watched, the person took a few steps closer to her car, crouching down as if to see inside.

Callie could just about make out a shape, dressed all in black or some other dark color. She tried to make out the features, but the darkness and falling snow on her windshield made that impossible.

Shifting in her seat, Callie tried to roll down the window to call for help, but it wouldn't budge. "Help!" she called, yelling as loudly as she could. "I'm stuck in here!"

But the figure was backing away from her car. Suddenly, the shape started running. Bright taillights flashed once again, blinding her. She blinked as the vehicle that had run her off the road sped away with a squeal of tires.

So much for help from the other motorist – she was going to have to find a way out alone. *What a jerk.*

Where was her phone? Groggily, Callie searched the seat next to her for her purse, but the phone wasn't in it. It was probably on the floor of the car. *Now what?*

Koukla whimpered and her little dog's distress galvanized Callie. She reached back into her purse and felt around for a pen or nail file. Bingo! Even better – she'd discovered a pair of nail scissors. She jammed them into the air bag and a whoosh of stale air rushed out at her. Coughing, she waited for the air bags to deflate, before being able to reach down and feel around the seats for her phone.

After a panicked search, she found it wedged into the side pocket of the passenger door, where it had apparently fallen as the car toppled into the ditch.

Her fingers shook as she dialed Sands' number. He didn't answer right away and her heart started to pound. She'd have to give up and dial 911. In fact, that's what she should have done in the first place.

She was just about to disconnect the call when he answered: "Sands."

Hearing his familiar voice caused a wave of relief to wash over Callie. "It's me. I'm, uh...in a ditch. With Koukla. Someone just ran me off the road."

She heard his sharp intake of breath and his words tumbled out. "Are you hurt? Where's Olivia? What about the dog? Where are you?"

"I'm just a few blocks from home, near Lake Shore. I was at my dad's and don't worry, Olivia is still at his house." Callie felt sobs starting in the back of her throat, she was so relieved that he'd taken her call. "I'm stuck in my car and I'm worried about Koukla. She seems okay, but we had a pretty rough ride down into the ditch. And get this," she croaked. "Somebody got out of the car and was looking at me. I couldn't see who it was. They just looked at me and then drove off."

Sands tone was steely. "I'm calling for an ambulance. In the meantime, a patrol car will be there soon. I'm on my way right now. " She heard him giving orders on a different phone, probably an office line. Callie squirmed, trying to get comfortable. She was relieved that help was on the way, though embarrassed at the fact that she'd had to call for rescue. Coupled with that unwelcome emotion was shame at the fact that she realized what a mistake she'd made in not reporting the incident when an SUV had nearly swerved into her car.

Her woozy head starting to clear, Callie thought it was possible that the large vehicle that had run her off the road tonight was the same one that had almost swerved into her a couple of days earlier. She tried and failed to call up any image of the car that had run her off the road, save the blinding blast of headlights that had filled her window right before she crashed.

Was the driver trying to run her off the road deliberately? Or was her terrifying, jolting near-rollover just an accident?

* * *

Red lights flashing gave Callie a headache as she warmed herself under a blanket in the back of an ambulance, Koukla snuggled next to her. A tow truck had removed her car from the ditch.

Miraculously, Callie had only a few bruises and scratches, though her face felt swollen where the air bags had smashed into it. The paramedics determined that she didn't appear to have any serious damage or a concussion, and one of them had even given the dog once-over. Koukla seemed to be fine, but they suggested that Callie take her to the vet for a check-up as soon as possible.

"Callie," Sands said, sitting next to her in the ambulance and putting his arm around her. She'd already given her statement about the incident to the officer on patrol and had been waiting for Sands to join her. "So you think the car that sideswiped you belongs to Mrs. Dayton," he asked. "Any idea as to why?"

Callie flushed, but decided the best thing to do was to come clean. "I didn't get a look at this car. But the other night, a woman driving a big white SUV almost swerved into me as I sat parked at the curb. I didn't say anything about it – I should have." Sands nodded, and murmured. "Don't worry about it. Too late now."

"In any case," Callie continued her tale, determined to tell what she knew. "I'm pretty sure it was Mrs. Dayton – Lexy's mother. Natalie told me while we were setting up for the bridal shower that the Daytons tended to be excitable – they get into fights. So I'm thinking that if it was Mrs. Dayton, maybe she was upset about something and distracted. Combine that with the slippery roads and – bam!"

"So you think the person in the car *tonight* was Mrs. Dayton as well." Sands delivered the line as a statement, clearly not trying to influence her answer.

"I don't know. It *might* have been but I didn't see the other car – or driver – clearly enough. Sorry. And goodness knows that anyone could be driving erratically, especially in the holiday season, and with this weather." She frowned and touched her jaw, wincing. "I wish that I'd gotten a better look."

"You're not seriously injured, that's the main thing." Sands was saying all the right things, but to Callie's foggy mind, he seemed distant. His chin was set in a firm line and his voice never wavered from its smooth intonations, but he seemed preoccupied.

Sands stood up, letting a rush of cold air into the warm pocket his body heat had created under the blanket. "We'll sort out your car. For now, someone will give you a ride home if you don't feel like you need to go to the hospital." He peered at her closely. "You sure you don't want a complete check-up?"

"Nah, I'll go to the doctor if I start feeling sick or seeing double – or anything else. But wait a second. You said 'someone?' will give me a ride home. Not you?"

Sands looked at her with a gaze she couldn't read. Or maybe it was just her head was still so fuzzy. "I'm sorry. I wasn't thinking. Of course I'll drive you home. Let me wrap things up here and we'll get you back in your warm, safe house."

It sounded good to Callie. Sands still seemed a bit reserved, though concerned for her health as he made sure she was safely in the car, Koukla in her arms. "I'm sorry I can't stay for a bit," he apologized. "But we're working late tonight on the Underwood murder. "

"I understand. Speaking of that, I'd like to share some things I've learned about Bix Buckman. Also, some odd details have come to light regarding The Daytons and Nick Hawkins, the long-suffering fiancé."

"How have you obtained all of this information?" Sands wanted to know.

"Oh, here and there. Don't worry – it's all in the course of a day's work, nothing out of the ordinary. I see and hear a lot of stuff just working in town all day."

"Right," Sands said with a sigh. "Well, what do you have for me?"

"Bix Buckman has some kind of money dispute with The Elkhorn Supper Club. I can't believe I forgot to tell you. He and the owner nearly got into fisticuffs the night of Natalie's murder. I was there with Sam – she was simultaneously trying to cheer me up – and anxious to watch Bix perform with his band. My dad of all people broke up the fight."

"I can believe it," Sands said. "What else?"

"Well, you know how we ran into Bix and Piper? She swears they're not involved romantically and told me that the reason they were at the pub the other night is because she's doing social media freelance marketing for him. Also, she thinks somebody was following her the other night at Crystal Bay College and wanted a bodyguard."

"That's interesting. Did she report it?" Sands looked stern.

"I don't think so," Callie answered. "She said that the person ran away when a bunch of students suddenly appeared in the parking lot."

"Do you believe her?"

Callie answered truthfully, glad that he wanted her gut feeling on the matter. "I do. She and Max appear to be awfully close. It's just that Bix seems like the type to prey on women – based on everything else we've heard."

"All right, Bix has a temper and he tends to bother women who don't reciprocate his romantic attentions. And maybe he plans to 'make a move' on Piper. You never know. Not a good look, I agree. Now, what's this about the Daytons and Nick Hawkins?"

Callie shared how she and Max had witnessed the couple fighting in front of her shop and how she'd taken Lexy for tea to talk things through while Max entertained Nick. She told him how Lexy thought Nick was in love with Natalie and how she'd seen Mrs. Dayton just sitting in her car, taking it all in and not making a move to stop the couple from their loud, public argument. She also mentioned Max's assessment of Nick.

"This is interesting, to be sure," Sands said slowly. "Good to know. But a money dispute and a couple having an argument don't give me enough to act upon right now. Still, I'll have them all questioned again. Let's see if it shakes any of them up at all."

They pulled up to her house, dark but for the porch light. She hadn't had time to string Christmas lights on the evergreens this year, although a festive wreath adorned her front door.

Sands walked Callie to up the walkway and apologized again for not being able to stay. "Please call me if you need anything," he said, kissing her on the cheek.

"I will," Callie agreed, but he made no move to hug or embrace her like he usually did. She cocked her head at him.

"Are you sure you're all right? You seem, I don't know, down or something."

He hesitated before answering. "It's just this case. I'm all worn out. You take care of yourself and I'll check in with you soon." He smiled at her, but his eyes didn't reflect much warmth.

"Thanks," Callie said, deciding she'd had enough drama for one night. Whatever was bothering him, he wasn't talking – yet. Hugging Koukla tightly against the cold, she hurried inside and shut the door, closing it perhaps more firmly than was really necessary.

Thirteen

Callie was moving stiffly around her kitchen the next morning, Saturday, still shaken by the car accident, not to mention Sands' oddly distant behavior, when the doorbell rang.

"Hi Mom," Olivia said, breezing in the door. "Pappou just dropped me off."

"Is he still here?" Callie asked.

"I don't know," Olivia shrugged. "Probably. He wasn't sure if you were home and he said he wouldn't leave until I got in safely." She snuggled Koukla in her arms. The dog looked perfectly fine, but Callie had already made an appointment at the vet's office for later that day. "What happened to your face?" Olivia asked, but Callie was already moving towards her front door, ready to confront George.

He sat in his truck, the plumes of exhaust white in the frosty morning air. Callie waved to him, wrapped her arms around herself and ran outside in her fleece slippers, carefully maneuvering around the icy patches on her front walkway. She scurried over to the driver side of George's car and he promptly rolled down his window. She could feel his car heater going full blast and the all-news talk radio station he listened to during the day was turned up to high volume.

"*Kalimera*. Good morning, Calliope –" George began, but then he noticed her jaw and he stopped short.

"*Kalimera*, Dad. I had a little fender bender," Callie said, thinking it best not to tell him that the car had nearly been hit by another vehicle twice the size of hers. "My car is at the shop right now but doesn't appear to be seriously damaged – and neither am I."

"Calliope! Are you sure you're all right?" George started to get out of the car, but Callie held up her hands in protest.

"I'm fine. Really. I'll get a ride to work today. Olivia is going to a friend's house for the afternoon and then she's going to Viv's."

"If you're sure? But your jaw – it looks swollen."

"My airbags deployed," Callie explained, starting to shiver without her coat. "One of the bags must have hit me in face, but it probably looks worse than it feels. Look Dad, thanks again for having Olivia over. I promise to give you a call later." She kissed his cheek and started walking back to the house. At the door she turned around and waved to her father, who hesitated before waving back. He gunned his motor, backed up the truck and slowly drove away.

Happy that she'd avoided a major confrontation about careful driving and icy roads, Callie went to join her daughter.

"How was your sleepover?" she asked.

"Great!" Olivia was lying on the sofa, with her legs stretched out in front of her and Koukla lying in a similar position right alongside of her. "Sweetie is so nice. She let me eat *koulourakia* for breakfast."

"She did?" Callie answered. "Did you eat anything, say, slightly more healthful?"

"Pappou made a feta cheese omelet." Olivia sighed and sat up. "I guess I'd better change my clothes – aren't you supposed to drop me at Grandma's in a bit?"

"Yes, and I'm going to ask her for a ride to work. Why don't you come in and get some food for you and Grandma to have for dinner. Then she won't have to cook."

"Can I pick it out?" asked Olivia.

"Of course. Within reason," Callie said with a smile.

"OK. But just once I'm going to have an all-cookie meal."

Callie laughed and kissed her daughter's cheek before the 10-year-old raced up the stairs as only 10-year-olds can do. Feeling slightly more energized, she made her way slowly into the kitchen for another fortifying cup of coffee and then called her grandmother.

Viv took the news of the accident somewhat similarly to George, but she calmed down when Callie explained that she seemed to be unharmed.

"Of course I'll drive you, dear. And I'll take Koukla to the vet while you're at work. You've been through enough."

"No, no, Grandma. I can take her."

"Nonsense. I'll take her and Olivia will help me."

"Olivia's going to a friend's house later."

"Oh that's right. Well, I'll just ask Sweetie. She's at loose ends if what she said last night is any indication."

"Grandma, you're the best. Thank you! But dinner is on me – I told Olivia to pick up some food when you drop me off."

* * *

Viv showed up in her champagne-colored SUV ahead of schedule and Callie packed both her daughter and dog in the car. She shuddered as she remembered the last time she'd strapped Koukla's kennel into the car – she was sincerely relieved that the dog seemed unhurt but would feel even better with a clean bill of health from the vet. Bless Viv's heart for taking care of that appointment.

The trio – well, quartet, if you counted Koukla – enjoyed each other's company on the way to work, and Callie was able to forget the unsettling events of the previous evening. And for once, Viv didn't mention the murder. Callie's grandmother stayed in the warm car with Koukla, while Olivia ran into Callie's Kitchen with her mother in search of a ready-to-eat dinner. She finally settled on Callie's special five-cheese mac-and-cheese – the top was sprinkled with a little feta – and a Greek salad. Some giant-sized chocolate chip cookies rounded out the kid-friendly meal.

Olivia kissed her mother goodbye. "Be good for Grandma. And don't forget to mind your manners at your friend's house."

"I know. Please and thank you!"

"You got it." She watched Olivia skip out into the snow with her goodies and then turned to her work for the day.

Max wasn't in until later, so Callie served some customers and then got to work on a few of her most pressing baking tasks. Gingerbread cookies and gingerbread cake dripping with a thick, lemony white icing were two of her best-sellers at Christmas, so she decided to get to work on the cookie dough first, before baking the cake.

The sweet, spicy and buttery smells of gingerbread baking permeated her shop within the next half an hour. Bit by bit, Garden Street's holiday shoppers were drawn in by the delicious smells and soon Callie's Kitchen was filled with people buying baked goods and choosing lunches and meals to take home.

With the soft sound of holiday music playing in the background, the cheerful sounds of a busy cash register and the soft, happy buzz of conversation all around her, Callie felt like she was witnessing an example of a Christmas miracle. A few months ago, when her business was in danger of being shut down, she couldn't have imagined this scene. Maybe people were still stress-eating or following the herd instinct, in search of comfort or at least, comfort food. However, at least for this brief time, it didn't appear that Natalie's unsolved murder was a topic of conversation inside of her shop and for that, Callie was exceedingly grateful.

Filled with a little bit of renewed Christmas cheer, Callie was only slightly startled to see Melody Cartwright and Kayla walk in. Both of them were bundled from head to toe in the bulky outerwear required by the cold and snow. She waited as they stomped off their boots and unwound their scarves, which were pulled up well over their faces in the bitter cold.

"Hi there," Callie greeted them. "It's nice to see you both. What can I do for you today?"

"Kayla and I bumped into each other while Christmas shopping, so I thought it would be nice to talk about what you could serve at my book launch." Melody's cheeks were pink and her eyes sparkled as she talked about her upcoming book.

Christmas shopping. Callie felt a pang of guilt. She hadn't even started her shopping yet and had absolutely no clue what to buy for Sands. It had to be just right – not too sappy and yet, not too casual. Though with the way he was behaving recently, she wondered if he would welcome a gift from her.

"Sounds good," she told Melody, tearing her thoughts away from her personal problems. "Do you have an advanced copy of your book with you? I'm happy to make any of the recipes in it – and as a bonus, I'll offer one or two Callie's Kitchen specialties."

"As a matter of fact, I do," Melody answered, handing Callie a thin book with a glossy cover. It read *"Teatime with Melody: A Guide to a Harmonious Tea Party."* Catchy. Pictured on the cover was a stunning photo of Melody in a pink sweater and pearls, seated at a beautiful table filled with tea pots, tea accessories, little sandwiches, cookies and cakes.

"Oh, Melody," Callie said, truly impressed. "It's just gorgeous." She smiled. "You must be so proud."

Melody blushed and ducked her head. "I am," she admitted. "I never really thought it would happen. But – here we are."

Kayla was peering in the glass case at one of Callie's freshly-baked gingerbreads with thick white icing. The icing had dripped down the sides of the cake in a tempting way. "What about this cake?" she asked.

"Oooh, it does look delicious," Melody answered, bending down to get a closer look.

"My gingerbread cakes would be perfect for your launch," Callie agreed. "And what about these?" she asked, holding out a jar of her newly-baked *paxemathia*. "These are basically a type of Greek *biscotti*. They're flavored with ouzo and they are great for dunking in tea, coffee or even hot chocolate."

Kayla and Melody each took a cookie and bit into it, getting crumbs on their coats. "These are a winner," Melody said, nodding her head. "Let's do it."

"What about some of those little sandwiches?" Kayla wanted to know.

"I'll make whatever is in your book," Callie answered. "Just tell me what you'd like."

"You have to make Melody's Greek yogurt scones," Kayla said. "They are to die for, with blueberries and a little orange flavoring."

"Oh my goodness," Melody said, laughing. She ate the last bit of her cookie and sighed. "That all sounds good. I really appreciate it, Callie. The thing is, my publisher hasn't really given me much of a budget. I can't pay a lot and I know you require a lot of work and time."

"We'll work something out," Callie reassured her. "After all, I asked you if I could help. Maybe you can just pay me the cost of supplies and the labor will be gratis. Or, you can do some social media posts or something, saying that Callie's Kitchen hosted the launch."

"Of course I'll do that," Melody said. "I would offer to plug your business anyway." She smiled at Callie. "Let's meet up in a day or two and we can work out all of the details."

Kayla was eyeing the *paxemathia* so Callie handed her a couple more cookies. "For the road," she said. She poured two cups of coffee into paper cups with lids and handed them to Kayla and Melody. "You need coffee with these, obviously." The two women sipped at their hot drinks and Callie decided she'd take a stab at seeing what Bix's coworkers really thought of him.

"Listen, I'm not trying to gossip, but you know my best friend Samantha is dating Bix," Callie began.

"I know," Melody answered. "I seem to remember Bix mentioning something. They make a nice couple."

"Yes, well, here's the thing. You two work with Bix and I've heard some things about him. I just wondered what he's like to work with, you know."

Kayla shrugged. "I only work part-time so I don't see him all that often. But he's always been fine to me. Polite, friendly. We don't chat much, but he seems like a good guy. And he's always busy working – he's not one of these people to slack off."

Interesting.

Melody looked a bit pained but surprisingly, she replied in kind. "Bix is a hard worker. He's actually been incredibly helpful since...uh, since Natalie's death. He's been more of a presence inside the hotel, keeping an eye on things, making sure reporters don't disturb the guests." Melody leaned forward, eager for details. "Why – what have you heard?"

Callie was uneasy. Maybe it had been a bad idea to bring it up, but she was worried about Sam and Bix's behavior had been downright strange. "Not too much," she said slowly. "Just that he dates a lot and has a bit of a temper."

"Oh, I get it," Kayla said. "You must have heard about Natalie. She was seeing him for a while but I think she met someone else. I never heard or saw anything unusual, though. They seemed to keep their relationship professional."

Melody chimed in. "I know that Bix and Natalie may have dated but she never complained about him to me. I thought it was a mutual decision for them to break up."

Melody suddenly seemed in a hurry to leave. She wound her scarf around her neck and thanked Callie for the coffee and cookies.

"I'll be in touch about the launch," she said. "Kayla, I'll see you at work." She swept out of the shop.

"I'd better get going, too," Kayla said, sipping the last of her coffee. "I sure hope they found out who did this to Natalie – and soon. It's horrible to think about a killer walking around out there."

Callie agreed. After the two women were gone, she realized that all she had accomplished was growing more confused about Bix – not less. Wouldn't Melody and Kayla have had something negative to report about Bix, given what she'd heard from Lina, the ballroom dance instructor and given the show of temper she'd seen at The Elkhorn Supper Club? Then again, Piper didn't seem to have an issue with Bix either.

Callie returned to her bakery cases and started arranging the cookies more neatly. Maybe Bix was a good guy after all and there was no reason to worry about Samantha.

Or maybe Kayla and Melody were afraid of him.

Fourteen

The respite following the departure of Melody and Kayla was short-lived. Soon Callie was practically roller-skating throughout the shop serving customers. She filled orders for eat-in dining, sold several jars of festive red-ribboned *paxemathia* and finally, got a head start on a new batch of Greek chicken stew for her dinner menu. Max had arrived and was prepping food in the kitchen when not serving customers. He seemed chipper enough, so she guessed that he didn't suspect that Piper was up to anything with Bix. Or maybe he just didn't know.

Viv had texted her after Koukla's visit to the vet. They'd done a couple of X-rays, but the little Yorkie appeared to have emerged from her ordeal in the car without a serious problem. Callie had been beyond relieved – Koukla was part of the family.

Callie's mobile phone "pinged" again and she wondered if it was another update on her dog. Instead, she saw that Piper had placed Instagram photos online within the last few minutes. Callie found herself smiling as she looked over the Callie's Kitchen Instagram feed.

Piper had taken some great shots of her food: crisp, buttery cookies, steaming *spanakopita* oozing with cheese, gingerbread loaf cakes dripping with sweet, white icing. It was too bad you couldn't scratch and sniff the screen. Plus, she was happy to note, Piper had kindly cropped her out of the picture where her hair was flying all over the place. Only her hands pulling cookie sheets out of the oven remained – and they were covered in oven mitts.

The bell over the door jingled and Callie looked up, eager to greet a customer who'd been inspired to come into the shop because of Piper's eye-catching Instagram photos. However, it was Christy, proprietor of Tea for Two, the new teashop across the street.

"Hi Callie," she said, strolling up the counter and peering into the nearest bakery case. "Mmmm. It smells wonderful in here. And it looks beautiful, with all of your Christmas decorations."

"Thanks. Well, thanks to my two employees. They did most of the decorating."

"It looks lovely," Christy said, smiling as she looked around the shop, taking in the lights, miniature trees, Santas and festive baked goods. Her face was rosy from the cold. "Pass along my compliments."

"I will. Now what can I get you? On the house – from one business owner to another."

Christy smiled and protested at first, but she finally agreed to a cup of coffee and a piece of iced gingerbread. Callie led her to a table in the front of the shop and sat down with her for a minute, since there was a lull in customers.

"You're sure persistent, but I'm glad you are," Christy said, taking a bit of cake. "This is delicious!"

"Thank you!" Callie said, flattered in spite of herself. "Anyway, good luck arguing with a Greek who's trying to feed you. We'll always win." The two women laughed, Christy less enthusiastically. She faced Callie, a serious look on her face.

"I don't mean to pry, but do you know how Natalie's murder investigation is going?"

"It's going. Why? Do you have some information?"

"No. I'm just really scared." Christy's blue eyes were wide with fear. "I wonder if I did the right thing by opening a shop in town. This murder just really makes me feel unsafe."

"Yes, I know what you mean."

"People are coming into my shop, which is great, but most of them seem to just want to sit over one cup of tea for hours and talk about the murder. It's really unsettling. And then, I had a strange incident the other day. Well, more than one."

Callie raised her eyebrows and encouraged her to go on.

"My store alarm went off the other night at about two in the morning. The alarm company called me and the police were there to check it out."

"Police?" Sands hadn't mentioned that, but then again, he didn't respond to those types of calls. "And?" Callie prompted.

"Well, that's it. But I found it odd. No one had broken in, that we could see. It could be that the alarm did its job and prevented a burglary. I have one other person who works there besides me and she swears she wasn't there, accidentally tripping the arm. I believe her. She'd have no reason to be there at that time of night."

"Who's your co-worker?"

"Her name is Kayla. She works part-time at the inn, where Natalie was killed."

Kayla? Working at Tea for Two? This was news to Callie, but of course, she and Kayla weren't besties. She was surprised she hadn't seen Kayla there before. No matter – she'd file that one for digesting later on, when she had more time.

"What was the other thing?" Callie asked, almost afraid to find out.

Christy ate more cake, but a dark look clouded her features. "It's a little awkward."

Callie nodded encouragingly and Christie continued. "Weren't you in the other day with that girl, what's her name? I'm sorry. I'm still putting names to faces."

"You mean Lexy Dayton?" asked Callie.

"Yes, that's it. The girl who was crying. Well, a woman who said her name was Dayton was in my shop the other day and she seemed a little...off. Is that her mother?"

"Was she well put-together, tall and thin?"

"She was tall and thin all right, and she had nice clothes on, but she seemed a little intense. She kept complaining that she had lost something and was looking all over my shop for it. Well, whatever it was, she never found it. I convinced her to have a cup of tea and then she left."

"Hmm. That's odd. Did she buy anything else?" Callie wanted to know.

"She said she was browsing. I get lots of customers like her – just browsing," Christy said. "I can only hope that they remember the place and come back to it when they really need something. And I hope this murder gets solved, soon. I don't mean to sound crass but it's not exactly good for business. And it's scary, as I said."

"I understand. Opening a new business and having a local murder is not exactly optimal timing. I know one of the detectives on the case and I know they'll get the killer – sooner or later."

Christy finished her cake and looked skeptical, so Callie continued her pep talk. "Your place is great. People will love it – you've created a beautiful space." Christy didn't need to have the high failure rate of new businesses pointed out to her.

"And what about this? Melody Cartwright told me you're helping with the book launch. I'm providing the food and you're providing the tea. Is it okay if we have it here? Bring any print advertising that you have – I'll display it near the books. That should help boost business for you."

"That would be really helpful," Christy said. "I think once people know I'm there, they'll show up. As you know, it's tough to be the new kid on the block."

"It sure is. Maybe we can even do some cross promotion – and not just for Melody's book launch."

"Definitely." Christy had already finished her cake and she took one last swallow of coffee.

"Thanks for listening to me. It really helped to share my concerns with someone who understands." She gave Callie a small smile. "Duty calls. I'd better get back to work."

Callie walked her to the door where the two women said their goodbyes.

"See you later," Christy called with real warmth in her voice. Callie smiled and waved, happy to have made a new friend.

Still, parts of their conversation had disturbed her. Kayla was now working at Tea for Two, right around the same time the store alarm was going off mysteriously in the night? It could be total coincidence but Callie was starting not to believe in those.

And what was going on with Mrs. Dayton? What was she looking for at the tea shop? And why was she seemingly always so agitated?

Callie understood somebody having personal problems, but the woman needed to stay off the road if she was upset. If not, the next person who she knocked off the road – if that was indeed her behind the wheel the other night – wouldn't be as lucky as Callie and Koukla were.

At her next thought, though, Callie felt chilled to the bone. Perhaps Mrs. Dayton was upset because she felt guilty – or afraid. Could Mrs. Dayton have killed Natalie in rage that had simply gotten out of control?

The phone rang, tearing Callie away from this unpleasant train of thought. Max answered. "For you," he said, holding the phone out to her. Then, he lowered his deep voice to a whisper. "It sounds like Bix Buckman."

Gingerly, Callie took the phone and cleared her throat before answering. "Hi, Bix? This is Callie. Can I help you?"

"Probably not," Bix answered, gruffly. The sounds of a loud and rapid conversation in the background made it difficult for Callie to hear him. She left Max to the customers at the front of the shop and went in the back room to hear more clearly.

"What's going on?" Callie asked, almost afraid to know.

"What's going on is that your grandmother and your cousin were found trying to break into the boathouse near where Natalie was killed," Bix said. "I told them I was going to call the police but they asked me to call you first. I'm only doing *that* because you're Samantha's best friend," Bix said, biting off each word sharply.

Callie's knees felt rubbery and quickly she sat down, holding her head in her hands. The large and luxurious boathouse was attached to the inn – how did they expect to break in without anyone seeing them?

"My grandmother?" she repeated. "And my aunt?"

"Yep. What the heck are they doing here, Callie? This is not acceptable. Don't they know what crime scene tape means?"

"Is there crime scene tape on the boathouse?" Callie asked, stalling for time. She had to prevent Bix from calling the police. Who would ever believe that she didn't put the two women up to it? And – horror of horrors – what would Emma say? Or Sands?

"No," Bix answered, exaggerating the word. "But other parts of the area have been roped off. You'd think they would have noticed."

Now Callie could hear Sweetie and Viv begging Bix to let them talk to Callie, not the police. Recovering from the shock, Callie spoke quickly. "I'll tell them to leave immediately," she said. "Please don't call anyone. I'm sure there's a reasonable explanation for what they were doing out there. Come on, they're harmless." Her throat constricted and she felt unexpected and entirely unwelcome tears start. She never should have discussed Natalie's murder with them. Who did they think they were? The Bobbsey Twins?

How could they have put themselves – and her – into such an awkward and suspicious situation? And what about the danger they could be in, with a killer still walking around on the loose, a killer who could very well be Bix himself?

At this last thought, Callie couldn't help it. She let out a strangled sob and quickly tried to hide it by coughing.

"Don't cry, Callie," Bix said, softening his tone slightly. "I hate it when women cry. Just a second." He must have put his hand over the phone because the voices were muffled. "Your grandmother wants to talk to you."

"Grandma! How could you?" Callie started in on Viv immediately and then regretted her harsh tone. Clumsy though her attempts may be she knew that Viv was only trying to help her.

"I'm sorry," Viv wailed. "It's a long story. You see..." she began but Callie shushed her.

"Please, Grandma. Not in front of Bix. Just get out of there – come straight to Callie's Kitchen. You can talk to me here. Can you put Bix back on?"

"Yes, dear. Here he is," Viv said, sounding relieved and back in control.

"Bix, please let them go. They were probably just looking at the water or something. I know my grandmother is interested in that Christmas Tea. Maybe she wanted to show my aunt how beautiful the view of the lake is from the boathouse. "At this last, even Callie had to roll her eyes. Bix would know she was bluffing.

"Oh, sure," Bix answered extravagantly sarcastic. "The beauty of the lake? It's 10 flipping degrees out here! You know what? *Some people* have to get back to work. This one time, I'll let them go. But if I catch them out here again, I am calling the cops. Maybe I'll start with your friend, that detective!" Bix exhaled noisily and hung up.

Callie hung up the phone in a daze. She had way too much work to do to deal with family members trespassing on private property.

Correction: her work load would be lightened because Viv and Sweetie could be kitchen helpers for the rest of the day. They might not like it, but too bad! She couldn't have them mingling with suspected killers.

Stomping back out to the front of the shop, Callie waited until a couple of groups of holiday shoppers had left their comfortable tables before filling Max in on Viv and Sweetie's plight.

Max burst into delighted laughter. "That's awesome!" he exclaimed. "They're tough. Did Bix know who he was messing with?"

Callie couldn't help but join in his laughter, but she was still annoyed with her grandmother and Sweetie –and concerned for their safety. "They are tough all right. And too stubborn for words! What were they thinking? I have no idea what they were even doing there. I think they've been watching too many episodes of *Murder She Wrote*."

Max wiped his eyes, still laughing. "I don't know. Jessica Fletcher could probably learn a trick or two from them."

"If they don't show up soon, I'm going to be the one who calls the police," Callie vowed. "What if the killer is watching the inn?" She started pacing around the kitchen until Max stood in front of her.

"Don't worry," he said, placing his hands on her shoulders. "If they don't show up, I'll go looking for them. It's going to be fine. Now let's get back to work." He pulled a few more jars of beribboned *paxemathia* out from behind the counter to replace the ones that had been sold. "And," he said, winking, "I'm thrilled to have some more kitchen help today."

Callie tried to keep her mind on work but her heart didn't stop pounding with anxiety until the two beloved ladies had made their way through the front door of Callie's Kitchen. From the time of the call to their arrival it had only been about twenty minutes, but to Callie's worried mind, it seemed like hours. Viv looked a bit sheepish but Sweetie held her head up as regally as a queen, almost like she was expecting to be greeted with congratulations for her caper. As if!

"Speak of the devil!" Max said by way of greeting. "I hear you two have taken up volunteer police work."

"Oh, Max," Viv said with a twinkly laugh, taking off her hat, coat and scarf and placing them on a chair. "It was all just a big misunderstanding."

"Yes," Sweetie repeated. "Big misunderstand."

"You two could have gotten arrested, injured – or worse!" Callie admonished them, even as she walked over and hugged first Viv, then Sweetie. "Don't do it again," she begged the two ladies. "You've got me worried sick. And just for that, I'm going to ask you to stay here a while and help Max and me cook. That way, I can keep an eye on you."

"Sorry, Calliope," Sweetie said, her pretty face flushed. "We no mean to get in trouble. We just look for something."

Viv shot Sweetie a warning glance, but in her enthusiasm to confess all to Callie and to be forgiven, apparently, she didn't see it.

"What were you looking for?" Callie asked, now thoroughly discombobulated.

"What else?" Sweetie asked, shrugging. "Murder weapon."

Fifteen

he murder weapon? Were they trying to get themselves killed? Callie mentally sputtered. She felt like she now truly understood the term "at a loss for words."

"Don't worry, Callie," Viv said, joining Callie behind the counter. "We didn't find anything. But I'll tell you what we did discover." She found a blue and white Callie's Kitchen apron and pulled it over her flannel shirt and jeans. Apparently, Viv had known she'd be outside and had dressed for the weather.

"What?" Max asked eagerly. Callie shot him a look.

"Somebody must have broken into the boathouse." Viv was continuing excitedly. "We saw scratches around the lock and it looked like the door had been forced open, and then hastily repaired."

"You mean, broke in before you did?" Callie said ironically, folding her arms across her chest.

"Oh, we never got to break in. Bix caught us. You know the rest."

"Grandma," Callie began, exasperated now. She took a breath and gazed at Viv's expectant face and found that she had rediscovered her ability to speak calmly. "Don't you think the police have been looking for the weapon? Don't you think they've checked the boathouse? Who knows, the lock could have been broken before Natalie's murder. No one has said what the weapon is, anyway. What makes you think you'll find it? Or that it's even a good idea for you to find it? What if the killer is watching us?"

"We smart," Sweetie answered, somewhat indignantly. "Why should we not find?"

Viv jumped in smoothly. "Callie, the police are doing a fine job, I'm sure. I just thought I'd take a chance and see if I could find any clues." Her grandmother pouted a bit and went to wash her hands in the hand-washing sink.

"Now Grandma, you know better than that. I appreciate the interest in solving the crime. I know my friend Emma is upset and worried. And we all feel terrible about Natalie." Callie put her hands on Viv's shoulders and looked her square in the eye. "But I don't want anyone to get hurt. Let me do any digging around if it needs to be done. Anyway, the killer could have tossed the weapon anywhere. Who knows?"

"Fair enough," Viv said briskly, choosing to let Callie's little diatribe roll off of her. "I'm ready to cook. What do you want me to work on?"

Callie looked at Sweetie, who seemed to be following Viv's lead and not pursuing talk of their "investigation" any further. "Yes, dear. What you want us to do?"

Relieved that the ladies had decided to stop talking about murder weapons and breaking into boathouses, Callie decided to let the conversation go for now. She explained the health and safety procedures for a commercial kitchen, made sure their hair was pulled back from their faces and got the two women started on some quick breads and cookies.

The kitchen regained its peaceful good cheer. To Callie, it seemed like the only place she felt safe anymore was in her kitchen.

Callie and Max worked even more efficiently with their crew of four. Max put some Christmas music on and they had a brief sing-along to "Rudolph the Red-Nosed Reindeer," in the lull between customers.

Before she knew it, Callie was amazed to discover that two hours had passed. Viv and Sweetie were taking a coffee break in the back of the shop. *Heaven only knew what they were plotting now.* Maybe now would be a good time to join them.

Callie strode into the back room, coffee cup in hand. "Grandma, Sweetie," she said, leaning against the countertop. "I'm sorry I got so upset with you. It's just that I don't want any harm to come to either of you. Or to me, quite frankly. Because if you two get into trouble researching this crime, Dad will kill me even if no one else does."

Viv made a face. "We're very sorry. And we do understand. We just want to help."

"I know." Callie sighed and folded her arms in front of her chest. "You know I care about the both of you. Anyway, I really appreciate the help today, and Max does too. Can you both do me a favor?"

"Yes, honey," Sweetie said, anxious to kiss and make up.

"Can you drive safely home and please, please don't go snooping around The English Country Inn again?"

The ladies looked at each other, then back at Callie. Viv sighed deeply. "Yes. But you will share what we learned, won't you? With your detective?"

Callie laughed weakly. "He's not 'my detective.' But are you sure that you want me to mention it? Bix was going to call the police and you didn't want him to."

"He say, he going to 'bust' us," Sweetie answered matter-of-factly. "Your detective, he want to help."

"All right, OK. But, likely the police have checked into it." The two women looked at her expectantly and stubbornly, Callie thought. She relented. "Yes! I'll tell him." She also had to ask him about Christy's burglar alarm.

The ladies looked pleased as they bundled back into their outerwear and said their goodbyes to Callie and Max. Viv said something to Sweetie at the door before rushing back to Callie's side and whispering in her ear. "He may not be 'your' detective. But he could be, if you want him to. I've seen how he looks at you." She waggled her fingers at Callie before re-joining Sweetie, the two of them giggling like a pair of school girls all the way out the door.

"What are you going to do with them?" Max asked, after they left. He was shaking his head and smiling.

"I'm not sure," Callie answered. "What do you do with family anyway? Love them, I guess. Tolerate them, at the very least. And try to keep them out of your business. Except, that last part doesn't usually work out so well for me."

"Hey, at least they're looking out for you." Was that envy in Max's eyes? Tough, tattooed muscled Max didn't talk much about his own family. Callie felt guilty for complaining.

"And I'm looking out for *you*," Callie replied. "Now, let's finish up here."

* * *

Luckily, Callie's car was ready when she called the garage during a lull at work. Max kindly offered to drive her there to retrieve it and she gladly agreed, only too happy to be back in her own familiar vehicle. All she wanted to do was to get home and attempt to relax. And sleep. Slumber had been in short supply these last several days.

With Olivia working on homework at the dining room table and Koukla nestled on her lap later that evening, Callie took a couple of ibuprofen for her jaw and daydreamed about taking a vacation as she did every year when Crystal Bay felt like one big icicle. It would have to be someplace warm. Palm trees, sun, cool drinks. Would Sands be with her? Come to think of it, she'd only had a text from him all day, asking after her health. Usually, he called at least once.

Retreating to more pleasant thoughts of warm climates, Callie imagined herself floating on her back in the water, not a care in the world. Crystal Bay in the summer was wonderful but it was hard to remember the warm, lapping waves of the bay when a gust of winter wind was whipping you in the face.

She must have drifted off, because soon Olivia was shaking her awake. "Mom. It's for you," she said. Her daughter picked up Koukla and kissed Callie on the cheek. "You look tired, Mom. You should get to bed soon."

Amused to hear her daughter repeating words she'd said to her so often, Callie smiled and sat up, rubbing her eyes before taking the home phone from Olivia's hand. "Thanks, Liv," she said. Then, into the phone, "Hello? Callie's Kitchen. This is Callie."

A warm rumble of laughter greeted her. "Callie's Kitchen? Aren't you at home?"

"Yes, sorry. Just a habit. I'm a little out of it. I was napping, if you can believe it."

"Oh no," Sands chuckled. "You must have had a rough day. Sorry to wake you, but I thought you'd want to know about the car that ran you into the ditch the other day."

Instantly, Callie felt alert. "Yes. What did you find out?"

"Later that same evening, a driver ran through a red light right near the place where your car wound up in the ditch. Are you ready for the driver? It was none other than Nick Hawkins, fiancé of Lexy Dayton."

"Nick Hawkins? Not Mrs. Dayton?"

"No ma'am. He was sober, by the way. Passed the sobriety test. We don't have proof that he was the same driver, so don't go spreading this around. But I know you're doing the food for that holiday party for Lexy so can you please be careful? Even better – can you cancel the event? These people seem a bit barmy."

Oh gosh. The Dayton party. Some of the baking was done for that, but not all of it.

Callie groaned with exhaustion. "Thanks for reminding me and no, I can't cancel," she said irritably. Belatedly, she smiled as 'barmy' sunk into her weary brain. "Sorry," she said with a laugh. "I didn't mean to snap at you. But there's no way. My reputation would be ruined."

"Better your reputation than your life, Callie. Think about it." He paused a minute, then changed the subject. "How are you feeling?"

"Sore, but OK. Thanks for asking." She hesitated. "Just so you know, Bix Buckman said my grandmother and my aunt Sweetie were snooping around near the boathouse. They said it looked like someone had been trying to break in. I promised them I'd tell you." She sighed.

"That's odd. I'll give it another look. In the meantime, will you kindly tell them to stay away from there?"

"I already did." Callie paused. "I wonder who did try to break in, though?" she wondered aloud. "It wouldn't have been someone who works at the inn. The staff would be able to get in there anytime, right?"

"You never know," Sands answered cryptically.

"Also, Christy, the new owner of Tea for Two said that her burglar alarm went off at two in the morning. Guess who's her part-time employee? Kayla, from The English Country Inn."

"You don't say," Sands said slowly.

"Had you heard anything about Tea for Two?"

"Yes, somebody mentioned something the other day but we get a lot of these calls this time of year. Anything can trip the door alarm – even rats or raccoons."

Callie shivered. "Yuck!" She decided to change the subject. "So, when do you think we can see each other again?"

"I'm not sure," Sands said, sounding preoccupied. She was pretty sure she heard him typing. "I'll call you. Got to dash. Cheers."

"Bye," Callie said into a dead phone. He was busy, after all, she reasoned with herself. He was working a murder case.

So why did she feel like he was avoiding her?

First her father, now Sands? Everybody was acting so weird. *Holidays*, Callie thought. They bring out the best – and the worst in people.

And by the way, what was it with Nick *and* Mrs. Dayton? Why were they *both* appearing to be using their vehicles as weapons – aimed directly at her?

Callie lay back down and sighed, desperately wanting to go back to her dream of floating along without a care. But that wasn't to be. Suddenly she shivered and it wasn't from the cold wind that was blowing the snow around outside of her windows.

* * *

Tired as she was, Callie welcomed the chance to forget her troubles at work the next day. After another near-sleepless night, she was happy to focus on the simpler, more wholesome tasks involved in baking, cooking and serving customers.

Talk of Natalie's murder was still a hot topic, but some of Callie's customers seemed anxious to move on to other, less depressing subjects. With a little prodding, she was soon chatting away with her regulars about the upcoming Christmas season and busying herself with planning food for each of three upcoming events: the Christmas Tea at the inn, the Dayton party and Melody's book launch.

Max worked alongside of her, busy and competent. Piper rang up customers in between restocking bakery cases and the refrigerator unit. It was wonderful to have extra staff and she even missed Sweetie and Viv working with her. Despite their troublesome investigative behavior, they were efficient bakers and cooks, not to mention pleasant and cheerful company.

During the late morning lull, Callie decided to take a break and check out the "Callie's Kitchen" Instagram and Facebook accounts. In the last few hours, Piper had posted one new shot of Max, who was beaming for the camera and holding up a jar of

what Callie was now dubbing "Spiced Greek Biscotti."

This post was going to be a sure-fire winner, Callie thought. With his edgy good looks, Max was certainly photogenic. The cookies didn't look half bad, either. Max didn't mind having his picture taken, unlike Callie.

Enough playing on the Internet. Putting her phone back in her pocket, Callie decided to get some food prep accomplished so that she could get a head start on her several holiday event items. But before she could bury herself in the kitchen work area, the door jingled and in walked Sands. Callie saw Max nudge Piper and the two of them beamed at her like she was about to go to her first prom.

"Hey, Detective," Max greeted him. "What can we get you today?"

"Hello, Max, Piper," he said, nodding. He was wearing his long wool coat and looked exhausted. "Just thought I'd pop in to see Callie," Sands said, clearing his throat. He stepped closer to her and lowered his voice. "Can we go somewhere private to talk?"

"Sure," Callie said, frowning a bit. "Come on, I was just about to go in the back room."

She ignored the interested stares of her co-workers and flinched when she thought she heard Piper make a soft "whoo whoo" sound. Callie would have laughed but she was pretty sure Sands wasn't here for romance.

Callie offered Sands a cup of tea while he took off his coat and draped it over a stool. He sat there, rubbing his face tiredly, but when she handed him the steaming cup of tea, he seemed to perk up a bit.

"So what's up?" she finally asked when she was seated across from him.

Sands stirred sugar into his tea. "I wanted to tell you about Bix Buckman. I've done some digging and apparently there have been some complaints about him. I'm worried about Samantha. Are they still seeing each other?"

"Complaints?" Callie wasn't entirely shocked. "You mean, from former girlfriends, or bosses – or what?"

"Girlfriends, unfortunately," Sands answered, taking a sip of tea.

"I can't say that I'm all that surprised," Callie replied, busying herself with a cup of strong coffee loaded with sugar and milk. "He seems to have a bit of a temper. The only thing I don't get is why Sam is still seeing him. It's not like her to tolerate a guy with a history of bad behavior."

"I'm afraid I don't know the answer to that one," Sands said, gazing at Callie with his hazel eyes. "So don't you want to know what his woman trouble is?"

"Of course!"

"Turns out that the trouble is in his more distant past. Apparently, he hasn't been violent but he has been "persistent." No restraining orders, but plenty of complaints regarding letter-writing, phone calls, that sort of thing. When the woman pushed back enough, he would back off."

Callie thought this over. "So maybe he snapped? I mean, it's possible."

"Anything's possible," Sands conceded. His sipped his tea and the color started to come back into his cheeks. "I don't want you to make this a public broadcast, but just let Sam know that he may not be the best choice in the dating pool."

"I'm surprised Sam doesn't know about his past," Callie remarked. "You'd think she would have checked him out. I mean, she does deal with criminals in her line of work."

"Who knows? She may have investigated him on her own and decided to take a chance. Isn't that what relationships are? A big gamble, all the way around."

Callie stared back at him. He was right, of course. But was he talking about the two of them? Or his ex?

Feeling a sadness emanating from Sands, she reached across the table and squeezed his hand. "I'll talk to her, definitely. It might help her to let her know I care – though she is a little defensive where Bix is concerned." She paused. "In any case, I hope you can get some rest – and soon. And thanks for stopping by. It's nice to see you. I miss you, you know."

"No rest for the wicked," Sands said, draining the last of his tea. He stood up and stretched. "I've got to get back to work. And I miss you, too." He seemed awkward and for the life of her, Callie didn't know why. Maybe she wasn't the only one with cold feet about their deepening relationship. Or maybe he felt badly about the potential for hurting Sam.

Callie watched as he shrugged on his coat and pulled a scarf tight around his neck. "Thanks for the tea," he said, his eyes sad but warm, and full of unspoken feelings. But then, he lightened his gaze and his tone and Callie wondered if she'd been imagining things. "I'll call you later. And remember what I said about the Daytons. They're an odd lot. Be careful, right?"

"I will," Callie responded. "I'll bring someone with me when I bring the food to their holiday party, if you like."

"Not a bad idea." Sands leaned down and kissed her on the cheek. She walked him to the door and he was gone in a flash, waving goodbye to Max and Piper before Callie could even offer him a Greek biscotti.

Callie's heart felt a bit sore when he left, but work beckoned. She could analyze the situation *ad nauseum* while she cooked.

And speaking of worries, she had to talk to Sam. She'd put it off long enough. Callie texted her friend, asking when they could get together, then put her phone away and returned to the safety and peace of her warm, fragrant kitchen.

Sixteen

Callie was still waiting to hear from Samantha about a potential get-together, so when her phone rang at the shop the next morning, she expected to hear her friend's familiar, throaty voice. Instead, it was Melody Cartwright on the line.

"Hi there," she said cheerily. "I was thinking that it would be nice to have you stop by and bring some samples of the food that you'd like to serve for the launch. We can have coffee and finalize the details for the launch party."

Callie surveyed her kitchen work room, which was full of dishes in progress on the stove and in the oven. The timing wasn't optimal, but she had to complete this task.

"Sounds good, Melody," she answered. "When do you want to get together?"

"I know this is short notice, but what about tomorrow afternoon? Does that give you enough time?"

"Sure," Callie answered readily. It would be tight, but she could always do Melody's baking at home. And some of the stuff, like the *paxemathia*, were already made and ready to go.

"This is going to be great!" Melody sounded exuberant. The tension and stress of Natalie's murder and the subsequent fallout at the inn must be taking a back seat to her excitement about her book. "Everybody will love the food."

"What time tomorrow?" Callie asked.

"I don't know if you can leave your shop, but what about four? I'm only working part-time at inn that day, which is fortunate. There's still a lot to do for my book debut."

Callie considered. That could be a busy time of the afternoon, but Piper and Max were both working that day. Maybe Sweetie would even help out. Still, she had the Dayton party to worry about in addition to regular cooking and baking. Evenings weren't much better – she considered that to be family time. And anyway, she was anxious to stay off of the treacherous roads in the dark, especially lately. She winced as she touched her jaw, still a bit sore from her trip down the ditch.

"All right, but I can't stay for very long. Sorry. It's a busy time of year."

"No problem, I won't keep you. Let's just get it done and you can get back to work," Melody agreed.

Callie headed back to the kitchen, where she put her head down for the next several hours and focused on finishing the many tasks on her list. With Max and Piper's help, she was able to complete several dishes and start on a few more baking tasks. The Dayton party was just two days away and Callie wanted to be prepared – in every way possible.

As she tried to focus, Callie's mind kept drifting to her friendship with Samantha and what she was going to tell her about Bix. She knew Sands meant well but she slightly resented him for putting her in such an awkward position. Finally, when Callie got the salt and sugar confused – luckily before she poured it into a bowl of beaten butter – she realized that her brain was not going to let her rest until she spoke to Sam.

Quickly putting the salt to one side, Callie wiped off her buttery hands. She would call her friend and see if they could meet up, even briefly. She hated to have to discuss any negative aspects about Bix over the phone – it felt too impersonal. Whatever was going on with Sam, Callie felt like she needed a face-to-face meeting with her. Grabbing her cell phone, she tapped out her friend's number and held her breath.

"Samantha Madine," her friend answered smoothly and Callie almost wept with joy. Samantha almost never answered her phone. Maybe things were looking up.

"Sam, it's me. I haven't seen you in ages. Can we get a coffee or something? I just want to touch base."

"Callie, it's great to hear from you. I'd love to see you but can you stop over here? I can't go out for coffee – too busy today, wrapping stuff up before the holidays. You know. But, we can have some in my office."

"I'll bring coffee and cookies. You just sit tight. I'll be there in a jiff."

Callie started packing up cookies and other goodies for Sam, but the ringing of the bell over her front door made her look up.

Jack Myers walked confidently into her shop. "Hi there," he said, smiling at her as if just the two of them were in the room. Callie glanced at Max, who was ringing up a customer but he didn't notice. *Thank goodness.* All she needed was Max teasing her about Jack.

"Hello, Jack. What can I help you with?"

"Just stopping in for some of your great coffee and more of those Greek doughnuts you make. I've got a long day ahead and I need sugar and caffeine."

"Well, I can certainly help you with that." Callie grabbed one of her signature blue and white bakery boxes and started filling it with warm, sugary *loukoumades*, aka Greek doughnuts.

"Callie," Jack seemed to caress her name with his voice.

"Hmm?" Callie said, searching for a paper coffee cup with a lid. She looked up, startled. Jack's face was mere inches from hers. Instinctively, she took a step back.

Jack backed up too, but slightly. For the first time since he walked through the door, Callie took stock of Jack's appearance. He was really quite handsome with dark hair, attractively stubbled cheeks and light grey eyes that sparkled.

He smiled at her again. "Sorry, just trying to get your attention. You seem a million miles away. Are you all right – especially after the other day, with Natalie?" He shook his head. "I still can't believe it. Nobody can."

Callie was warmed by his concern. "I'm not great, but I'll be fine. Working helps." She handed Jack his coffee and bakery box and rang him up on the register.

"I hear you'll be helping out at the Christmas Tea. Melody told me."

"That's true. Are you going to be there?" Would flannel shirt-wearing, rugged Jack show up at a tea party?

"I'll make it a point to be there now." He winked at her, took his change and gave her another saucy smile before sauntering out the door.

Callie stared after him. She'd thought he was interested in Melody. *Oh, dear.* Could he be interested in *her*? She felt herself blushing. Of course, he hadn't done anything more than be a little flirtatious. And she was involved with Sands – didn't Jack know that? Callie's heart gave a little catch. Things with Sands weren't exactly smooth sailing these days. But how would Jack know that?

Well, whatever. Jack was probably flirty to every female under 90. Callie continued packing up goodies for Sam and headed out the door.

The short drive to Sam's office was slippery but thankfully, Callie stayed firmly on the road. She couldn't help but look in her rearview mirror, remembering the glaring red headlights that filled her rear window right before she crashed. Cringing, she kept her eyes on the road and her thoughts positive as she geared herself to tell Sam about Bix and his problems with previous girlfriends.

When she finally arrived at Sam's law office, Sam came out to the waiting room herself, steering Callie past reception as she gratefully accepted the proffered coffee. She looked a bit tired, but as always, she was polished in a gray suit with a pencil skirt, her feet in sleek ankle boots. Callie felt a bit dowdy next to her in her "Callie's Kitchen" t-shirt and well-worn jeans paired with practical waterproof boots.

"What's up?" Sam asked, taking a Greek biscotti and a Christmas-tree shaped butter cookie to go with her coffee. "There goes my carb count for the day, but who cares? Thanks for stopping by to see me."

"I'm happy to take a short break. I'm going to be spending pretty much ALL of my time in the kitchen between now and New Year's. I have to get some fresh air and sunlight when I can."

The two friends smiled at each other and made a few more pleasantries before Sam brought up the topic of men.

"So how's the detective?" she asked. "He's cute, I'll hand you that. But have you had a chance to see him much? This Natalie Underwood murder has to be taking up a lot of his time."

"We've seen each other a bit," Callie said, warming up to her topic. "He's busy, true. But I have to say – I like him. A lot. I'm not sure how I feel about that."

"Yeah, I know what you mean. When you like them a lot they can hurt you." She frowned and sipped more coffee.

"So how's Bix? Seeing him much these days?" Callie ventured, taking a sip of her own coffee for fortification.

"Yes, but not as much as I'd like to. He's busy with work and his band. Plus this thing at the inn – ugh. It's been awful: tourists asking questions, business falling off. He's been acting as kind of a bodyguard over there." Sam shook her head.

Callie took a deep breath, feeling like she was about to jump into an ice-cold swimming pool that was filled with sharks. Still, wouldn't she want to know if they guy she was dating had a history of stalking?

"Sam, I wanted to talk to you about Bix. This is kind of hard to say, so I'm just going to say it. I've heard a few things and I thought you should know."

"What kind of things?" Sam asked, her eyes narrowing slightly.

"I heard that he has been reported by previous girlfriends for stalking-type behavior. Coupled with what I saw at The Elkhorn, I'm worried about you."

Sam didn't reply for a moment and Callie did what she always did when she was nervous – she filled the void by talking too much.

"Please don't be upset. It's just that Sands said..." Oh no. Now it would sound like she and Sands were gossiping. Sam cut her off.

"Callie. I can't believe you were sitting around and discussing my relationship with him. I feel really stupid. Why would you two want to do that?" Sam's eyes blazed and two spots of red flushed her cheeks – and they weren't from blush.

"I – uh – well," Callie stammered but found her voice. "I care about you. We both do. I just don't want to see him do the same thing to you."

"Bix is a good guy. And you know what? He told me about his ex-girlfriends. Did Sands also tell you that this all happened a long time ago – like when he was just out of college? Look, he may have a temper but he's matured a lot since then." Sam stood up, leaving her half-eaten cookies on a paper napkin. "I think you should go. I've got to get back to work." She wouldn't look at Callie.

"Sam," Callie pleaded, taking a step towards her, but Sam held up her hand, palm out: The international sign for "stop."

"I know you mean well. But to think that you think I'm too dumb to handle my own life and to know you've discussed me with Sands is hurtful. Right now, I think it would be good to have some space. We can talk later."

Callie took a step back. "Got it," she said softly, nodding. She quickly left Sam's office, her cheeks burning. *Way to go, Costas.*

* * *

Driving to Melody's the next day with some of the book launch foods carefully secured in the car, Callie was still smarting from her encounter with Sam. She knew she'd done the right thing by confronting her but it didn't feel good. She'd texted Sam another apology and a plea to talk to her in person, but Sam hadn't responded.

Maybe Sam was right and Callie and Sands were being overzealous. After all, Sands saw the bad things that people did to each other in his line of work. To Sands, maybe people couldn't change.

It *was* possible that Bix had put his past with women behind him. Still. The conflicting reports about his lecherous behavior, not to mention the fight Callie had witnessed, seemed enough to support the theory that Bix was bad news.

Callie was listening to the 24-hour Christmas music station as she drove along, so she tried to focus on the cheery if squeaky sounds of "Alvin and the Chipmunks," doing a rendition of the song "Christmas Don't Be Late." She was even able to smile a little bit at the Chipmunks antics as she pulled into Melody's driveway. What would Melody think if she showed up to discuss her book launch party looking like Ebenezer Scrooge?

Callie parked the car and got out, the cold hitting her hard. It must be well below freezing. A bundled-up postal worker on the opposite side of the street made her grateful that she was able to spend most of her time inside of a warm kitchen.

Melody came to the door wearing softly flared black yoga pants and a grey off-the-shoulder sweatshirt, her feet in fleece ballet slippers. She welcomed Callie inside the house, taking her coat and offering a cup of freshly-made coffee.

At Melody's behest, Callie carried the foods she'd brought into a small but beautiful dining room, complete with a sparkling chandelier. The walls were painted a pearlescent grey color, a pretty contrast to the white crown molding. Soft draperies accented the windows. A large, dark wood and antique buffet with a built-in wine rack stood along one wall. The dining room opened into a cozy living room with a sparkling Christmas tree right at the center. In the stone fireplace, a fire blazed and crackled. The whole house smelled like pine and cinnamon.

"You have a beautiful home." Callie put down her foods and accepted a cup of coffee.

"Thanks." Melody looked around, a small wrinkle of a frown marring her otherwise smooth forehead. "Come on, let's sit by the fireplace," she offered. She would have been wonderfully relaxed in a home like this, but Melody seemed stressed out. Must be book launch nerves.

Callie joined Melody on the sofa. She put her coffee cup down on the table and relaxed back into the cushions. "Thanks for the coffee. What about the food I brought? Do you want me to go and make up a sample plate for us?"

"In a minute," Melody answered. "I'm kind of...exhausted today. Let's just sit here a minute first."

"Fine by me," Callie agreed. The two sipped their coffee companionably in silence before Melody ventured some conversation.

"I wonder when Emma is going to be back," Melody wondered, plucking at her yoga pants. "You two are friends, right? Did she say anything to you?"

Callie stopped drinking her coffee in mid-sip. Did she know that Emma had appointed her the unofficial spy of The English Country Inn? She answered in what she hoped was an innocent way.

"I don't know when she'll be back. I think the snowstorm is preventing air travel. And now she's having trouble getting booked, so I guess she decided to extend her stay in Arizona. What have you heard at the inn?"

"I've heard the same thing," Melody answered, fidgeting with her cup. "You know what, let me run to the restroom and then let's go ahead and discuss the book launch party. I'll be right back."

"Of course," Callie answered, finishing her coffee and heading back into the dining room.

Callie slowly removed her festive foods from their protective wrappings. She couldn't help but stop a minute to admire the buffet in the dining room. She'd love one just like it, she thought, running her hand over the smooth, glossy wood. And the built-in wine rack was a perfect touch. Callie leaned down to check out Melody's wine collection and saw what looked like a crumpled piece of paper stuck wedged in next to one of the wine bottles. Deciding she'd help Melody by doing a bit of housekeeping for her, she carefully pulled out the paper so that she could throw it away.

But it wasn't a piece of scrap paper. It was an envelope, typed, no return address and post-marked yesterday. The envelope was crumpled in half. It was addressed to "Sandy Madison," same address as Melody.

It must be a mistake, just a piece of mail sent to the previous owner or to the wrong address. So why was it wedged inside what appeared to be a hasty hiding place?

Seventeen

Callie quickly shoved the envelope back into its spot and straightened up just as Melody swept back into the room. "Sorry to keep you waiting. Let's see what you brought."

Callie's hands shook a bit as she plated some of the items and handed then to her hostess. Melody was being so gracious and it wouldn't do for her to be discovered snooping – even if it had been accidental. She was getting as bad as Sweetie and Viv.

Talk soon turned to cake, cookies and tea, safe topics all. Callie bit into one of the scones Melody had made. It was tender and flavorful with just the right amount of sweetness. "This is delicious!" she enthused. "If all of your recipes are as good as this one, your book will be a big hit."

"I sure hope so," Melody answered. "This book has been a long time coming. I've worked so hard to build up this part of my career. In fact, if things go well, I'm going to make writing books and doing tea parties my full-time job. Adults like them too, not just kids. Don't tell Emma," she said hastily. "It all depends on how many books I sell." She frowned. "A murder at the inn isn't exactly going to help my image." She looked up, a sheepish look on her pretty face. "No offense."

"I completely understand," Callie answered. "But look – you've achieved your dream. Writing a cookbook sounds like fun, though I'm sure it's a lot of work, too."

"You should write one," Melody said, picking up a square of iced gingerbread. Thick white icing dripped off of the sides and a candy version of holly berries and leaves completed the decoration. "Your food is amazing. Not just the Greek stuff – everything."

"Oh, I don't know. Is there room for more than one cookbook author in Crystal Bay?" Callie joked and both women laughed.

"What about Christy from Tea for Two?" Callie asked. "I thought she might be here today to talk about the launch."

"I asked her, but she begged off. Apparently, she's really busy with gift orders for Christmas and anyway, she's only serving the tea. I figure she's got that part down pat. I already know what teas pair well with what foods. In fact, I make suggestions in my cookbook."

"Kind of like pairing food with wine? Or even, these days, with beer?"

"Exactly," Melody answered. "It's part of the fun. Of course, everyone has their personal taste preference, but a lot of people appreciate the suggestions."

Callie had finally relaxed and was pleased to find that she was enjoying herself, but a quick glance at the clock on her phone made her realize that she'd lingered at Melody's long enough.

"I've had a wonderful time, but I've got to get back to work," Callie said regretfully. "I've got a bunch of stuff to finish making. Max and Piper will wonder what happened to me."

"Of course! Listen to me – I've been talking your ear off!" Melody blushed. "Thanks for stopping by and for offering to help me out." Her voice wavered a bit. "You have no idea how much this book means to me. It is real a dream come true and I just want everything to go well." Melody's large, beautiful eyes had tears in the corners of them.

Callie impulsively hugged her, moved by Melody's obvious joy in her new venture. "I'm sorry to be so emotional," Melody said, wiping her eyes. "I know it seems silly."

"No it doesn't," Callie countered. "I know you've worked hard. Now it's time to enjoy your success."

"Sure, Callie. You're right."

But she didn't sound all that sure, Callie thought, after she had taken leave of Melody and was driving her car on the icy roads back to Callie's Kitchen. Something was bothering Melody and Callie wanted to know what it was. She'd been on edge since Natalie was killed.

But truthfully, who wouldn't be? Callie shook her head. All of this stuff was making her paranoid. Time to focus on food.

* * *

Snow was falling thickly by the time Callie was putting the finishing touches on the baked goods for the Dayton party. Hardy Crystal Bay-ers were still coming in to buy dinner foods but they were leaving dirty wet slush in their wake. Piper had volunteered to clean the entryway while Max and Callie boxed up meals and sold baked goods at a nice pace. The herd instinct and stress-eating among Crystal Bay residents seemed to be continuing. Combined with the normal uptick in business that accompanied the holidays, Callie hoped that maybe she'd be able to make up for some of the money she'd lost when she'd been under suspicion for the death of Drew Staven.

When she thought of Drew, she felt sad and helpless. Callie wondered if maybe that was why she was so reluctant to let herself fall too hard for Sands. She didn't have the greatest track record.

The phone rang in the back room and Callie picked it up, hoping it wasn't somebody calling to tell her that Viv and Sweetie needed to be bailed out of jail. She hadn't spoken to them all day and had no idea what they were up to.

"Callie! It's Emma. Can you hear me?" the line crackled with static.

"Hi! Yes, I can hear you. Well, pretty much. What's up? When are you coming home?"

"All I could get were standby flights and even those flights have been cancelled. The big storm must be headed your way – brace yourself."

"Yes, I know," Callie answered, not wanting to contemplate what debilitating snow would do to her business. "So if you're not able to come home yet, what's the plan?"

"I found a time share," Emma explained, "which I probably wouldn't have done if I'd had to leave earlier. I'm just going to stay in Arizona awhile longer until the weather permits me to finally get home. My hotel bill is astounding, but what can I do?"

"Yeah, that's tough. But on the bright side, congrats on your new vacation spot!" Callie said.

"Thanks. I certainly hope you'll join me out here sometime."

"I'm going to take you up on that – if I ever get a vacation. In the meantime, let me catch you up on things at the inn."

"That was my next question. How does it seem over there? When I call, they tell me everything's going great, but it's hard to believe, given all that's happened."

Callie held her breath – had Bix refrained from telling Emma about Viv and Sweetie's aborted attempt to find clues? It seemed like it. She felt almost disloyal for telling Emma about his checkered past, but she'd promised. Could it jeopardize his job? What would Sam think of her then?

"I don't have too much to report right now," Callie said, deciding at the last minute to leave the Bix stalking problem alone for the time being. After all, the police knew about it – let them tell Emma. She just couldn't do that to Sam right now – even if she didn't want Sam and Bix to be together.

"It seems like the staff are working hard and keeping things to-gether. I hear Bix Buckman has been helping keep the hotel secure and relatively free of nosy onlookers." She winced at this last state-ment, thinking of Sweetie and Viv's clue-finding caper. "And I'm busy working with Melody Cartwright on the Christmas Tea. In addition to that, I'm hosting a book launch party for her at Callie's Kitchen."

"That's actually a big relief," Emma admitted. "I wanted to do something to help celebrate but obviously, I can't now. Thanks for helping her. You're the best." Callie wondered what Emma would think if she knew Melody was looking to leave the inn and work at a new career as author and party planner. But again, she'd promised Melody not to tell Emma about any of that.

Callie was starting to feel uneasy. It was a compliment to be seen by others as someone to confide in – but it certainly created some interesting situations. Luckily, Emma was anxious to end the call.

"I've got to go," she said. "That's my realtor on the other line – we've got a few details to iron out. Thanks again and I'll be in touch."

In something of a daze, Callie walked slowly over to a pot of *avgolemono* soup and checked it to make sure the delicate egg-lemon and chicken soup concoction wasn't curdling. She turned the flame a bit lower and stirred the creamy, fragrant soup with a huge wooden spoon. Closing her eyes, she inhaled the familiar, homey scents of succulent chicken and tangy lemon. No doubt about it, the soup was reviving her spirits.

Determined to put thoughts of Emma's troubles at the inn, her issues with Sam, Natalie's unsolved murder and an impending blizzard from her mind, Callie found herself thinking about the crumpled envelope addressed to "Sandy Madison." It probably had nothing to do with anything – and in fact, she was a bit ashamed of herself for snooping. She couldn't even justify investigating the inn and its staff anymore if she wasn't even going to tell Emma what she learned.

Still, she thought, stirring the steamy pot of soup: Would it hurt to find out whom Sandy Madison was – if only to satisfy her own curiosity? Then again, as Viv would say, "Curiosity killed the cat."

Callie looked up as Max burst into the back room, his muscular and tattooed arms full of empty bakery trays. "We sold out of *loukoumades*," he said proudly. "Plus, gingerbread. And the *paxemathia* are pretty low, too."

"That was quick!"

"Yeah, no kidding. Every time somebody comes in and wants to discuss the murder, people just start stuffing their faces with sweets." Max grimaced. "Who knew that murder would be good for business this time around?"

"Oh, Max! What a way to put it." She thought a moment. "I've got some butter cookie dough in the freezer, so let it thaw. We'll bake some of those while I get going on more cakes and *paxemathia*."

"Sounds good," Max said, already striding to the freezer.

"Max," Callie ventured. "Have you ever heard of someone named Sandy Madison?"

The back of Max's neck turned bright red and he nearly dropped the cookie dough. He coughed a bit before turning around.

"Uh, yeah. I have. Have you?"

"No, Max," Callie said, growing exasperated. "That's why I'm asking."

"Sandy Madison, if it's the person I'm thinking of, was a center-fold in the '90s for a men's magazine. She was pretty well known in certain circles."

"The '90s! How do you know about her, then? You were probably barely even alive."

Max cleared his throat while his face grew red to match his neck. "My dad kind of collects these old magazines. I may have seen a few, you know. Once or twice."

"Don't worry," Callie laughed. "I'm sure you read them for the articles." But inside she was thinking – *why would Melody be getting mail for Sandy Madison?*

Max laughed too, a little uncertainly. "Why do you ask? Do you know her?"

"No!" Callie answered, a little too loudly. "I just sort of...heard the name the other day. This Sandy Madison that you're talking about – did she ever live in Wisconsin?"

Max seemed on more secure ground now that the embarrassing part of the conversation – at least for him – had passed. "I don't think so," he answered. "I thought she lived in L.A."

"My, my, Max," Callie said, teasingly. "You certainly know your men's magazine models."

"Not really," Max answered, turning red again. "But would you please *not* tell Piper about this conversation? I'll never hear the end of it." He had placed the cookie dough on the counter and had stacked some clean cookie sheets next to it before turning to face Callie, his face now only slightly pink.

"If you don't mind, I've got customers to wait on. I'll be back to scoop out the dough when it's thawed." With dignity, Max walked out to the front of the room and Callie waited until he'd gone before she burst out laughing.

Poor Max. Sandy Madison was a common enough name, of course. It was just a coincidence.

Wasn't it?

Eighteen

Hugh dropped Olivia off at home the next evening, but he stalled in the entryway instead of going through his usual drop-off routine, which was to give his daughter a hug, maybe pet the dog and exchange brief – but civil – remarks with Callie.

Tonight, though, instead of leaving, he shifted from foot to foot.

"Hugh. You're jumpy as can be. If you need to use the facilities, please feel free. Down the hallway and first door on the left."

Callie knew something was up when he didn't even take the bait at her mild jibe. "I need to talk to you about something," he said, looking into her face with an expression that was part excitement and wait a minute – could it be pity?

"Raine wanted to join me," Hugh was saying in gentle tones, "but I told her it was better if I spoke to you first, alone. Can we sit down for a minute?"

Callie closed her eyes and steeled herself. "Yes, of course. Come on in." She led the way into her front room and perched uneasily on the edge of a chair while Hugh flopped down on the well-worn sofa.

"Raine and I have decided to put in a bid on a house, right here in Crystal Bay. We've thought it over and it's the right thing to do for a lot of reasons. The number one reason, of course, is that I really want to be closer to Olivia."

"What about work?" Hugh worked as a bank manager but she knew he'd been somewhat unhappy with the job for a while.

"I'll commute, but I'm keeping my options open. In fact, Raine and I have both been looking for new jobs."

"Well, it may have escaped your notice, but we seem to be having an uptick in homicide right here in good old Crystal Bay."

"Yes, I know. Kathy told us you were the one who found the body. Sorry. But it's all the more reason for me to want to be closer to my daughter."

Callie was running out of objections. Of course she wanted her daughter to keep a close bond with her father. She'd even resigned herself to Raine, his new wife. However, Callie had come a long way. She finally felt free, independent and in charge of her life – well, most of the time. What would it be like to keep running into her ex and his new wife while grocery shopping, going to the mall – heck, they could even be customers at Callie's Kitchen. It would be odd, to say the least.

"Where is the house?" Callie heard herself ask faintly, but already bracing herself for the answer.

"That's the beautiful thing about it, Callie. Just two blocks from here. I'll be able to see Olivia just about every day!"

* * *

"Do you have a personal beef with that cookie dough or is it just that you now hate all dough in general?" Max asked Callie a few hours later as they worked side by side, prepping for the next day's baked offerings.

Callie looked up from her work station where she was using a rolling pin to smack a piece of hardened, refrigerated dough repeatedly, so that she could roll it out.

"What?" she asked absently.

"You're beating the heck out of that cookie dough and I just wondered what was wrong."

"It's nothing." Callie went back to whacking the dough with the rolling pin.

"Bull." Max walked over to her where he gently, but firmly, yanked the rolling pin away from her. "Sorry, boss," he said. "I can't stand the racket. Why don't we let the dough thaw a few minutes more while you tell me what's going on. Bonus: this way we might just save the rolling pin from cracking in two."

Callie half-laughed. "OK, OK." She wiped her floury hands on her apron and leaned against the counter, amused that her protégé was offering to listen to her woes. It was actually kind of refreshing. "I'll tell you what's bothering me, but no judging. I already feel like a jerk."

"I'm all ears," Max said, folding his arms in front of him, the colorful tattoos on his forearms providing a visual feast for the eyes. Piper was out in front serving customers, so apparently Max thought he had all the time in the world to play psychologist.

"It's just that Hugh told me that he's buying a house with his new wife, just a few blocks away from where I live. I know it's good for my daughter, so I feel guilty for being upset. I'm unsure about how the move is going to affect my daily life. No wait: correction. I know it will impact my daily life and I'm not too happy about it."

"Wow. No wonder you're beating up on your cookie dough." Max looked thoughtful. "I wonder what Detective Sands will say about it."

Callie's heart gave a painful jolt. She hadn't even thought about Sands and his response to the news. He wouldn't feel threatened, surely. Not someone as confident as him, or as open about some of his feelings about his past relationship.

As Callie reasoned with herself, she suddenly felt very overwhelmed. The kitchen seemed overly warm. She went to the tap and got a drink of water, gulping it down greedily.

Max followed her to the sink and put a hand on her shoulder. "It isn't the greatest news, I get it. You don't want to keep running into your ex. Don't beat yourself up about your feelings. And don't beat up any more cookie dough while you're at it. I'm sure you'll find a way to work it out. Besides, Olivia will be happy."

"Yes," Callie said, smiling as she thought of her 10-year-old daughter. "She's ecstatic. It's just – I've moved on. It's hard to be reminded of the old mistakes."

"I know. And then there's your dad. I can't imagine he'll be thrilled."

Callie felt some anger return as she thought of George. Her father and Hugh had a surprisingly good relationship – even after the divorce. George could be surprisingly open-minded about life's ups and downs, perhaps as a result of his own struggles as an immigrant, not to mention losing his wife at a relatively young age. However, even if he did bear resentment towards Hugh, what could George say about it? He had been squiring Hugh and Raine's realtor aunt all over town, giving the appearance of not only tolerating the move, but endorsing it.

Callie sighed. Max was a sweetheart but he just kept bringing up even more issues for her to be worried about. She decided to change the subject. Walking over to her beaten up cookie dough, she touched it gently with her forefinger to check its consistency.

"I think it's ready to roll out," she said. "Thanks for your concern, Max. I promise – no more errant rolling pins."

"If you say so," Max said, giving Callie a sidelong glance. They got back to work.

Quietly, this time, Callie rolled out dough and cut festive Christmas shapes. Some of these cookies were going to be served at the Dayton holiday lunch. *The Daytons.* Callie couldn't even make herself think about them right now – that was going to be one awkward gathering, given all the vehicular near misses she'd had with that group lately.

Her mind drifting as she worked, Callie had finally relaxed when she heard the familiar sounds of her father's voice as he said hello to

Piper at the front of the shop. Callie tensed, waiting to hear the soft tones of Kathy's modulated voice, but none came.

"Callie!" Piper called but she was already walking out of the back room, ready to greet George.

"Calliope! *Hrisi mou.* I came as soon as I heard." George's weathered face looked anxious, his brown eyes crinkled at the corners.

"Oh no!" Callie, exclaimed, concerned. "What's wrong? Is Olivia all right?"

"Yes, of course. Well, as far as I know. What are you talking about?"

"I don't know," Callie said, now thoroughly rattled. She didn't mean to be so protective of her daughter, but her daughter had asthma, and occasionally, she experienced a bad attack that required emergency treatment. It was a constant source of worry. Callie composed herself and asked her next question in a more measured tone. "What did you hear?"

George looked around. "Let's sit down," he said to his daughter. "Piper, dear," he said smiling at the young woman who stood looking quizzically at them behind the register. "You bring us *loukoumades* and coffee, OK?"

"Sure, Mr. Costas," Piper answered, already pouring the coffee. She plated about a dozen of the small, Greek doughnuts and handed them across the counter. Callie accepted the plate gratefully and took a whiff, the cinnamon and honey glaze making her mouth water.

Finally, George was seated with Callie at a snug table in the corner, presumably for privacy. He dug into the *loukoumades* with relish before looking up at his daughter.

"I hear that Hugh is moving to your neighborhood with *Raine*," George said her name with emphasis.

He brushed a crumb from the corner of his mouth and sipped his coffee, a slight frown creasing his already-lined forehead. "Kathy told me this news. Calliope, I'm sorry that I let you down."

"What are you talking about, Dad?" Callie felt a headache starting right behind her left eye. George seemed to be speaking in riddles since he walked through the door.

"This whole time, I've been trying to convince her not to sell the house to Hugh." George twisted a paper napkin in his callused hands. "I tried to help you because you're family. I know you don't want to be near Hugh and his wife. He sees his daughter and he's a good father, even though he didn't work out so well as a husband. But living so close to you – it's too close for comfort. I did my best." He patted Callie on the hand.

Callie was utterly confused. "Wait a minute. You mean that you were only going out with Kathy because you thought you could dissuade her from selling a house to my ex-husband?" Part of Callie's heart was doing a little dance. Maybe she wouldn't be related to Raine one day, after all.

But the other part was none too happy with her father's antics. Whether or not Callie liked the situation, Kathy had feelings. George definitely liked to interfere, but being a "player" wasn't his style – at all.

Callie's emotions barely had time to settle before George hit her with his next bombshell.

"Not exactly true. I started out wanting to know more about this woman trying to bring your ex-husband back to Crystal Bay. But, well...." He stopped speaking and turned several shades of red while he busied himself with the *loukoumades*. Callie took pity on him. He really was one of a kind!

"Dad," she said gently. "I think I know what you're trying to say. You started out wanting to sabotage the house-hunting but ended up really liking Kathy. Is that it?"

George's face was as red as the Santa hats that Piper had displayed around the shop. He nodded, his lips pressed together. Callie felt a rush of love for her father.

"It's all right, Dad. Really. I'll be fine with Hugh and Raine moving nearby. I've just been acting silly. It was a shock, that's all." Maybe if she said it enough, it would become true. "Anyway, Olivia deserves to have her father in her life as much as possible." That last part was definitely true.

"Dad," she said, leaning forward, now genuinely curious. "How long ago did you decide that you like Kathy? Does she feel the same way?"

Fortified with doughnuts and coffee, George had recovered enough to be a little gruff. "Who 'decides' to like someone? You do or you don't. You know, like with Sands. You like him, yes?"

"I do," Callie said slowly, impressed with his skill at deflecting an issue away from himself. "But we were talking about you."

"I told you before. She's a nice lady. We have fun together. Who knows what will happen?" George shrugged, but his eyes twinkled at Callie.

"That's great, Dad. Seriously, I am happy for you. Just so you know: you didn't let me down. You don't have to keep protecting me, you know."

"You'll learn, Callie, mothers are the same as fathers. Will you ever want to stop protecting Olivia?" He had her there.

"Probably not." She smiled at him and he smiled back. He laughed his big-hearted laugh.

"So, you see? It's normal to protect and to worry."

Customers were starting to trickle in for their afternoon snacks and evening meal pick-ups. "You're busy, so I'm going. Say hello to Olivia for me. And to Sands."

George enveloped her in one of his rib-crushing hugs and left. Callie wiped up the table and took the plates to the back room in a daze, avoiding Piper's interested gaze.

Say hello to Sands? Callie thought. *That was a new one.*

George must be in love.

Nineteen

"**S**weetie, Viv, why don't you go ahead and get in the car. I'll join you in a minute."

The day of the dreaded Dayton holiday lunch had finally arrived and Callie didn't feel ready for it. The *food* was ready – with Max and Piper's help, she'd been able to make the baked goods they'd asked for, along with *spanakopita, avgolemono* soup and *pastitsio* – a fragrant meat and macaroni dish topped with a luscious cream sauce. This was going to be a Greek feast, for sure. Regarding the status of the complicated family hosting the lunch – Callie wasn't so sure she was ready to deal with *them*.

"I take those boxes," Sweetie insisted and Callie gratefully handed her the last two boxes they needed to pack – those were filled with Christmas cookies and traditional Greek baked goods.

In this case, Callie was thrilled that her business only delivered the food to the guests and that serving was not required. She didn't want to be around the Daytons longer than was necessary, given the fact that Mrs. Dayton and now, Nick Hawkins, Dayton son-in-law-to-be, seemed to have a thing for reckless driving. Especially, it would seem, when Callie was the only other motorist on the road.

In the end, she'd asked Sweetie and Viv to come along for the ride. She would have preferred the extra muscle offered by Max, but he was holding down the fort at Callie's Kitchen.

"I can bring the food to the Daytons," he'd persisted, but stubbornly, Callie had refused. As much as she didn't want to face that group, she didn't want them to think they'd gotten the best of her. Besides, she wanted to gauge their behavior for herself.

168

"Are you ready, dear?" Viv asked, all bundled up, her cheeks bright red from the cold. "I told Sweetie to stay in the car since it's already warmed up."

Callie darted her eyes around the kitchen. "I think so." All of the other food had been kindly packed into her car by Max.

"I won't be gone long," she told him as she walked out the door with Viv.

Suddenly, Callie had second thoughts. Would she wind up counseling Lexy and Nick once again – or would she wind up in a ditch? Maybe she should have taken Sands' advice and made an excuse regarding the Dayton party.

No way. Callie squared her shoulders. Cancelling without notice would be fatal to her business. She'd stay on her guard and she'd be fine! Anyway, Callie was deeply curious to see how the Daytons behaved around her. The good news was that if they were all seated and eating, they wouldn't be on the road.

Icicles dripped from the eaves of the modest older homes that Callie and her crew passed as they made their way along Lake Shore Drive. The Dayton address was in a neighborhood of large, newer homes that were set far apart from each other and well off the road. Callie knew that the homes in that neighborhood backed up to an inlet that fed into the bay, to accommodate the boating mania that most Crystal Bay residents shared. Callie wondered if the Dayton family had ever had any incidents on the water or if their vehicular troubles were relegated only to dry land.

Viv and Sweetie kept up a rapid and lighthearted chatter throughout the drive that Callie found soothing. That is, until they wanted to know all about the new house that Hugh and Raine were purchasing and how she felt about it.

"Well," Callie said, striving for diplomacy. "At least Hugh gave me some warning. It will be strange to be living in the same neighborhood with him. I'd be lying if I said otherwise. I'll get used to it." She said all of this in a firm tone, hoping that would settle it, but she should have known better.

"Callie, you can tell us the truth," Viv said. "I know it can't be easy for you."

"I know, Grandma, but we do have Olivia. We have to work things out for her sake. Anyway, I can't tell him where to live!" *Unfortunately.*

"Oh, I know," Viv nodded her head vigorously. "Still, the man sometimes doesn't seem to have the sensitivity that God gave a goose when it comes to people's feelings."

"Or squirrel," Sweetie pointed out, as one of the furry brown rodents shook its fluffy tail at them as it ran across the road in front of the van.

Callie had no desire to denigrate her ex-husband, but even she had to laugh at that one. She just shook her head and said "Hugh means well. We'll all adjust."

Fortunately the ladies were changing the subject of their own accord as they started to point at and exclaim over the elegant homes along the tree-lined road. Soon, the Dayton house loomed in front of them, at the end of a lengthy drive. The snow-covered trees and rooftop of the large, rustic home made a pretty picture as the three women emerged from the car.

The sun was bright despite the frigid temperatures and patches of snow were turning to slush. "Be careful, both of you," she told Viv and Sweetie. "I don't want you to take a tumble out here."

"Don't baby us," Viv chirped back and Sweetie nodded, a little less certainly. She was probably missing the mild, warm air of Greece right about now.

Callie gave each of the women a pastry box to carry and a stern warning not to carry anything else or risk slipping and falling. Carefully, they all made their way up to the front door and Callie rang the bell. Of course, it was Mrs. Dayton who answered the door. Callie almost didn't recognize her; she was wearing glasses with large, squarish frames. They looked out of date, which was very unlike the well-dressed, fashionable Mrs. Dayton.

"I was wondering where you were," she said by way of greeting, glancing at Sweetie and Viv with a dubious eye. Today she was decked out in a silvery grey sweater and black skirt, a red and green Christmas tree pin placed jauntily near her shoulder. "Who do you have with you today?"

Well hello to you, too. Callie only smiled and shot her two helpers a warning glance. "This is my grandmother and my aunt who's visiting from Greece. They're just along for the ride – and to help me carry a few things." Mrs. Dayton looked stern. Was she going to invite them in or not?

Callie took a deep breath and tried a different tack. "Sorry if we're a little late. The roads are slippery and we don't want to risk an *accident.*" No doubt about it, Mrs. Dayton's cheeks flushed a bit at that last line.

"Greece?" she said, nodding at Sweetie, a hint of a smile on her face. "How interesting. I've always wanted to visit the island of Santorini." Sweetie nodded and beamed, her dimple clearly on display.

"All right, no use standing around in the cold," Mrs. Dayton's frosty demeanor had thawed ever so slightly – thank goodness. "Come in." *Finally.* She stepped back and held the door open wide for Callie and her small but motley group.

The trio looked at each other and then followed Mrs. Dayton into a large entry way that led to a long hallway, and behind that, the kitchen.

"Wipe your shoes, if you please, then follow me," Mrs. Dayton instructed. The three ladies took turns wiping their slushy boots on the door mat so as not to track anything into the beautiful space. The gleaming hardwood floors were covered in plush area rugs and Callie could only imagine Mrs. Dayton's reaction if they tracked in snow and mud.

Viv and Sweetie were speaking in whispers, almost like they were in church. Callie didn't blame them a bit. Despite its rustic appearance, the house had what could only be described as an expensive "hush" over it.

The Dayton home was truly a lovely and welcoming space, with high ceilings, exposed beams and casual, but expensive-looking furniture. It reminded Callie pleasantly of an upscale ski lodge. She longed to be able to sit and read near the large fireplace she noticed in the airy front room. Instead, she followed obediently behind Mrs. Dayton's broad-shouldered frame.

"Just put everything over here," Mrs. Dayton said. Callie was surprised when her client took some of the boxes from her and arranged them on the granite countertop. Mrs. Dayton definitely didn't seem like the type to be helpful to "the help" but maybe she was just in a hurry.

"Thanks," Callie said with real gratitude. "All of the instructions for reheating are taped to the front of each box. Should be a snap!"

"All right," Mrs. Dayton said briskly, fidgeting with a huge emerald ring on her finger. "Is that everything?"

"Yes, you should be all set." Callie wondered where the dining room was – no doubt, it was a beautiful space and she found her desire to get in and get out was overridden by her curiosity about the lovely home. Mrs. Dayton was being fairly gracious. As long as she was here, why not take a look around?

"Can I take a peek at the set-up?" she asked Mrs. Dayton. "I just wondered if there's anything that I – or we – should help you with in the dining room. Then we should be going. We don't want to be in the way."

"Yes, let us help," Viv agreed and Sweetie nodded. Mrs. Dayton seemed distracted and she gave them her assent.

"Go ahead. It's just through there. I should go and check on Lexy. She's *still* getting ready." Mrs. Dayton rolled her eyes and pointed at a doorway next to the homey eat-in kitchen – also rustic and ski-lodge like. Callie liked the space very much – it radiated warmth and comfort, unlike its owner.

The trio made their cautious way to the dining room and Callie heard their collective intake of breath at the sight. The scene was pure holiday glamour, but in a casually refined way. Again, the high exposed beams provided a rustic touch and large windows framed the now-frozen inlet and sparkling snow outside.

The long dining room table was set with aplomb. Grudgingly, Callie had to admit that Mrs. Dayton had an eye for decoration. Each place had some evergreen clippings and pinecones strewn artfully by the plate. The centerpiece was a tiny live evergreen tree, trimmed with silver and gold Christmas ornaments.

"Is beautiful," Sweetie said, gazing around her with appreciation. She smiled at Callie. "And your food is perfect touch."

"Here, here," agreed Viv. "It doesn't seem like there's much for us to do." She sounded regretful and Callie knew it was because her grandmother was dying to take a better look around.

Callie scanned the room once more. The buffet was empty, just waiting for Callie's rich Mediterranean-style lunch. Stacked on one end of the expensive-looking buffet was a stack of fancy-looking plates.

"I'm going to see if Mrs. Dayton wants me to put these cookies on a plate for her, and then we really should be going," she said to the two ladies who were now chattering about how much they would enjoy a dining room just like this one.

"Yes, dear," Viv said. "We'll just enjoy this gorgeous room a moment longer and we'll be right out." She blinked her eyes innocently at her granddaughter.

Callie was uneasy. She trusted herself to be discreet about snooping – Sweetie and Viv, not so much. "I'll be right back," she warned them. She hurried back to the kitchen but Mrs. Dayton was gone – Lexy must be doing some serious primping. From upstairs, Callie could hear the distant whine of a hairdryer and Mrs. Dayton's voice urging her daughter to hurry up. Oh well. Better leave well enough alone.

She walked to the foot of the stairs so that she could call "goodbye," but almost ran smack into Nick Hawkins. When he registered who she was, his face did a strange thing: it slowly turned red, like those pens that gradually change color when your turn them upside down.

"Callie, hi," he said, looking at her, then away. "I didn't know you were here. I'm just on my way to run an errand before the party."

"I'm on my way shortly, too," Callie replied, her tone light. But her gaze was sharp as she tried to decide if Nick looked like a man who would leave a woman and her dog stranded by the side of the road.

Just then, a crash sounded from the impeccable dining room, followed by what sounded like a cry and a muffled curse. Callie watched in horror as Nick brushed past her and into the dining room. Quickly, she followed him, her heart in her throat. *And to think, we were just inches from a clean getaway.*

"Who are you?" Nick demanded. A crystal pitcher lay on the floor at Sweetie's feet. Or what was left of it. It looked like it had shattered into a million pieces. Viv was crouched on the floor, plucking at glass shards and muttering to herself.

Callie rushed to Viv's side and pulled her to her feet. "I'll sweep it up – no use getting cut," she told her. Then she turned to Nick, a smile plastered to her face. "Just a little accident, Nick. I'm so sorry."

"Accident?" Nick said, his voice deep and menacing. "That 'accident' was a Waterford pitcher given to Lexy and me for our engagement." He glared at the three of them, turning his gaze first to one, then the other. "Do you have any idea how much those things cost?"

"I'm very sorry," Viv said firmly, standing up tall and facing Nick. "I'll pay for the damages."

Nick pressed his lips together and was silent but the red color of his face only intensified.

"Take it up with my mother-in-law," he said finally. "I don't have time for this!" He swept past Callie and out the front door. Great, he was back behind the wheel.

Callie started when she heard footfalls, but it was only Mrs. Dayton or Lexy moving around upstairs.

"Quick!" she whispered. "Let's find a broom and then let's get out of here! I'll send Mrs. Dayton a check."

Locating a broom in a small closet off of the kitchen, the three women teamed up to sweep every last shard and tiny bit of glass from the floor. Thankfully, it was polished, uncarpeted hardwood. Callie sent Viv and Sweetie to the front door while she did one final inspection. It looked good to her.

She took a cautious step to the foot of the staircase once again and called up to Mrs. Dayton. "We're leaving! Enjoy the party!"

A moment's hesitation, then Mrs. Dayton called down. "All right. See yourselves out."

But of course. The trio walked to the door. When they were finally safe in their car, Callie realized she'd been holding her breath. Boy, those people made her tense and it wasn't only the fact that her group was responsible for breaking an expensive pitcher.

Callie had dealt with rudeness and brusqueness before, but truthfully, she'd never dealt with clients who had such barely suppressed anger.

"Am I glad that's over," Callie told Viv and Sweetie, as she exhaled in a whoosh. "Thanks for being my bodyguards."

"Some bodyguards," Viv protested. "I could just kick myself."

"What were you doing, anyway?"

"Oh, I don't know. I picked up the pitcher, just to admire it, you see. I love Waterford. The darn thing just slipped out of my hands."

"It's OK, Grandma. Stuff happens. I'm just glad we got out of there when we did. I have insurance – should pay for the breakage. You don't owe a dime."

Callie backed down the driveway, on the lookout for Nick Hawkins and his potentially wayward driving.

Something wasn't quite right at *Chez* Dayton. That much was clear.

Twenty

Still somewhat troubled at the show of rage from the normally docile Nick Hawkins, Callie went to her shop early the next morning to finalize her food for the Melody Cartwright book launch/tea party. She had a few things to make fresh, but she figured that the more she finished early, the better off she'd be.

As the sumptuous, spicy scents of gingerbread cake – to be topped after baking with a creamy glaze that dripped down the sides – filled her warm, bright workspace, she found herself thinking about "Sandy Madison" and any possible connection that she could have to Melody Cartwright.

Callie checked the timers and saw that only 10 minutes remained on the gingerbread cakes. They'd have to cool before being topped with the rich glaze, so she had a little time after they came out of the oven.

Looking around to make sure no one was watching her, Callie tapped the search "Sandy Madison" into her cell phone. Several entries came up and Callie scrolled through them looking for likely matches.

Soon she'd clicked on a promising link. Filling the screen was the photo of a young, blonde woman wearing bikini bottoms and nothing else. Callie blushed. Fortunately, the model was facing away from the camera so none of her "naughty bits" showed. Callie squinted at the small image. It was hard to make out the woman's features.

She clicked on the next link and this time, the face of "Sandy Madison" stared out at her. She blinked. The woman did look just a little bit familiar. The eyes, the face ... they looked quite a bit like a certain cookbook author.

Could it be? *No!*

Callie started to take another look but the jingle of the bell over her door startled her. Quickly, she tried to click off of the image. In her haste, her phone slipped right out of her hands and clattered to the floor.

With a small whimper, Callie picked it up, almost afraid to look. Sure enough, the screen was shattered. Well, that's what she got for looking at salacious web sites.

Sighing she tested the phone and found that it still was useable – but only for calls, not for anything else. The screen was barely readable. Who knew when she'd have time to replace it – not to mention the expense? With Christmas gifts looming, she would have to wait until after New Year's.

Callie put the damaged phone back in her pocket and focused on serving her customers. But inwardly, her curiosity was beyond piqued. Without access to her private screen, where could she continue her research? Her home computer was tempting, but she shared it with Olivia. She really didn't want to take the chance of her daughter stumbling across any inappropriate images.

As she was wiping crumbs off the counter, she had lightbulb moment.

There was a large antique shop just a block away from Callie's Kitchen and she vaguely knew the owner, since it was a spot she enjoyed browsing in, when she had the time. They carried everything, even vintage men's magazines. She'd always walked right by those displays – until now.

Determined now, she grabbed her shattered phone out of her pocket and tapped in a number before she could lose her nerve.

"Hiya, Callie. Howya doin'?" asked Earl, the manager when Callie identified herself. Along with his wife, a 70-something with bright red hair named "Ginger," they had been selling vintage and antiques to Crystal Bay's residents and tourists since the 1970s.

"I'm looking for some, uh...reading material."

Earl cut in cheerily. "I just got a bunch of those vintage cookbooks you like. You want me to hold them for you? I've got Betty Crocker from the '60s, even a Good Housekeeping from the '50s. Good condition, not a bad price."

This was going to be more difficult than she thought. "No, Earl, this is a bit different. I'm looking for men's magazines. You know, the kind with centerfolds. I'm looking for stuff from the 1990s."

"Callie, don't tell me George sent you on this wild goose chase. I'll whip him myself!"

"No, no. It's just for a, uh, friend." Why did she keep explaining herself? What friend would send her on an errand like this?"

"Yeah, no problem, Callie." Earl was apparently used to discretion where his buyers were concerned. "As a matter of fact, I've got all kinds of stuff like that. But believe it or not, I just sold out. Just a second –" Callie heard a muffled bit of conversation and Earl was back on the line.

"Yeah, Ginger said a woman came in the other day and bought the lot of them. She wasn't around for that particular transaction; one of the other sales girls was working that day. Sales girl didn't know the lady – she just happened to comment on it to Ginger because it's unusual to sell out of that stuff in one fell swoop. Still, collectors are nutty. You never know what they'll buy. Thank goodness, they are, 'cause a lot of 'em will pay high prices for something like that. We did okay."

Callie stammered a bit. This wasn't what she was expecting at all. *Strike one.* "Thanks, for the info, Earl. I appreciate it. And while you're at it, go ahead and hold the Betty Crocker for me."

* * *

That night at home, Callie realized that the Christmas cheer she'd felt just a few days ago was rapidly diminishing. She was anxious to see if her hunch was true and knew that she could ask Sam or Sands, or even Max to look up Sandy Madison for her online. Briefly she wondered if Max's dad would let her take a peek at his magazine collection and then she colored beet red. No way could she ask that of him. For one thing, Max would probably be mortified.

And what if her hunch did prove true? Callie didn't know if she was ready to expose Melody – she cringed a bit at the term – when it could damage her reputation right before her book launch. If she was wrong about Melody – well, then, she'd look ridiculous. Plus, rumors could get out and that could hurt Melody's chances.

An even more unwelcome thought occurred to Callie. If Melody had assumed a new identity, it was just possible that Natalie had discovered it and that was why she was killed. Callie tried to picture gentle Melody killing someone and shook her head.

No, for right now Callie would do the investigating on her own.

Besides the aches and pains from her minor car accident, and the strike-out on the "Sandy Madison" magazines, Callie realized that her brooding had not only been about Melody – she was also worried about her fall-out with Samantha.

Checking to see if Olivia was safely in her bedroom upstairs, Callie decided to phone Sam and see if she'd cooled down at all. Her entire body felt tense as she waited for her friend to answer.

"Hello?" Sam said, her voice sounding thick and strange.

"Sam? It's Callie. Are you all right? I was just calling about the other day. I feel terrible."

"No, I'm not all right, actually." Sam was silent a minute. Then, "You were right about Bix."

"What do you mean? He didn't do anything stupid or hurt you in any way did he?" Callie was aghast.

"He hurt me all right but not in any physical way. More of a psychic way. He dumped me. I can't believe I'm so upset. I mean, I'm a big girl, right? And it's not like I wasn't warned." Sam blew her nose loudly.

"Oh Sam, don't do this to yourself. I am sorry, you know, despite what I'd heard about him. What happened?"

"He left it kind of vague. My guess is that he met somebody else. I really liked him – it feels like a gut punch." Sam blew her nose, loudly, into the phone.

"I'm sorry," Callie repeated. "I'd come over there but I can't leave Olivia right now."

"Don't worry about it. I look awful and I should probably be alone. My plan right now is to lie around, eat potato chips, watch old movies on TV and feel sorry for myself. After a brief period of that, I'll get back in the saddle." The two of them laughed.

"Anyway, I haven't been very nice to you lately." Sam sighed. "Well, you were right. You can say 'I told you so.'"

"Sam, come on. You know I'd never say that to you."

"Yeah, I know." Sam paused. "Let's get together when I've emerged from my self-pity cocoon."

"You bet. Stop by anytime. Or come visit me at work."

The two friends rang off, and Callie was relieved that Bix and Sam were no more, but she was also concerned. She certainly hoped her best friend wasn't now going to be the target of the odd behavior he'd exhibited to other girlfriends.

Callie sat there a moment, cuddling Koukla who had jumped on her lap. Sam's love life was one thing – but what about Callie's?

Ever since her car accident, Callie had sensed a tension in Sands. He was still kind and friendly but there was an aloofness that hadn't been there previously. It worried her a bit, but at the same time, she didn't want to assume the worst. She had been enjoying the easy, non-stressful relationship they'd seemed to be developing and the last thing she wanted to do was push it.

"Let's face it, Koukla," she said, rubbing the dog's ears. "I'm a little gun-shy when it comes to guys." Koukla just stared back at her, an adoring look on her face. If only humans were as simple to get along with as dogs.

Callie's ruminations were interrupted by her daughter who suddenly materialized in front of her, her cheeks flushed. "Mom," she began breathlessly, "I have to go to the library. Can you take me – like now?"

Callie peeked out the window – it was snowing, but lightly. "I don't suppose it can wait until tomorrow?" she asked ruefully.

"No. I'm sorry, Mom. I have a project due and I need a certain book. I thought it was due the day after tomorrow, but I checked the calendar and it's due tomorrow!"

Callie sighed. "And this isn't something you can get off of the Internet?"

"No," Olivia, said, growing a little more agitated. "We need to use this certain book for the report. It won't take long. Come on, Mom. Please."

Callie heaved herself off of the sofa, dislodging Koukla in the process. "Sorry, Koukla," she said. "I'd rather stay inside but it's not to be."

"I'll get the car warmed up," Callie told her daughter. "You get your coat."

"You're the best mom in the whole wide world!" Olivia chirped, relieved that her mother was now taking action on her behalf.

"Thanks for the vote of confidence," Callie laughed. "Last-minute school projects are my specialty."

Soon the two of them were bundled up and powering along in the icy darkness towards the library. It didn't close for another two hours but the cloud cover cloaked the streets in darkness and not even a star could be seen – it felt like the middle of the night. Callie found herself glancing surreptitiously in her rearview mirror a couple of times trying to gauge if anyone was suddenly speeding up, but they passed only one or two cars on their journey.

Callie parked in the sparsely-populated parking lot and looked around as an idea struck her. Maybe she could use this unexpected trip to the library to do a little additional research on Sandy Madison.

Despite the cold and her tiredness, Callie found that the small and charming Crystal Bay Library was a balm to her spirits. The structure was designed in the 1950s by a student of Frank Lloyd Wright, the famous Wisconsin resident, and it had a beauty and charm that made you want to sit down and stay awhile. Tall windows on one entire wall of the building framed picturesque views of the bay and offered a changing panorama of the seasons.

Olivia marched in and shed her coat, which Callie took from her. Olivia knew her way around the library and took off in the direction of the young adult department in search of her book, so Callie sauntered over to circulation desk to talk to a librarian she recognized. Bev Anderson was a frequent customer at Callie's Kitchen and one of the best-read women Callie knew.

"Hi, Callie," she offered cheerily. "Cold night to be out. Can I help you find anything? We just got a bunch of new paperbacks in stock."

"No, not tonight, although that does sound wonderful. I just need to use one of the computers." You had to sign in to use them, so Callie handed over her library card. You had only an hour at a time but that was plenty. She didn't plan to linger.

Before heading over the computer station, she checked in with Olivia who had found her book and was already avidly reading it. "I have to research something real quick," she said to her daughter. "Can you sit here and read while you wait?" Olivia nodded without looking up and Callie smiled to herself.

The library was relatively empty, but for a few high school kids studying, their brows furrowed over thick textbooks, and older folks gathering reading materials to fortify them for the cold winter days. It wasn't long until Callie found the links she was seeking, including a few more on auction sites. The library blocked any sites that were too explicit, thank goodness, but the auction sites showed only "appropriate" images and some of the links looked promising.

She took a closer look: Earl was right when he said that collectors would pay top dollar for their favorites. Depending on the issue, the prices were surprisingly high.

Scrolling quickly before Bev or anyone else busted her looking at this "adult" merchandise, Callie felt her heart do a little flip in her chest when she saw a thumbnail photo with the heading "featuring Sandy Madison" on it. Quickly, she clicked on the thumbnail.

The face of a beautiful, twenty-something woman stared back at her, a sultry look in her heavily made-up eyes. The woman was blonde and her nose was a little bigger, but Callie felt herself gripping the edges of the desk as realization dawned slowly. Her hunch had been correct.

Put on a dark wig and some glasses and you had the spitting image of Melody Cartwright.

Twenty One

Callie sat a minute, absorbing this information. In her astonishment, however, she had let the screen – now showing an enlarged title of the said men's magazine for everyone to see – sit for too long.

"Why, Callie," said a voice at her elbow and she whirled around. "*What* are you looking at?"

Quickly, Callie clicked off of the site, her face feeling like it was on fire despite the cold evening. Kayla, coat check girl and Melody Cartwright co-worker from The English Country Inn was smiling down at her, a quizzical look on her face.

"Uh, nothing," Callie stammered, thoroughly angry at herself for being caught in such a compromising position. A weak explanation occurred to her and she grabbed at it. "I must have clicked on the wrong thing. I was actually looking for a Christmas present and it took me to that page."

Kayla looked bemused. "Yeah, you really have to be careful on the Internet," she said pointedly.

Callie clicked off the site and stood up, gathering her purse and outerwear. "I'm sure I'll see you at Melody's book launch," she stammered to Kayla.

Another mistake. Why on earth had she brought up Melody? Her face flamed again, but Kayla was losing interest and gazing vaguely around the library.

"I'm hoping to make it. I might have to work. Well, stay warm," Kayla advised, raising an eyebrow. She sauntered off towards the section marked "Romance."

Face still burning, Callie collected Olivia and then retrieved her library card from Bev, making small talk, but barely able to meet her gaze. Olivia checked out her school book and Callie hustled them both out of there, feeling like a thief in the night.

Besides an embarrassment that threatened to smother her, she was blown away by the photo she'd found of "Sandy Madison." It was Melody Cartwright, Callie was sure of it: same face shape, (basically) the same facial features, just different hair color and all of that make-up. To the indifferent observer, she supposed they would look very different.

As she drove, Callie listened to the excited chatter of her daughter, grateful for the distraction, but her brain was churning and she had to force herself to focus on the road. Living in a small town was generally a wonderful thing, but you couldn't do anything without running into somebody – or in this case, somebodies – that you knew. How unfortunate to have run into Kayla when she was almost home free!

Fleetingly, Callie wondered if anyone would talk about what items they'd seen her perusing. Why was she even debating about it? Of course somebody would talk. This was Crystal Bay, after all. Well, at least they wouldn't know she'd been researching Melody Cartwright.

With a chuckle she wondered what types of books would Bev might have waiting for her on her next library visit.

* * *

Despite a text to Sands telling him that she had some new, "delicate" information, Callie couldn't find time to visit him personally before heading to work the next day. Instead, she found herself overwhelmed with the business of getting ready for Melody Cartwright's launch party.

Callie felt like she was in a daze as she rolled out cookie dough, cleaned pans and packed up ready-made meals for customers. She wasn't one to judge people for what they'd done in the past. What was dawning on her, with chilling reality, was that if someone knew that Melody had led a previously very different life, then that might affect Melody's squeaky clean image. Being on the brink of success, someone might very well want to kill in order to keep this information from the general public.

Anyone with a computer could put two and two together about Sandy Madison and Melody. However, it wasn't an obvious connection to make. You would probably have to be pointed in that direction in the first place. It appeared that Melody had worked very hard to change her name, identity and image – and so far it had worked. Who did it benefit to unveil her?

Callie knew she should just focus on the book launch, her cooking and the surprising – and welcome – uptick in customers she was currently experiencing at Callie's Kitchen. But she couldn't. Images of the sultry visage of Melody/Sandy were interrupting her thoughts.

She'd even asked Max if he'd heard anything about Sandy Madison, the model, moving into the Crystal Bay area and he'd blushed to the tips of his spiky hair. "No way, Callie," he'd said. "I have no idea." He gave her a pleading look. "Can we please close out that topic – forever?"

Callie had agreed. However, as she stirred soup, rolled dough and took food in and out of the oven, her brain churned with questions. She sighed as she put the last batch of *paxemathia* in the oven for Melody's launch. As soon as it came out of the oven, she was going on a brief field trip to Earl's antique shop to see if they knew who had purchased the magazines. It could have been an innocent collector or it could have been the person who sent the note to Melody. In any case, it was worth checking.

Piper was taking pictures of the bakery cases when Callie emerged from the kitchen thirty minutes later, her Greek spiced biscotti cooling on a rack. A delicious scent of butter and anise wafted from the cookies and Callie almost stopped to take one, but she had no time to waste.

When Piper saw Callie looking at her, she smiled and said simply "Instagram." Well, at least Piper was taking her job seriously. It seemed to be working, too, judging from the amount of customers in the shop.

"I won't be long," she called to Max and Piper, biting her lip. She promised herself she'd only be gone ten minutes.

Earl wasn't in his usual spot behind the register when Callie walked into the large, slightly dusty antique store, but Ginger and a petite, dark-haired woman were chatting animatedly. They stopped talking when they saw Callie, but when Ginger recognized her, she greeted her warmly.

"Hi there, Callie. How are things?"

"Pretty good, you know. Busy," Callie answered, uncertain how to begin. Might as well just come out with it, she decided. "You know those magazines I called about the other day?" She noticed that Ginger was suddenly all ears.

"Sure do. But hon, we sold out of them. I heard Earl telling you on the phone."

"I know. That's not what I came for. I wondered if the person who sold the magazines is working today – or when I can find them. I...uh, have a question for them."

The petite woman standing next to Ginger had been diligently listening to Callie speak, and now she smiled broadly.

"That was me, toots," the woman said. "Name's Elsa. I sold the magazines. What kind of question do you have? If you're looking for more of the same – though I don't know why you would be –" at this, Callie felt her face turn pink – "you might want to try a store in Milwaukee. Or even the Internet, though it pains me to say it. They're going to put us right out of business one of these days."

"No, I just wondered if you remember who you sold the magazines to."

"I remember all right," the woman said, frowning. "But I don't know her name. She was kind of tall, not sure about her age. At my age, everybody looks young to me."

"It was a she? You're sure of that?"

Elsa looked at Callie in amazement. "Darling, I may be getting up in years, but I'm not addled. Of course I know it was a woman!" she exclaimed, glancing at Ginger, who only shrugged.

"Sorry," Callie muttered. "I was just checking. What about this: Did she wear glasses?" Callie asked. "Or have long dark hair?"

"She had glasses on, but I couldn't see her eyes. She had sunglasses on and she kept 'em on. Also, she had on a ski hat and most of her hair was hidden in it. I only remember because it was a cold day, everybody was bundled up. She was wearing a heavy coat and pants with boots. She looked like a lot of people around here." The woman squinted at Callie. "You know her?"

"I don't know," Callie admitted. She felt a little bit defeated. She'd been sure she could uncover answers by finding out who had bought the magazines. The description of the buyer could have been Melody, but based on Elsa's description, it could also have been dozens of women in town.

Time was ticking away, baking was awaiting Callie and anyway, Ginger and Elsa were looking at her like she was a kook. "Thanks for answering my questions," Callie said. "I'd better get back to work."

"Suit yourself," said Elsa, shrugging, but Ginger smiled and pulled a book out from under the counter. She handed it to Callie. "Here's that vintage Betty Crocker that Earl found for you, hon," she said. "That'll be $15."

* * *

Callie trudged back through the snow, feeling childish pleasure in stomping into slushy mud puddles. A weak sun tried to peek through the overcast skies. If her shop wasn't too packed when she returned, she realized it was time to clue in Sands on what she'd learned about Melody. This time she wasn't taking any chances – she'd speak to him in person.

"Where is everybody?" she asked Max, who was wiping crumbs off the countertop near the register. "It was packed in here a few minutes ago."

"We got them all taken care of, boss. It's a lot easier with Piper here to help." Callie surveyed the remaining few who were sipping coffees and eating *loukoumades* or who were staring into the refrigerator cases, looking for meals.

"All right, then I've got to go somewhere. I'll be back in twenty minutes, tops. When the *paxemathia* are cool, I'll box them up. Just leave them where they are for now." She paused. "I'm sorry to keep going in and out of here. It's just that what I have to do can't wait."

"No problem," Max assured her. "I'll do it for you now."

"Thank you," Callie said gratefully. "Back in twenty minutes," she repeated. But Max had already turned to ring up a customer with a carton of Greek stew in her hands. He gave Callie a wave and she dashed out the door to her car.

The short trip to the Crystal Bay Police Station seemed to last an eternity. Sands usually returned to his desk to complete paperwork in the afternoon and Callie prayed that's where he was now. She should have called, she fretted, but with the distant way he was acting, would he even have agreed to see her? Better to make a surprise visit.

Callie fluffed her wavy hair into a better semblance of order as she walked into the warm building. It smelled like coffee and paper.

She asked to see Sands, saying she was a 'friend.' The officer behind the reception desk showed no visible reaction, and Callie was relieved. She'd hate to think she and Sands were a topic of gossip at the police station, even though, she told herself truthfully, they probably were. Everybody knew her at the station after the Drew scandal.

Minutes dragged by and Callie debated heading back to work but just then, she heard the familiar voice of Sands and she whirled around. "This is a surprise," he said, raising one eyebrow in the sardonic gesture he had. "How are you? Everything okay?" he asked in a softer tone.

"Yes, of course," Callie said, looking into his hazel eyes. They were warm and gentle as always. Maybe she'd imagined him being distant. After all, the man was trying to solve a murder.

Well so am I, she thought. She squared her shoulders. "I'm here to talk about the text I sent to you. Can we go and talk somewhere less public?"

"Yes, yes, of course." He took her by the elbow and started leading her back to his office. "You caught me at a good time. I just got back."

"Investigating?" she asked, hoping for some good information.

"Always," was all he said, smiling down at her. She sighed in frustration. Of course he wouldn't share more details.

When they were seated, Callie carefully averting her eyes from the picture of his young daughter that Sands kept on his desk, he suddenly appeared stern. "What's this delicate matter you have to talk about?"

"You know Melody Cartwright from the English Country Inn? It seems that she's been living a double life. She used to be known as 'Sandy Madison.'" Callie sat back and waited for Sands to make the connection.

But he only looked puzzled and Callie was amused at herself for being relieved that he didn't know the name.

"Fine, I'll bite. Who is 'Sandy Madison?'" he asked.

"That was the name Melody Cartwright used when she was a nude centerfold model in a men's magazine in the '90s!"

Sands tried to hide a smirk but didn't succeed. "Callie, my dear. What have you been up to? Nude model – Melody Cartwright?"

"I know it sounds funny, but just hear me out," Callie said.

"All right." Sands assumed a serious expression. "You've got my interest, that's for certain. What have you learned?"

Callie took a deep breath and told Sands everything, from the envelope she'd found, to the discussion with Max, that led her to the antique mall and finally, to the online auction site selling the magazines.

"And you're sure this is really Melody Cartwright?" Sands looked skeptical. "The tea and cookbook lady?"

"Yes!" Callie exclaimed. "She changed her hair color and maybe her nose. But the Sandy Madison picture looked like Melody, no question! I looked her up again on a library computer – it looked like the same person to me."

"I think I know where you're going with this," Sands observed drily. "You think that perhaps Melody would kill to keep her identity secret – and that perhaps, Natalie, being a coworker, found out?"

"The thought did occur to me," Callie admitted. "However, it may have nothing to do with Natalie's death. I just thought you should know about it. What do you think?"

"I think this is an interesting piece of the puzzle," Sands said. "And I'm glad you told me. I'm not sure what it means, but I will find out."

Callie exhaled loudly. "Melody seems like such a nice person," she said, suddenly uncertain of her decision to cast aspersions on the woman. Still, she was glad to have passed this burdensome knowledge onto a detective. She knew that Sands would be thorough, but discreet. "On a completely different note, Bix and Samantha broke up."

"Oh, really?" Sands replied. "His loss, I guess. A good woman is hard to find." He smiled at Callie and she was suddenly emboldened to speak.

"If that's true, why do I get the feeling you're being a bit distant with me lately? Aren't I a 'good woman'?" she blurted. *Why did I say that?* she thought. For a second, she considered bolting out the door.

Sands face suddenly grew serious once again. "Callie," he said. "I didn't know you'd noticed how I've...seemed lately." He sighed, deeply, and Callie grew alarmed. "But of course, you'd notice. You do tend to notice things. Hence, your visit today." He smiled weakly at her.

"So you *have* been feeling differently," Callie said. She sat back in her chair feeling drained, then stared at her lap. She should have kept her big mouth shut.

Sands took her hand in his. "I have been a bit of a prat, lately. Sorry," he said, as she looked up, unfamiliar with the term. "UK word for well, 'jerk' would be the nicer term."

"You haven't been," she protested. "I didn't mean that."

"No, it's all right. I've been struggling a bit and it's not your fault. Well, maybe it is, but not in the way that you might think. When you had that car accident, it brought back a lot of bad memories for me."

"What are you talking about?"

"My daughter was killed in a car accident. That's how she died, Callie. I never told you because I just didn't want to think about it."

"You mean..." Callie couldn't finish. One of Sands' mysteries had just been solved – and it was heartbreaking. "I'm so sorry," she murmured, stunned. She got up and walked over to him. "I wish I'd known." She put her hand on his arm and squeezed, unsure of what to say or do.

"Thank you," he said quietly. He took her hand and held it briefly. "I do care about you, you know. It's all maybe just ... a little overwhelming for me."

"Of course it is," Callie said, tears making her eyes sting. "I'm glad you told me. What a secret to keep."

Sands sighed. "Yes, it's been difficult but I...well, I don't know." He shrugged. "Life goes on, but I find that it's best now if I take one day at a time."

Maybe Sands was feeling overwhelmed because he was realizing that he just didn't want to be in a relationship and become vulnerable again after all he'd been through. She couldn't say she blamed him, but it was still painful.

The combination of the news she'd just heard and the prospect of losing him suddenly flooded her with sadness. She didn't want Sands to see it – if she was feeling this way, what must he be feeling? With all the strength she had in her, she kept her face and voice composed.

"I should let you get back to work," she said quietly and Sands nodded his head.

Having recovered from his show of emotion, Sands, ever the gentleman, saw her to the door. "I'll check into the Melody Cartwright situation," he said, trying to smile. "And thanks for letting me know."

As Callie walked back to her car, hunched inside her heavy coat against the biting cold and brisk wind from the bay, she realized he hadn't said he wanted to see her again or that he would call her, as he usually did. The tears that burned her eyes weren't just from the wind.

Twenty Two

"Callie, we need more coffee!" called Max. Callie was already fumbling with her large coffee urn and she grumbled under her breath as she spilled coffee grounds onto the floor. Melody's book launch was buzzing in the front of her shop and so far, so good, despite Callie's misgivings about Melody at this point. She hadn't heard any more about her previous identity from Sands and she didn't know if this was a good sign, or a bad one.

"On the way, Max!" she called. The enticing beverage varieties from Tea for Two were still flowing, but a lot of the book launch attendees were clamoring for coffee instead of tea, especially the men. Callie could sympathize. It was only by virtue of several cups of coffee that she was still standing at all. It had been another nearly sleepless night as she tossed and turned, thinking about not just Sands, but Natalie's murder. The killer was still out there.

Still, the show must go on and Melody's book launch appeared to be a hit. Sands had said he'd stop by – but that was before yesterday's tense interaction. Callie hoped he'd make an appearance, if for nothing else than to get a better look at Melody Cartwright aka "Sandy Madison."

Carefully maneuvering through the double doors with another platter of gingerbread cakes, Callie set down the treats and took a surreptitious look around her shop. Fortunately, none of her inner turmoil was reflected here. It looked like a picture of holiday cheer with its white Christmas lights and warm, homey decorations.

Groups of book launch attendees were chattering away in groups and eating the delicious foods she and Melody had provided. Max was wearing a Santa hat perched jauntily atop his spiky hair and his tattoos were covered up by a bright green sweater with a reindeer design. A gift from Piper?

Piper, meanwhile, was wearing a white cardigan sweater with puffed sleeves, and a red and white polka dotted wool skirt. She looked like The Elf on the Shelf, but in a charming way. Callie was amused and gratified that her employees were embracing the Christmas spirit for the launch.

Along with plenty of under-eye concealer and some bright red lipstick to give her face a little color, Callie had let her long, wavy dark hair hang loose, with a red poinsettia pin holding one side back behind her ear. A red sweater, black slim-fitting pants and a retro Christmas apron from Earl's antique shop completed her look.

As Callie surveyed the room, she sighed a bit with relief that she and her co-workers had been able to pull it all off. She smiled as Christy, Tea for Two proprietor, walked up to her, a cookie in hand.

"It all seems to be going well," Christy remarked. "Melody looks happy."

"She does, doesn't she?" Melody, though beautifully outfitted in a winter white sweater dress, her sleek dark hair pulled back in its signature bun, appeared a bit preoccupied as she chatted with the guests, posed for pictures and signed copies of her book.

Callie turned to Christy, unwilling to share her observations about Melody. "You've been a big help. We should team up again sometime."

"I'd like that," Christy said with a smile.

The two were interrupted by the arrival of Bix and Jack Myers who entered the shop, stomping snow off their boots. Callie nodded at them. "I'm happy to see some of Melody's co-workers supporting her," she remarked to Christy. "Bix works part-time at the inn and

Jack supplies the food, among other things. At least somebody showed up for her."

"Yes, it's important to have support." Christy eyed the two good-looking men appreciatively. *Uh-oh.* "I'm so glad we could do this for Melody."

Suddenly, there seemed to be a bit of commotion while a pair of women appeared to be trying to drain an empty tea urn by turning it at a precarious angle. "Oops, better get a refill, stat, before somebody gets burned," Christy said, scooting towards the women.

Callie took this opportunity to speak to Bix and Jack who were waiting in line to talk to Melody. "Hi guys," she said. "Thanks for stopping by." She was a little leery of Bix, given his debacle with Viv and Sweetie, not to mention Samantha. She was also shy around Jack, who had been so flirtatious with her the last time he'd stopped by her shop.

"Of course," said Bix, nodding at Callie in a relatively civil way. Callie was relieved that he appeared to be in a calm mood. "It's not every day someone you know gets a book published," he said, looking over at Melody.

"Melody must be really proud," Jack observed. He and Bix looked like lumberjacks in their puffy coats and heavy boots worn with jeans. He gave Callie one of his dazzling, intimate smiles and Callie blushed. *What was it with him?*

Nervously, she glanced at Melody, who was chatting brightly with a cookbook fan, seemingly unaware of her co-workers' arrival. When she looked at Jack again, he was eyeing the platters of food, not Callie. *Thank goodness.*

"We can't stay long," Bix was explaining. "I've got to get back to work soon. Kayla's working the front desk alone. She volunteered to hold down the fort, but she's sorry she had to miss it. I think Melody told her she'd give her an autographed book."

Callie noticed that her platters of food were emptying. Time to excuse herself from the conversation. "You're here and that's the important thing. I'm going to put out some more food – it's going fast! Be sure to have a bite to eat and a hot drink before you go."

Bix and Jack nodded at her and shuffled towards the line of people waiting for Melody to sign their books.

The rest of the launch went swiftly. Callie couldn't believe it when she checked the time – 6:30 pm. She was exhausted but exhilarated. She had sold lots of food and gift certificates for Callie's Kitchen, so the day was a success by her standards. Gathering up some empty platters, she swept them into the back room so she could do a quick wash-up.

When she emerged just a few minutes later, many of the guests had left. Callie looked around for Melody and didn't see her. She checked the restroom but Melody wasn't in there, either.

"Piper," Callie said, as the young woman dashed by her with a tray full of empty tea cups. "Where did Melody disappear to?"

"She said she had to go and that I was to say thank you." Piper frowned, remembering. "She *did* say something about calling you later."

"Oh," Callie shrugged. "Fine. She was probably tired and I don't blame her."

What a day. Callie's shoulders slumped a little bit when she remembered that Sands had never shown up, either.

Oh, well. She'd worry about him tomorrow. All she wanted to do now was take a hot shower and sleep for about twelve hours. It probably would be more like seven, but she'd take what she could get.

Max and Piper offered to stay and clean up and Callie gratefully accepted. She hadn't realized how exhausted she was until she was sitting and pulling on her boots like an old woman. Suddenly, her phone buzzed in her coat pocket. Sands! It had to be him.

"Hello!" she said eagerly, not even bothering to look at the number on the screen.

"Callie it's me, Melody. Listen, I'm at the inn and I wanted to know if you'd bring those cookies by for me tonight. I know you're tired and so am I. But Emma called to ask how things were going and I thought it would be good if I could at least tell her that I had secured your cookie delivery, so to speak."

Callie was silent for a minute, wondering if she even had the energy required to pack up more cookies and drive to the English Country Inn.

"You can trust me. I'll have the cookies. Can't it wait until tomorrow? Emma will never know!"

"Please, Callie. Bring whatever you have. It would really help me out. I think Emma is really on edge."

In her tiredness, Callie was losing patience

"All right, fine. I'll be there. Just give me a few minutes to pack up and then I'll stop by. I can't stay long though," Callie warned. "I'm about dead on my feet."

Callie packed up the *kourabiethes* for the Christmas Tea party, willing herself to keep alert and awake. It wasn't that late, after all.

Christmas cheer, Christmas spirit, she kept telling herself, feeling a bit like Scrooge. True, she'd had a long day, but she was fortunate to get the additional business at the inn's celebrated holiday tea event, wasn't she? Plus, she was exceedingly lucky that her business seemed to be on the upswing. For whatever the reasons, people were starting to frequent Callie's Kitchen once again. These were all good things, no doubt. So she had to make another delivery – it was a small price to pay. She was ashamed at snapping at Melody on the phone.

Before she could make her exhausted way out the door, Piper had insisted on snapping a picture of Callie holding the boxes of cookies. "It will be great to show you contributing food to something as elegant and popular as the Christmas Tea," she gushed.

Callie had relented, applying a fresh coat of lipstick and doing her best to smile. "I'm posting this now," Piper had chirped as Callie was leaving her shop. "Your customers are going to be impressed!" *I hope so.*

As Callie drove the short distance to the inn, the snowfall seemed to be growing thicker. Callie drove slowly and carefully, the headlights of her car highlighting the wall of white flakes that were swirling out of the sky. Had the imminent blizzard finally arrived? Callie gripped the wheel tightly. Despite being a lifelong Wisconsinite, she still didn't care for driving in a snowstorm. Her recent trip down a ditch hadn't helped matters.

At a stoplight, Callie texted Sands and told him where she was going and why. Since she didn't yet know if Melody was a threat, the more people who knew she'd be at the inn, the better.

As usual, the inn made a pretty picture. Tonight, it was aglow with lights and its signature cheerful Christmas décor. Bright white lights sparkled under the thick layer of freshly fallen snow. Angels with bugles hung from the eaves and wonderfully piney-smelling fresh Christmas wreaths adorned nearly all of the inn's windows. Despite her weariness and her apprehension about Melody, it truly was a winter wonderland.

Stepping gingerly over half-hidden icy patches, Callie made her way to the door of the inn without falling. As soon as she crossed the threshold, Melody was practically falling over herself to take the cookie boxes from her hands.

"Callie, I'm so glad you're here. Let me bring you to the kitchen so that we can put these away."

"Sure thing. Can I take off my coat first?" Melody was certainly eager to get moving – just as well. Callie was feeling more exhausted by the minute.

"Of course. Sorry – I'll take it for you." Melody hung Callie's coat behind the reception desk and bustled back to her side.

"My goodness, you brought quite a few boxes," Melody remarked. She looked at Callie, who was yawning, despite her best efforts to look perky.

"Thanks for coming out here. You must be exhausted."

"It's fine," Callie said, stifling another yawn. "It's an honor to contribute to the tea."

The two women distributed their boxes between the two of them and made their way down the hallway, past the dining room and to the clean, white kitchen.

"Hello, anybody here?" Melody asked, hesitating before entering the room. She nodded at Callie to follow her inside. Hesitantly, Callie did so and stood on the threshold of the door. She watched as Melody placed the cookies on a shelf and then motioned for Callie to join her.

"I didn't want the staff to see us bringing in boxes of cookies or they're going to be asking us to taste-test them."

Callie chuckled. "Yep, that happens. Where do you want these?"

"Let's put them in the walk-in refrigerator," Melody suggested. "They'll stay fresher in there, plus, the kitchen staff may not be as tempted to sample them if they're not lying around on the countertops."

"You bet," Callie answered. The two of them stacked boxes on the shelves, shivering a bit with the cold air of the fridge. The fridge was tidy but packed full of food – it was difficult to wedge the boxes in place.

"Well, hello there," said a familiar voice. Callie looked up to see Jack Myers standing outside the door. He was holding the remainder of the cookie boxes. "Can I help?"

"Thanks, Jack!" Melody said, smiling at him. "Just put them in here." Jack stacked the additional boxes and they all walked back out to the warmth of the kitchen.

"Is that everything?" Jack asked.

Callie started to nod, but Melody shook her head. "I left a couple more boxes near the reception desk," she said.

"I'll get them," Jack said with a grin. "As long as I can have a few of whatever's in here – it smells great!"

"You see what I mean?" Melody said to Callie.

"I'm sure we can spare a few cookies," Callie answered, grateful for the help. She was fading fast and happy that her errand was nearly complete.

Looking to expedite her homecoming, Callie ventured back into the walk-in and started looking for space on the shelves – which was a mistake. The second she tried to move a stack of frozen food, several parcels spilled out onto the floor. Sighing, Callie leaned down to pick them up, Melody joining her when she heard the noise.

Callie picked up the first package of food and recoiled at the label: "*Lake Perch. 2010.*" What was 6-year-old fish doing in the walk-in?

"Yuck!" Callie said, showing the package to Melody.

"What in the world?" Melody sniffed the package and started to unwrap it. "I'm sorry, but I need to show this to the chef. It's unthinkable that someone would keep this in here."

"Just be glad it has a date," Callie remarked. She wasn't at all sure she wanted to see a petrified fish.

Suddenly, Melody gave a little gasp. "Callie," she whispered. "Look."

Not really wanting to, Callie forced herself to look at the object in Melody's shaking hands. Horrified, Callie recognized a heavy pipe wrench. Sticking to it was blood and bits of hair ... long, red, curly hair. *Natalie.* Callie felt her stomach lurch.

"We've got to call the police. Now." She felt her pockets but her phone wasn't in any of them. "Darn, I must have left my phone in my coat or in the car. Let's go call from reception." She started toward the door but nearly bumped smack into Jack Myers who was carrying the remaining boxes. One of the boxes had an open lid and Jack had apparently taken the liberty of sampling the cookies already. Any other time, that might have annoyed her, but right now she had bigger fish to fry, so to speak.

"Jack!" she shrieked. "We need help. Melody found something in the freezer. I think it's the weapon that killed Natalie."

Slowly, Jack set the cookie boxes on the counter and walked over to a stricken Melody, who was holding the wrench gingerly, trying to touch only the ends of the paper.

He took it from her hand and gently turned it from side to side. When he looked at Callie, she couldn't believe she had ever thought his eyes were attractive and warm. He gazed at her with intense hatred.

"Bad luck just seems to follow you two around," he said. "I knew I should have gotten rid of this a long time ago. But there's always somebody hanging around here."

Melody stared at Jack, stricken, as he pulled something out of his pocket and pointed it at her. A Taser gun. In seconds, she was unconscious on the floor. That must be how Jack had been able to stun and kill Natalie.

Callie was horrified, rooted to the spot. *Move*, she told herself. *Maybe you can outrun him.*

Smirking now, Jack turned to Callie, his eyes like steel. "Don't even think about it," he said. "I have a three-shot Taser."

She looked wildly around her but there was no one to help. Her body jolted, then froze as the Taser went off. Callie flopped to the floor, just like a freshly caught lake perch.

Twenty Three

Callie was unable to move or talk as Jack dragged her into the walk-in. She watched with horror as Jack dragged Melody inside the refrigerator and let her drop unceremoniously to the floor.

Jack muttered to himself as he arranged each of them inside the walk-in. Callie felt him sit her up and prop her against a shelf. Her legs splayed uselessly in front of her. He did the same to Melody.

"I thought we had a nice thing going," he was saying to Melody, but very softly. Callie had to strain to hear. "You don't tell anyone that Natalie and I were skimming off the top here at the inn and in exchange, I don't tell everyone about your torrid past as Sandy Madison. Oh yeah, and unlike, Natalie, my would-be whistleblower, you get to live. It was only my bad luck that my partner in crime ended up having a *conscience.*"

He spat the last word as if it tasted bad. "So much for honor among thieves." He practically snorted before continuing to castigate Melody, who was looking distinctly out of it. Could she even understand?

Jack's voice rose, dripping with venom. "But no. You had to be so inquisitive. And then you drag Callie into it with you. Too bad you're so active on Instagram, Callie," Jack turned to her with a sneer. "That's how I knew you'd be here." Callie groaned and tried to move but Jack went on, relentlessly.

"You should be more discreet in your investigative techniques. I've been keeping an eye on you and I knew you had figured things out about Melody. It was only a matter of time until you figured out the rest. Was I right or what?"

Terrified by his attention turning to her, Callie struggled to move once again. Jack snorted with derision.

"Well, ladies, get ready for a nice long slumber party. Real long. *'Such a shame those nice women got locked in the walk-in. Accidents happen.'*" He paused and looked at the two of them, shaking his head. "Too bad Emma didn't upgrade the old door to have a safety latch, but she was always looking to save a buck. Your loss." He slammed the door, leaving Callie and Melody in complete darkness.

Callie wanted to cry for help but she couldn't. It was like one of those nightmares where you want to scream loudly but nothing came out.

Inside the walk-in, the darkness was almost palpable and the cold was astonishing. Callie sat on the icy floor, willing her fingers and toes to move, move, move. She was unclear how much time had passed before she heard Melody moaning a few feet away from her.

"Melody. We're stuck. In the walk-in," came out weakly, but at least she was talking again. "We've got. To get out of here." Callie found that she could slightly move her arms and she braced her hands on the floor before slowly rising to a kneeling position. Every movement felt like she was in slow motion.

She crawled at a snail's pace to the door of the walk-in and started trying to ram against it with her shoulder to make noise. She was too weak. Callie felt warm involuntary tears flow down her cheeks. With longing, she thought of her cell phone, left in her coat pocket near the reception desk.

Would Sands get her message about the inn – and when she didn't answer his texts, would he think of coming to find her? Or would he assume she had only texted him about her nighttime visit to the inn in a rather lame attempt to get his attention?

Callie heard a small cry escape her lips and she bit them, hard. Crying would do nothing. She and Melody were in serious danger. Their only hope was to make some noise and try to get out.

Once again, Callie tried to scream but her voice was still too weak. And she was getting colder. She envisioned taking off her coat when she entered the inn and wished she hadn't. What could she do to stay warm?

Callie remembered that the most heat escaped your body from your head. Crawling around on the floor of the walk-in, she felt around the walls for an apron or anything that somebody might have left behind. Nothing. Frozen food clattered to the floor and Callie felt something hard hit her shoulder. She grunted in pain.

Well, she would just have to use what she had. She pulled at her sweater until it covered her head – leaving part of her abdomen exposed, but she wore a knit camisole and at least that offered some protection. As Callie struggled with her clothing, a memory struck her like a thunderbolt. The day of Natalie's murder, she'd barely recognized Jack, all spiffed up in a suit, so unlike his usual lumberjack-style attire. She remembered that she'd found it slightly odd that he was so dressed up, but now she knew – he'd gotten his clothes wet killing Natalie and had to change.

Now able to sit up, Callie called to Melody, who was babbling incoherently. Maybe she was regaining consciousness, Callie thought, clinging to any hope she could.

"Melody, we're locked in the walk-in," she repeated. "Jack Myers put us here." Callie's ability to speak was getting stronger. "Our only way out is to make some noise! Do you think you have the energy to yell?"

"I don't think so," Melody rasped in a whisper. "Sorry." She tried to scream but it only sounded as if she were gargling. Her body must have reacted more strongly to the Taser, Callie thought. Drat.

"I'm going to find something to hit the door with," Callie said. "Will anybody hear us? Is there a cleaning crew here tonight? Will the guests hear us? Anyone?"

"Guests...not allowed...back here..." Melody rasped. "Cleaning crew...gone."

"Fine. Then we're going to have to make a heck of a lot of noise and hope that an insomniac guest is hungry – or that one of the cooks forgot something. Let me find something to bang on the door. It will work better if you can help me." Talking felt like speaking through a cotton cloth but at least she was communicating again.

"I can't...." Melody said, whimpering. "Sorry, Callie. For getting you ... in this...mess."

"Melody, I'm not dying in here, okay? Now, please. I know you can do it."

Without any lights, it was difficult to see. Still, this was a commercial kitchen. Callie knew that there had to be some heavy stainless steel containers in the walk-in, since that's what she used at her shop.

With fingers that were beginning to cramp up from the cold, she felt along the shelving unit until finally she hit pay dirt – a huge, heavy container. She nudged it and felt liquid slosh inside. She would just have to dump out whatever was in there, she thought grimly, and hope for the best.

Next to her, Melody was starting to move. "I'm trying to stand," she told Callie.

"Good," Callie told her, gritting her teeth as she struggled to get to her feet. She braced herself against the shelving unit and grabbed the heavy, liquid-filled container.

"Look out!" she cried as she tipped it over, more clumsily than she would have liked.

Callie smelled beef broth and yelped as some of it washed over her pant legs. Cold and wet – this was not going to be good.

"Is that beef broth?" Melody asked weakly.

"Yep. Just be glad it wasn't clam juice. Now I'm going to ram against the door with this thing. Can you find a container and help me do the same?"

"I don't know." Callie heard Melody flop to the floor. "I'm not feeling so good."

Callie's fear was starting to choke her but she tried to remain calm. "I guess I'm on my own, then. Yell with me, if you can."

With all of her strength, Callie rammed the door repeatedly, again and again. "Help!" she called in her weakened voice. "Help!"

Again and again, she rammed the door, stopping with only minutes to rest. Nobody came. In fact, the silence that greeted Callie was absolute.

Shivering, Callie crawled back along the floor until she found Melody, who was making frightened sounds. "Let's huddle together for warmth and then I'll try again," she told her. Melody agreed and the two women clung to each other as if they were floating on an iceberg. Well, Callie reasoned, that's about accurate.

She was terrified. If they didn't die of cold, the lack of air would become an issue very soon. With two of them in there, the oxygen was going to be used up even more quickly. Her sense of time wasn't great. Being Tasered had made everything foggy. If they could get out soon, they would be all right. If not..... Callie didn't let her brain continue the thought.

"I'm trying again," she told Melody. With what strength she had left, Callie struggled to get up and rammed the stainless steel container against the door once again. Over and over, she hit the door, losing all sense of herself and focusing all of her thought and concentration on her task. In between thuds she yelled as loud as she could, which wasn't very loud.

Callie felt herself grow dizzy as she kept up the racket, but she couldn't stop, she could never stop. What about Olivia, and George and Koukla, Viv, Sweetie and Sam? She saw all of their faces in her mind's eye and desperately wanted to see them again.

And Sands. His face came to her last of all and the image stayed.

Over and over she hit the door, oblivious to Melody at this point and only vaguely registering the other woman's frightened tears. She felt her eyes closing in exhaustion, she couldn't keep going, and she was falling forward, falling, falling...

"Oof!" Callie said as her body made impact with a solid – and warm – floor. Light and warm air washed over her. Forcing herself to roll over, she looked into the wide eyes of Kayla. She was free!

"Callie!! What's going on? I was in reception and I started getting phone calls and complaints from guests about a loud clanging through the vents." Kayla did not sound happy. But then she peered into the walk-in and saw Melody lying there, not moving. She stared at Callie, horror-stricken. "Is she – dead?"

"No, not yet. Just cold. Let's get her out of here." The two of them helped Melody out of the walk-in and led her to a chair.

Callie turned to Kayla. "I've got to call the cops. This wasn't an accident. Jack Myers locked us in here."

"Jack Myers?" Kayla looked skeptical. "He's in the parking lot right now trying to get his car out of the snow. Why would he lock you in here?"

Callie gasped and suddenly adrenaline rushed through her like a tidal wave. "He's still here?" She felt her anger surge and suddenly she felt like George on a rant – all she could see was red!

"Call 911!" she yelled to Kayla as she darted past her and down the hall. Still feeling weak, she stumbled a bit, but as she spotted Jack's car in the parking lot, she felt her rage return. Blindly, she burst through the doors and ran to his car.

Jack was gunning the engine but the wheels of his car spun uselessly in the snow. Plumes of white exhaust made her choke. The killer was looking straight ahead, so she knocked on the driver's side window and enjoyed seeing him jump at the sight of her. He looked like he'd seen a ghost.

"Yes, Jack. It's me!" Callie hollered so that he could hear her. "Melody and I escaped and the cops are on the way. Too bad you didn't get out while you could!"

Jack gunned his engine once more and his tires continued to spin crazily. There had to be another six inches of snow on the ground, at least, since she'd first arrived at the inn. This must be the infamous blizzard that Emma had predicted was headed their way. What a time for it to arrive in Crystal Bay!

Jack gunned his motor one more time, but the wheels continued to spin. Suddenly, Jack slid his body in a snakelike motion to the passenger side and darted out the door. He started running.

Her body numb from cold and the Taser, Callie ran after him, determined that he wouldn't get away. Snow was falling thickly and it was difficult to see Jack in the dark. Icy cold snowflakes stung Callie's eyes and nose but she kept on.

Jack stumbled and slipped on the snow and ice as he skittered like a scared rabbit, first starting one way, then the next. Suddenly, he raced towards the waterfront and Callie followed from a safe distance, not wanting to be Tasered again. In her adrenaline rush, she felt like her feet had wings. "Help!" she called, "Help!" Her voice echoed in the cold, empty night.

With a surge of anger, Callie saw that Jack was running for the woods that bordered the water. If he got lost in there, he just might be able to escape.

No. Way.

Suddenly, Callie noticed Bix's truck, with a snowplow attachment, parked near the patio that held the inn's diners in the balmy summer months. Bix had probably stored it there, out of sight of the guests, most of who would not be venturing out onto the snow-covered patio.

Callie raced over to the vehicle. She touched the hood of the truck and discovered that the engine was still warm. Perfect. Opening the driver's side, she saw the keys in the ignition.

With about two seconds of thought, Callie jumped behind the wheel and started chasing Jack in Bix's truck. In the rearview mirror, she saw Bix running after her, shouting but she didn't stop. Shaking her head, still foggy from her recent ordeal, she bore down on Jack who was now looking from side to side, obviously trying to find an escape route. He hesitated a minute before darting in the direction of the lake path. Callie gunned the engine and followed.

Jack looked behind him when he heard the rumble of Bix's large vehicle, coming straight at him, with Callie bent over the wheel like a racecar driver. She didn't stop. She didn't even slow down. Bix's truck rumbled onto the lake path and Callie held her breath as she gained on him. She couldn't run him over – what would she do?

Jack appeared frozen to the spot but at the last minute, he dove into a thick copse of snow-covered trees by the lake path.

No! If he got lost in the woods, they'd never find him. Callie jumped out of the car, planning to chase him on foot, and Bix was at her side in a moment.

"Have you lost your mind?" he sputtered, but Callie cut him off. She pointed wildly in the direction of the trees.

"Bix, Jack killed Natalie. Don't let him get away! He's got a Taser – be careful!" she warned, aware of the hysterical note in her voice. Bix stared at her, stunned, before breaking into a sprint and heading in Jack's direction.

Snow continued to fall, large, fluffy flakes that seemed to float to the ground. It was like someone had opened a huge feather pillow. Callie slipped and slid as she tried to keep up with Bix and Jack, panting and determined. She was freezing and shaking but so angry she could barely feel the cold.

Suddenly Callie heard shouts and she followed them. She caught up to the two men in time to see Bix tackle Jack and pin him to the ground. The words that were flying out of Bix's mouth were not any that she'd like Olivia to hear.

Callie stopped to catch her breath and remembered Samantha mentioning to her, in the early days of her relationship with Bix, that he had played football at Crystal Bay High back in the day.

"Do you have him?" she called to Bix, brushing her hair, now wet with snow, out of her eyes. Her long, wavy hair felt like wet, cold seaweed. Cold rivulets of melted snow ran down her neck and she shivered.

"What does it look like?" Bix asked, struggling to keep Jack still. "Hurry – get help!"

Callie nodded and staggered back towards the inn, bone tired, cold and triumphant. Jack wasn't going anywhere, she thought, as the flashing blue and red lights of the Crystal Bay police surrounded the parking lot.

Twenty Four

"**S**o let me get this straight," Samantha was saying. "Jack and Natalie were in some kind of scheme to cheat the inn out of money?"

Several days had passed and Callie was at the inn's Christmas Tea celebration, slightly bruised, perhaps a little sniffly, but extremely happy to be alive. She, Samantha, George, Kathy (!), Sweetie, Viv and Olivia were seated at a cozy table piled high with delicious teatime treats: little sandwiches, tiny cakes and many varieties of cookies. Sands was expected to join them any minute.

"Unfortunately, yes," Callie replied. "Natalie and Jack worked out a deal. For example, Natalie would supposedly order $5,000 worth of goods from Jack, but he would only deliver, say $4,000 worth. They'd split the difference between them so over time, they were developing a nice little side business."

The tea had been postponed for a few days to recover from the latest crime, but Emma had been given the go-ahead to reopen. Newly returned from Arizona, she was determined to host her yearly event. The snowstorms had finally abated, allowing her to travel. Crystal Bay was once more sunny and serene.

Sipping tea and munching on festive foods – including Callie's *kourabiethes*, aka Greek snowball cookies – her audience was rapt as they listened to the motives behind Natalie's senseless murder. Feeling exhausted from her ordeal, Callie had asked her friends and family if she could recite what she knew only once, to the group as a collective whole. Surprisingly, they'd agreed.

Of course, Callie thought, the draw of a Christmas Tea at the scene of the crime may have had something to do with their agreeing to wait to hear the complicated story of Natalie's murder.

"How long did they think they'd get away with it?" asked Viv, sipping from her cup of Earl Grey.

"Who knows?" Callie said with a sigh. "Obviously, Natalie was helping to cook the books, and it worked well, for a while. Sooner or later, though, Emma was going to notice that she was being shortchanged. In fact, it seems that she and Jack had overestimated their little plan. Staff and vendors were starting to realize that something strange was going on. In fact, that's why Melody ended up asking me to contribute food to the tea today."

She took a deep breath before continuing. It was difficult to think about Natalie's fate. Her death seemed like such a waste.

"Poor Natalie," Callie resumed her story after a moment. "She had second thoughts and was planning to throw herself on Emma's mercy and ask if she could repay what she'd stolen instead of being reported to the police. However, she made the mistake of telling Jack about it and asking him to go to Emma with her so that they could make a full confession. He didn't want to do that and he panicked."

The group was silent for a minute as they took in this sobering information. Sweetie even stopped piling goodies on her plate and looked downcast.

"And then there was Mrs. Dayton. While she might not be the easiest person to deal with, it turns out that she had lost her eyeglasses and that's why she was driving erratically. She wasn't trying to hit me with her – in fact, just the opposite."

"Who told you about her eyeglasses?" Viv wanted to know.

"Christy, from Tea for Two. She found a pair of glasses on one of her shelves and held onto them. Mrs. Dayton came in looking for them."

"I'm interested in hearing about Melody. How does her "center-fold" past tie into this?" Sam asked abruptly.

George cleared his throat and cast a sidelong glance at Olivia, who was sitting, placidly sipping a cup of tea. Callie decided to keep the explanation short and sweet for her daughter's sake.

"Somehow Melody figured out what Jack was up to with the shortchanging of supplies and being the kind of guy he is, he did some extensive research on her." Callie shook her head. "When he threatened to expose her past career right before her book launch, she agreed to keep quiet about the fraud. I think she started to suspect Jack had gotten rid of Natalie and she was afraid. I don't blame her. She didn't want to be the next victim, I suppose."

It had come to light that Melody herself had bought the stock of magazines at the antique mall, in an attempt to stave off Jack's threats about unveiling her previous identity. Unfortunately, there was nothing she could do about the Internet.

George was growing perturbed. "Why would Natalie do such a thing in the first place? It seems like a foolish plan."

"Greed," replied a deep voice and Callie looked up to see Sands standing next to them. "Pure greed. Jack and Natalie enjoyed nice things. Jack wanted to move to a warm climate and Natalie – well, she just wanted to have the things that money can buy."

"Money no buy everything!" Sweetie piped in, indignantly. She smiled and grabbed the hands of the two seated on either side of her – Viv and George. "Like friends. Family. Love."

Callie snuck a glance at Sands at this last comment from Sweetie, but he was only nodding his head gently.

"Too true," he agreed and sat down next to Callie who moved over a bit to make room for him, then back next to him, comforted by his warm, solid presence.

Viv set down her teacup and clapped her hands together briskly. "Now, then! That's enough depressing talk for one tea party. Let's be grateful that all of us are here together. Safe, healthy and happy!"

"Here, here!" George said. They all cheered and called "Merry Christmas" and Sweetie chimed in with *Kala Christouyenna*" before they resumed their eating with renewed vigor.

Callie was relieved when the conversation moved on to lighter, happier topics, like the beautiful holiday décor that graced the room and how much butter to use in Sweetie's favorite cookie recipe. She'd had enough death and destruction in the last few days.

Sands filled his plate with sandwiches and cookies from the tea tray at the center of the table and scooted even closer to Callie. He took a bite of gingerbread cake and his face lit up.

"I love this one, did you make it?" he asked. She nodded, still a little shy around him. He'd arrived at the scene and wordlessly hugged her for several minutes before attending to Jack, Bix and the rest of the witnesses on that terrible evening. She'd been so happy to see him, she almost cried.

"Don't do this again," he'd said, after he'd gently released her. His gaze was more serious than she'd ever seen it.

"Do what?" Callie asked, bracing herself for a scolding.

"Make me think I'm going to lose you," he'd answered and embraced her again. Callie had been wrong – he didn't want to stop seeing her. Like everything else in life, it was just a little complicated.

"The cake is great, but the best part is the icing," Sands said, breaking into her dreamy recollections. He took another bite of cake.

"Don't even say the word 'icing' to me," Callie said, only half-joking. "After my time in the walk-in refrigerator, I don't know if I'll even want to eat ice cream anymore."

Sands set down his plate. "That's it. Right. You need cheering up. I've got an early Christmas present for you." He reached into his coat pocket and Callie felt her heart start to pound. Did he have a ring box? Was he going to propose?

In a panic, Callie darted her eyes around the table and noticed that her friends and family had stopped talking and were listening intently to Sands. Even in her excitement, Callie took note of the various facial expressions worn by the group: George was frowning, Olivia was wide-eyed, Viv and Sweetie looked as if they could barely contain themselves and Samantha was beaming.

Sands blinked as he realized that the hubbub had stopped and he faltered. His hand stayed inside his coat pocket before, fumbling, he pulled out an envelope.

An envelope? Gently, Sands handed it to her and she opened it slowly. "To: Callie Costas from Ian Sands. This is an IOU, good for one trip to a warm climate, when we both get time off of work. Merry Christmas!" It was signed, "Love, Ian."

A smile slowly spread across Callie's face until she was laughing. "You've got a deal!" she said. His gift was much better than the ordinary sweater she'd ended up buying for him, but that was alright. Callie realized that the table was holding their collective breath and decided to put them out of their misery.

"It's just an invitation for a vacation to a warm climate, at some later date," Callie told her assembled onlookers, waving the piece of paper. "Everybody can relax now!"

"Better if it's for a honeymoon," George said under his breath, but he was smiling at Callie and Sands. She saw him squeeze Kathy's hand.

"I figured Callie needed some sun and hot weather after her time in the freezer," Sands explained, chuckling.

"So, who need time in freezer to want warm climate?" Sweetie asked, hugging herself. "I like it here, in Crystal Bay, but I miss warm Greek weather."

"When are you going back to Greece, Sweetie dear?" asked Viv. "We'll miss you."

"I miss you too, but time for me to go. I stay until New Year's and then go back. You visit me, sometime, yes?"

They all rushed to reassure Sweetie that of course, they would visit her and they asked her to come back to Crystal Bay, too. In the chaos that ensued, Callie thought about how she felt when Sands reached into his coat pocket.

It was exciting, but she wasn't ready, yet. And he probably wasn't either. But as she looked at him, laughing and joking with her friends and family, she knew that she wanted him to be in her life for a long, long time to come.

The food was nearly reduced to crumbs when Emma, newly returned from Arizona, came over to their table.

"How was everything, today?" she asked, deeply tanned and looking spiffy in a green dress. "We wouldn't even be here today if not for Callie and of course, Detective Sands."

"Don't forget about Kayla," Callie added. "She's my hero. Where is she today?"

"Oh, she's taken over for Melody – in fact, I think she might be planning the Dayton wedding." Melody had resigned from the inn as soon as she'd recovered, but the discovery that she'd been a centerfold had done nothing but boost interest in her new book. To wit: she was off being interviewed for a national morning show later in the week. Callie was happy for Melody – she had suffered enough, thanks to Jack.

"So the wedding is still on?" Callie said, surprised and pleased for Nick and Lexy. It turned out that Nick hadn't been trying to run her down, either.

"Seems to be," shrugged Emma.

Nick had bought a new SUV for Lexy. The sleek new vehicle had lots of bell and whistles and Nick was unused to driving it when he ran Callie off the road. His irrational behavior at the crash scene and his burst of anger at Mrs. Dayton's house was a combination of embarrassment, guilt that he had endangered Callie and her dog and fear that he'd be charged with reckless driving. Sands had filled her in on most of this the day after Jack's capture.

"I hope they both go to remedial driving school – maybe there's a package deal," had been Callie's irritated response.

"Well, Nick is in a bit of trouble for leaving a crash scene." Sands had given Callie a warm gaze. "Chalk it up to wedding jitters. But luckily for him – and me – you were mostly unharmed."

Even though she didn't trust them behind the wheel, Callie was happy for the Nick and Lexy. She hoped that they would work out their differences and that Mrs. Dayton would be a support to her daughter and not a source of problems. She also hoped that she would get a chain for her eyeglasses and use it!

"So, listen, you two," Emma said conspiratorially, leaning close to Callie and Sands. "I figure I owe you one. I'd like to treat you both to a free dinner at the inn tonight. It's the least I can do."

Callie thought about the last few days she'd spent dealing with the English Country Inn – Natalie's death, Melody's trials and tribulations, the Dayton bridal shower disaster and finally, her near death by refrigerator.

She knew Emma meant to be kind, but Callie wanted to take not only a vacation to a warmer climate – she wanted an extended vacation from the inn.

She glanced at Sands and it was if he could read her mind.

"Sorry, not tonight," they said in unison.

THE END

Recipes from Callie's Kitchen

Spiced Greek Biscuits (*Paxemathia*) (Greek biscotti)

Ingredients:

1-½ sticks unsalted butter, at room temperature

¾ cup granulated sugar

3 large eggs, beaten

1 tbsp olive oil (or canola oil)

2 oz. of ouzo (Greek liqueur) or 1 tbsp pure anise extract

3 cups flour (if using 2 oz. of ouzo) and 2-3/4 cup if using anise extract

½ tsp baking powder

1 tsp baking soda

Preheat oven to 350 degrees F.

Mix together flour, baking powder and baking soda. Set aside. Cream butter until light and fluffy and gradually beat in sugar. Mix in the beaten eggs, oil and ouzo or anise extract. Add dry ingredients gradually until incorporated. The dough will be sticky, but should not be too loose. You should be able to form loaves with it.

Spray a large baking sheet with Pam spray or use baking parchment paper. You need one of your bigger baking sheets, as the dough spreads out during baking.

Pat dough into two loaves, about 1 inch high and 1-1/2 inches wide. Don't place loaves too close together, or they will join together while baking. Bake for 30 minutes. Remove baking sheet from oven and allow the loaves to cool undisturbed for 15 minutes.

Using a sharp knife, slice each loaf diagonally into slices ½ inch to ¾ inch thick. Lower oven temperature to 250 degrees F. Turn biscuits on their sides on their baking sheet and dry slowly in oven for an additional 50 minutes, turning biscuits over once.

Allow cookies to cool completely, then store in airtight container or Ziploc bag for up to 3 weeks.

Greek Snowball Cookies (*Kourabiethes*)

These are the festive cookies on the cover of SPICED AND ICED. They are a family favorite and a Callie's Kitchen bestseller.

Ingredients:
1 lb. (4 sticks) unsalted butter, very soft
1/4 cup confectioner's sugar, plus more for sprinkling on cookies
1 egg yolk
1 tsp vanilla
1 oz. ouzo (Greek liqueur) OR 1 tsp anise extract or 1 tsp orange extract
5-6 cups all-purpose flour

Preheat oven to 350 degrees.

Beat softened butter until very light and fluffy. Add confectioner's sugar, egg yolk, vanilla and ouzo (or extract), beating thoroughly after each addition. Add flour a little at a time until soft dough is formed that can be handled easily.

Taking about a teaspoonful at a time, (or use a small ice-cream scoop) roll into a small ball about the size of a walnut. Place on a non-stick cookie sheet and bake for 15-20 minutes. Cookies should be light golden brown on the bottoms.

Roll in powdered sugar while still hot. When cool, sprinkle liberally with powdered sugar again.

Makes about 5 dozen.

Blueberry Greek Yogurt Scones

Courtesy of Karen Owen, creator of *A Cup of Tea and A Cozy Mystery* blog

Ingredients:

2 1/2 cups of all-purpose flour
1 tsp salt
4 tsp baking powder
1/4 cup of white sugar
Zest of one medium sized orange
Juice of one medium sized orange
1/2 cup of cold butter or margarine
1 egg
1/2 a cup Greek yogurt
3 tsp pure vanilla extract
1 cup of fresh or frozen blueberries (in Wisconsin, in wintertime, it's easier to find frozen!)

Preheat the oven to 400 degrees F.

In a large bowl, combine flour, sugar, baking powder, and salt. Zest orange and add it to your dry mixture. Squeeze the juice from your orange and set it aside.

Cut up the butter and add it to the rest of the ingredients. Blend it with a pastry cutter until the consistency of bread crumbs.

In a separate bowl, beat eggs. Add your yogurt to eggs, then add vanilla and orange juice. Fold the wet mixture into the dry mixture and gently combine. Add blueberries, folding them gently.

Use a spoon to drop the size scones you wish to enjoy (smaller for an afternoon tea or larger for a coffee shop sized scone) on to parchment lined baking sheets. Bake until golden brown edges and tops appear.

Depending on the size, makes a dozen or more scones.

Sweetie's Spinach Squares aka Lazy *Spanakopita*

Author's note: this tasty recipe is a creation of my husband's "Thea" Beth Partalis, a wonderful cook and beloved aunt. Spinach Squares are a family favorite and they are often served at parties.

Ingredients:

2 packages chopped frozen spinach, thawed and drained

2 bags Monterey Jack cheese

4 8 oz. boxes of feta cheese, crumbled (Odyssey is our preferred brand – and it's made in Wisconsin)

4 eggs, beaten

1 stick of butter, divided in half and melted

1 onion, chopped

2 cups milk

2 cups Bisquick

Salt, pepper to taste

Preheat oven to 350 degrees F.

Sauté onion in a half stick of the butter. In a large bowl, mix all ingredients together until thoroughly incorporated and season to taste.

Put in a large glass pan (9 x 13) and drizzle with the rest of the melted butter. Bake for about 40 minutes or until sides begin to brown. Turn down oven temperature to 325 degrees F until the mixture looks set. Put under the broiler to brown the top. Cut into small squares and serve as an appetizer, warm or at room temperature.

Makes about 24 squares.

Wisconsin Supper Club Cheese Spread

A signature cheese spread is frequently served at Wisconsin's supper clubs, along with a relish tray. Serve this with your favorite crackers, breads or pretzels. Some supper club patrons even use it on their baked potatoes.

Ingredients:

1 container cheddar cheese spread (such as Kraft Old English spread)
4 oz cream cheese
8 oz sour cream
1 tsp salt
¼ tsp cayenne pepper

In large bowl, blend ingredients using a hand mixer (or use a Kitchen Aid standing mixer). Chill at least one hour and preferably longer, to blend flavors and ensure that the mixture sets and is spreadable. Keep leftovers covered in the refrigerator. Great with crudité, crackers, bread or even on baked potatoes.

Spiced and Iced Gingerbread

This is what the customers clamor for in Callie's Kitchen at Christmastime. The lemon icing provides a nice contrast to the spicy cake (and lemon is a very Greek ingredient). However, if you prefer, see the variation for vanilla icing (below).

Ingredients for the gingerbread:

½ cup unsalted butter or shortening such as Crisco. Callie would most likely choose butter – she does live in the Dairy State, after all.

½ cup sugar

1 egg

½ cup molasses, regular, not robust. Note: For a darker cake with even more molasses flavor, use ¾ cup.

1 cup boiling water

2 1/4 cup all-purpose flour

1 tsp. baking soda

1/2 tsp. salt

2 tsp. ginger (you can grate in some fresh or crush in some crystallized ginger for even more ginger flavor)

1 tsp. cinnamon

Have a ready a greased and floured 9-inch by 9-inch pan, available at a reasonable price in kitchen stores and any place that sells bakeware. A smaller pan will create a deflated spot in the middle and the edges will cook too soon.

Preheat oven to 325 degrees F.

In standing mixer or a large bowl with a hand mixer, beat shortening, sugar and egg until well blended. Blend in molasses and water. Gradually add the dry ingredients, and mix until well blended.

Pour into prepared pan. Bake for 38-45 minutes; do not overbake! Check the cake before end of baking time. The cake is done when toothpick inserted in the middle comes out clean, but a few moist crumbs clinging to the toothpick is OK. You don't want a dry cake.

Let cool on wire rack until completely cool while you prepare the icing.

Lemon Icing Ingredients:

2 cups confectioner's sugar, plus more if needed
2 tablespoons lemon juice
1-2 tablespoons warm water

Whisk the lemon juice into the confectioner's sugar and then add water slowly – you want a nice, thick icing, so you may not use all the water. If the icing looks too thin, add a little more confectioner's sugar.

Vanilla Icing Variation:

Follow lemon icing directions, but omit lemon juice and substitute with 1 tsp pure vanilla extract.

Let the icing set a bit and then spread on the cooled gingerbread.

Makes 12 squares.

Acknowledgements

I'm grateful to so many people. I'd especially like to thank:

Linda Reilly, for your support, encouragement, enthusiasm and friendship. You always give me the boost I need.

Loretta Nyhan for your unfailing support, astute critiques and wonderfully generous heart. I'm lucky to have you as a friend.

Susan Furlong, for your support, encouragement and charming editorial review of my first Callie's Kitchen Mystery.

Renee Barratt, for delivering an exceptionally beautiful cover under some difficult circumstances.

Julia Lightbody, fellow Midwest Mystery Writers of America member, for answering my Wisconsin pier questions so quickly and generously.

Karen Owen, for allowing me to use her delightful recipe in my book.

The wonderful book bloggers who've reached out to me and welcomed me into the world of cozy mysteries with open arms. Thank you for your support!

The readers! I couldn't do it without you. Thank you for buying my book, writing reviews, spreading the word about my books and most of all, for welcoming Callie Costas and crew on to your bookshelves!

My family and friends, for their love and support, as well as their efforts in helping me to spread the word about my books.

My two daughters, Alexandra and Zoe, for encouraging me in my writing efforts.

Last but not least, my wonderful husband, Jim, for his tireless tech support, editorial acumen and positive encouragement and love all along the way.

For anyone not mentioned here who helped me in some way with my writing journey – thank you!

And finally, a special note to readers: If you enjoyed this book, will you consider leaving a short review on Amazon? The more reviews that a book has, the more readers will see it. This helps writers keep writing books! Reviews need not be long and complicated – a simple "I liked it" means so much.

To those of you who have already taken the time to write a review, thank you! It is very much appreciated.

About the Author

Award-winning writer and blogger Jenny Kales worked for years as a freelancer, but fiction writing has always been a dream. Kales' marriage into a Greek-American Midwestern family inspired The Callie's Kitchen mysteries, featuring Calliope Costas, food business owner and amateur sleuth. The setting of the story, "Crystal Bay," is inspired by a favorite family vacation spot - Wisconsin's beautiful Geneva Lakes. Ms. Kales is an avid reader, cook and baker and she's addicted to mystery TV, especially anything on Masterpiece Mystery or BBC America. She lives just outside of Chicago with her husband, two daughters and a cute but demanding Yorkshire terrier, and is hard at work on her next book. Visit the author's web site at *www.jennykales.wordpress.com*. To keep up with author news, giveaways, recipes and other fun stuff, sign up for a FREE newsletter at *tinyurl.com/huv5pof*.

Made in the USA
Middletown, DE
25 September 2017